SECOND POCKET FIRST

GREGORY GROSVENOR

Black Rose Writing | Texas

ISBN: 978-1-68513-564-5
PUBLISHED BY BLACK ROSE WRITING
www.blackrosewriting.com

Printed in the United States of America
Suggested Retail Price (SRP) $21.95

Second Pocket First is printed in Garamond Premier Pro

*As a planet-friendly publisher, Black Rose Writing does its best to eliminate unnecessary waste to reduce paper usage and energy costs, while never compromising the reading experience. As a result, the final word count vs. page count may not meet common expectations.

PRAISE FOR
SECOND POCKET FIRST

"In the tradition of the great comic novels. Original, quirky, bighearted, I loved this book!"
–Janet Peery, National Book Award Finalist

"A lighthearted jaunt alongside a lovable loser whose rise and fall will keep readers turning pages."
–*Kirkus Reviews*

"Catches the reader's attention with its simplicity and humor from the very first chapter to the very last page and an ending that is unexpected but wholly satisfying."
–Bernadette Longu, *Readers' Favorite*

"Subversive in its usage of the English language, and always hilarious, *Second Pocket First* offers an absurdist, ultra–stylish window into the declining mind of a professional thief. Unpredictable to the last. Underneath its calendar beauty, New England never really makes up its mind about outsiders."
–Del Blackwater, author of *Dead Egyptians*

"*Second Pocket First* is a twenty–first century picaresque novel. In the guise of gentleman thief Issey, Gregory Grosvenor has created an interesting protagonist whose peculiarly wayward moral compass marks him out as not quite of our times."
–Craig Jones, *IndieReader*

"With all the serious news and tragedies taking place, *Second Pocket Firs*t provides a light, fun diversion."
–JD Jung, *Underrated Reads*

"A delightful read for those who enjoy literary fiction infused with comedic undertones and eccentric characters."
–Carol Thompson, *Readers' Favorite*

To my mom and dad for love, humor, and tenacity.
And to Randi, my goose. *Why, bébé?*

SECOND POCKET FIRST

PART I

CHAPTER ONE

Issey was a lousy thief, but a good son. The vases he stole usually found their way to his mother's doorstep in Vermont, and the few items he did sell, Issey got hustled by pawnshop owners and their children. The high-end hot stuff went to his fence, but the fence was a talker and also lousy. Anyway, Issey kind of knew—he just wanted to help the guy out. So, Issey never did much time in county and the fence was eventually retired in the ol' cold meats way.

And Issey had been at it all night. He was stealing without technique, without curiosity, without *feeling*. It wasn't just the *Grüppe's* upcoming Faneuil Hall heist that crowded his thoughts. And it wasn't finding something special for Mary Anne Loggia or Bianka Fröhlicher or Gwenni Von Maxi. No. It was here in these East Cambridge apartments that bugged him out. One apartment felt too fragrant. Another apartment felt too stale. The next apartment was too month-to-month. The following apartment was too MIT. The next too leopard print. Too delivery food. Too litter box. Too laundry basket. Too fragrant—was Issey already back inside the fragrant dump? What a waste.

And it had started as an inspired night, a night tasked for gifts. Jade cigarette holder for Mary Anne Loggia. Museum gloves for Bianka Fröhlicher. Bedazzled phone case for Gwenni Von Maxi. In the North End during the tourist rush, he stitched the thoroughfare cheek-to-jowl, engaged in some light pickpocketing, and romanced a late-October mist hanging over the Charles River. It gave the night courage. And his outfit—his outfit! He was absolutely luxe in classical thief-wear: slimming gray blazer, heightening turtleneck, nailhead Sheridan scarf, double gloves made of veal, and black boots with an ankle zipper and Cuban heel. *Witty Rogue in the Autumn.*

But by the end of the night, his black thievin' bag carried nothing more than a desk lamp, a phone charger, a stainless-steel ladle, chopsticks, a penlight, and a set of teacups that had been broken by the ladle. And the penlight was already his. There was also some blood on the bag from the beating he had taken in the MIT apartment, but he could take this to the cleaners.

Issey returned to Den12, the empty woodworking studio in Winter Hill where Berger managed the *Grüppe's* activities. Grumpy faces were coming in and out with hand trucks. They ignored Issey and were on the business of unloading storage containers and cases on wheels for the Faneuil Hall job. The only bright face was Berger's, who wore an open gingham shirt, revealing the early stages of a Côte d'Azur tan. His shoes were loafers and Italian. He was good taste embellished with occasional acts of terrorism.

Berger led Issey into his office. The space was empty except for a dusty metal desk, two metal office chairs, and a lobster tank that housed about twenty live lobsters. The sound of Issey's boots echoed in the office. Berger leaned his thin backside on the desk and pointed at Issey's boots.

"Is that a Cuban heel?" Berger asked.

"Indeed!" Issey beamed. "They're stunning, right?"

"We're letting you go."

"What?"

"Yeah. You're out."

"Out of the *Grüppe?*"

"Stop calling it that," Berger said.

"I thought we were calling ourselves the *Grüppe.*"

"No. No one's ever said that." Berger looked him up and down, disappointment on his French-cut face. "Those boots are so loud that I can hear you coming a mile away."

"I can wear different boots."

"And you have blood all over your face. Were you in a fight?"

Issey pulled a handkerchief from his inside pocket and wiped his upper lip and cheeks and forehead and teeth and jacket. Blood was everywhere— that MIT guy really went to town! As Issey cleaned himself, the lobsters stared at him. They were bewildered. They floated in their tank like they were on drugs.

"You're just terrible at this," Berger said. "And you never bring in anything worth having."

"It's the neighborhood," Issey pleaded. "The North End is sacked."

"McCauley's from the same neighborhood. He's cleared the place out."

"That's what I'm saying! He's left no meat on the bone."

"Look," Berger stood upright from the desk and threw an arm around Issey's lumpy shoulders. "You've slopped out a pretty good career for yourself. And even though we're basically the same age, I've always thought of you as a son. But there's too much going on with Faneuil Hall."

"I have good ideas for Faneuil Hall! You ever heard of the famous French bank robber Albert Spaggiari?"

"No."

"He had this code of no weapons, no violence, no hatred—"

"I'm going to ask you to stop talking."

Berger stared him down.

Issey drooped. His chin felt heavy.

"You're a Vermont guy," said Berger, facing him square. "I know you did your apprenticeship in Montreal with Claudia, but that's... French Canadian country. Different place, different time, different Claudia."

"That was a whole week of nothing but Murano glassworks."

"Still..."

"And what about Claudia? She's our connection—"

"That's off," Berger laughed, then laughed some more. "That's way off. From what I heard, she and Erik got tangled in the tinsel last December, and she's been nothing but a disaster ever since."

Issey placed a hand on his hip. "But my lockpicking. Berger. My *lockpicking.*"

"Hm."

"And I have a great temperament. Think about who you have going into Faneuil Hall. McCauley's psychotic. He's unpredictable. He carries a gun. And Triple B drinks *all the time.*"

Berger considered these points. When someone was talking to Berger, he made them feel like the most important person in the world was listening. Berger was a big deal. He could turn a suitcase into a storage locker.

"The hell of it is, Issey, you *are* a quality lockpick... But McCauley's gun gets him in places. And Triple B has that one good glass cutter."

"One more chance..."

Berger sniffed around Issey's bag.

"Fine," Berger relented. "But you've got to steal something. *Something.* Something that shows like you know what you're doing. Not these crumbs. Something real. Then we'll revisit your future."

Issey sucked in his tummy and nodded. He picked up his bag with its rejected stuff.

"Oh, and Issey," Berger said before Issey left the office. "Help yourself to a lobster on your way out."

Going into his bag, the lobster squirmed and hissed, fanned its claws and swimmerets. And it wasn't all that thrilled two hours later when Issey's fat fingers wrapped around its carapace and lifted it from the bag. Its antenna had gotten tangled in phone charger wire, and there was a little dance between lobster and Issey when it swiped at the charger again and again until the animal came loose and fell onto the grass. "I'm doing this for you, stupid," Issey said. He dropped the lobster into the first decent body of water he could find, somewhere on the border between Arlington and Cambridge.

Like all gentlemen thieves, Issey was a vegetarian, and he could walk the night to his Porter Square hideaway attic with a clear conscience.

Clear conscience, sure, but now that it was nothing but night and walking, night and clacking Cuban heels, the drift of Berger's last words finally caught up to him. "You're just terrible at this." And Issey had only ever been good at one thing. And that was being a thief. It was all he had ever wanted to be good at. Even as a child in Bell River Valley, being a thief was the *absolute business*. You had access inside the big homes, access inside the tuckaways, the fat barns with the gambrel roofs, the bungalows hanging off declivities, the neighborhoods on hooks, banks, and slopes. Inside the dumps, the trailers, the rat-houses, the junko-miniums, the narrow complexes and suplexed duplexes. From the richos high in the mountains to the wreckage frontloaded off Exit 10—none of it mattered just so long as he was inside. He wanted to open closets and refrigerators. He wanted to see the insides of junk drawers, medicine cabinets, armoires, pie safes, piano benches. He wanted to touch things, hold things, see how they fit into his hands, pockets, and life. And then there was the planning, the props, and the outfits—shapewear, ankle boots, tortoiseshell sunglasses, blueprint canisters, fingers of port. He was heavy on the swank and full of high drama, mama!

But:

"You're just terrible at this."

What a blow—a real gut punch! He felt his gut. His body was becoming the shape of a bowler hat. Good thing for the shapewear.

He arrived at his hideaway attic a little after one. There was a note taped on the door. The note was folded in half, with "Issey" written in boarding school cursive. Some lovely had him on her mind. Mary Anne Loggia? Bianka Fröhlicher? Gwenni Von Maxi? Maybe Berger writing to whisk him back into the *Grüppe*? A briny smell from came floating up from his bag.

"Doll," the note began. Mary Anne Loggia.

Doll,

My doll, my Issey. You don't take No for an answer and you don't take Yes for an answer either. You're easily confused. You're stupid. And this is the part of our story that reaches its feral end. My doll, my Issey. May you soar!

-M.

Issey turned the note over, the part he had already seen with his name on it, and then turned it over and then read it again. "Doll, my doll, my Issey."

Ah, well. Here, there—whatever. Issey entered his attic space and placed the note with the other notes and went on drafting for the Faneuil Hall job. He sketched a lot of different outfits, shoes, accessories, walking sticks, umbrellas, caution tape, orange traffic cones. Crumble, crumble—all junk. Maybe Berger was right. He dropped ice cubes in a towel and pressed it against his battered face.

CHAPTER TWO

In the custom of a good steal, Issey felt most safe. Hiding in ceilings and in plain sight gave the Cambridge nights a well-pronounced sweetness. "'My good fellow,'" Issey drew on a cigarette that dangled in his dreamy lips, while threading his stubby fingers through doubleskin gloves of ibex, "'plans for the night?' 'Oh, just thievin'. Don't mind me, neighbor. Just thievin'.'"

But no matter how much he looked forward to thievin', Berger's words followed him, rattled his confidence, his fingers, his lockpickers. And when he finally got inside, broken out in sweat and adrenaline, the place had nothing in it. There was some unread mail on a side table. Jury duty notification. A letter that looked personal. Junk mail. Credit card statement. He pocketed the jury duty notification. It was like the old Bell River Valley days, "*let petit jours*," he said aloud, the days when he lacked a philosophy, when he simply stole for the sake of stealing, pushing his little-boy mitts into Old Man Brill's box. His weakness for stealing mail stayed with him into adulthood. But it didn't make him any more secure tonight.

Keys jangled, the door swung open, and the people entered.

"Jesus! Call the police!"

Hah! Issey thought. Joke's on you two: I've snipped your telephone wires.

The woman, plump, whipped out her cell phone and the boyfriend, plump with a beard, whipped Issey with fists and brown shoes. Issey was getting beaten up a lot these days. More than usual. Was he just terrible at this now?

But luck bounces both ways, and it came with a phone call from his brother Rohel who had news: their mother had remarried again and moved out of state, and Issey was told get to Vermont to "clear out all these vases."

Issey paused.

"Why are you pausing?"

"I was just thinking."

"Why are you thinking?"

Issey slid his finger on the rim of a Murano glass sculpture.

"Look," Rohel said, "We'll fly you up here. What's your email? I'm going to forward you these tickets."

"Email? Why not just pop them in the post? When's the wedding?"

"We already had the wedding."

"Hm."

"What is the humming?"

"It would have been nice to have known about the wedding, Rohel," Issey said. "I have a really good wedding outfit that I never get to wear."

Rohel whispered in the background: "Honey, Daddy is talking." Then he returned: "So... what's happening? You're coming up here."

Issey put a finger to his bruised upper lip. "I could hot-wire a car."

"You don't know how to do that."

"I do. I can do a lot of things that you don't know about. Just the other night, I saved a lobster from the old boiler when I dropped it in Spy Pond. And it was really out of my way."

"Iseey, you can't put a lobster in a pond."

"Really?" Issey thought about it out loud. "No, I think you can."

"No, Issey. Lobsters live in saltwater."

"Isn't that a pond?"

"A pond is freshwater."

"Oh," Issey said. "Is there a big difference? Lobster-wise, at least?"

"Lobsters die in freshwater."

"Oh," Issey said again. "How do you even know how to find saltwater?"

"Okay," Rohel put an end to it. "Look. Just go to Logan, find the ticket counter, and I'll have 'em in your name."

"Ah, yes—thanks, brother!"

But Issey paused again.

"You're pausing again."

"For arrangements... I'd rather it be train travel. You know, the sliding compartment doors, lacquered teacarts, *chef de train,* food served under a dazzling cloche. I've also made the acquaintance of the most stunning indigo travel case."

"It's not *Murder on the Orient Express*, Issey."

"Then aeromobile it is—up, up and away!"

His brother ended the conversation and Issey closed his pre-paid phone with a slap. Issey circled the phone's body with a sort-of manicured finger.

"Sweet Ptolemy!" Issey shouted. He saw this as a kind of cosmic ticket. And he already had his hands and neck outfitted with the nailhead Sheridan scarf and vealskin gloves. Heavy rain beetled on the eaves, so he reported to his brolly stand and chose in accord to occasion. Onyx handle for their mother's many mood swings and black-and-white plaid for their mother's new marriage. He was happy about his mother's marriage, surely, maybe, arguably. Life is a circle and eventually that becomes the shape of your body. Issey sucked in and posed in front of the mirror.

But his mother had some *good stuff* tucked away in that old bolthole of hers. Good enough to get him back in Berger's good books!

The prospect of Vermont and the return to Bell River Valley excited him. His childhood was a fond recollection. Everything for Issey was fondness and optimism. He was never in a bad mood. And as he moved freely through the Cambridge night looking for the *right vase*, he carved time for nostalgia: the harvest markets he toured as a child where his face was painted, the choo-choo mailboxes he had marked as a beginner thief, the worrying country roads that were unlighted and crunchy in the dark. Perhaps one day in his twilight years he too would marry in the valley, in a three-season sunroom overlooking Mount Mansfield. But then he saw the lobster in the pond, and it wasn't the kind of thought he welcomed. How would he know if a pond had saltwater or regular water or what kind of water is good for a lobster? Who knows these things? Stupid lobster and science and nature.

Enough of that. Most of his worries could be resolved with some light burglary. And after a night of inspired break-ins, Issey awoke the next morning with a rejuvenated sense of purpose, body and hair shined with *crème de menthe*. He left the hideaway attic with his indigo suitcase and strode into Boston Logan humming "Moonlight in Vermont." At the airport bar, he ordered a finger of port, and was given a roast beef sandwich instead. He ate in tidy bites, avoiding the clutch of animal parts, and thought about his brother Rohel. Ah, brother Rohel. Oh, brother Rohel. Sigh, brother Rohel. The eight-year age difference between them was to Issey's great fortune. Sure, Issey understood he was something of a biological error (his mother was forty-six on the mid-afternoon laugher of Issey's conception), but from all that sick, orange treacle spilling out of her nine months later came smooth boundaries between Issey and brother, between Issey and mother, between Issey and Yes and No. Issey and Rohel hardly knew each other. Issey couldn't remember the last time he had seen him. There was some kind of dinner thing five years ago? Or was it a brunch? Or was it ten years ago? People were sitting, the wife was there, and there had been lots of food. Whatever it was, Issey had been impressed when Rohel paid for the whole thing. Nevertheless. At the last wedge of his sandwich, Issey blew a kiss for all the people in his brother's life. Rohel was some bigshot dud of an architect who played by the rules and was championed by those who made them. He was compassionate and straight and generous in the worst possible way—the societal way, the familial way, the career way, the handsome way. Yawn, brother Rohel. The sandwich sucked, but on the bright side, Issey stole the bartender's tips.

And then he stole a carry-on bag from an airport boutique. The flight was delayed and during the wait, Issey outfitted the new bag and its new bag smell with magazines, razors, candy, and a stuffed animal for his brother's daughter, all of which he had stolen during the delay. Air travel—who would have thought!

After landing, de-boarding, and picking through a few passenger pockets, Issey opened his phone to the broken English of Bianka Fröhlicher on his voicemail. "Oh, Issey. *Mein* Issey. I'm—I'm here at the Back Bay Excelsior. I'm needing a total reset. On Saturday, I'm flying to Abano. Maybe after my spa, we can lunch? Or maybe if we don't, my new friend, would... would it be breaking your heart if I never saw you again? *Aber ich liebe Dich doch...*"

And on she went, mostly in German. Issey pressed DELETE and wondered: *Was* she German? But certain details, like so many good romances, are best left to the imagination, or ignored forever.

There was Rohel, standing at the luggage carousel.

Under an REI down vest, Rohel's Oxford button-down was wrinkled. His eyes were glassy. His thousand-dollar jeans looked cheap. It wasn't the Rohel he knew, but the generous hand on Issey's shoulder was familiar. "Good to see you, pal."

Issey spotted his indigo suitcase and then lifted a black suitcase that was too good to pass up. On the way, Issey gave the black suitcase a good tapping.

"Handy's Pawn and Gun Shop—still open? I'll slide you a percentage point."

"Just, let's go. And put that back."

But Issey did not.

The drive from the airport to Bell River Valley was a long one. All Vermont drives are long ones. All Vermont nights are long. The air has a purity that cuts through scavengers and liars.

This wasn't the Rohel that Issey knew. Rohel had always been something of a babe, a cheerful face. Behind his eyes was every compliment he had ever received. Contrasting Rohel's eyes were Issey's eyes and you couldn't see behind Issey's eyes. One was black from the beating he had gotten from the MIT dweeb. The other had nothing behind it.

Face and all, Issey tried to lift everyone's spirits. In Rohel's home, a disgusting white clapboard, Issey showed off his indigo suitcase and the new black suitcase to Rohel's wife, an attractive idiot with high cheekbones under longish honey-brown hair. The daughter was something of an idiot, too.

The Rohels had expensive tastes. Double Gaggenau oven. Farmhouse sinks. Soapstone countertops. Scandi pendant lights. Tube amplifier and mahogany record player. Entire living room wall covered with massive art collage thing.

The four of them ate in a post-and-beam dining room.

Issey asked the little girl, "Did you score well on Hallow's Eve? Were there any pranks of the stinking variety on Cabbage Night?"

The little girl picked her nose.

Issey asked the wife, "How is your writing coming? Any hot new stories?"

The wife rolled her eyes.

Issey asked his brother, "Is Old Man Brill still among the living? Remember him?"

Rohel shook his head. "What kind of shit are you trying to pull?"

"Rohel," the idiot wife said, "Not in front of M-A-D-I-S-O-N."

Since all conversations were duds, Issey's thoughts turned to Berger and next plans, which were still murky. But in the past "next plans" had comprised of nothing more than a smile and a set of lockpickers, qualities that won out: repartee, optimism, and a tool to invade someone's home.

"Ah! Wonderful meal." (It wasn't.) "Brother Rohel, perhaps the gentlemen could retire to the library for port and a game of cribbage."

"Where do you think you are?"

The wife gave Rohel a married look.

"But..." Rohel said, "if you want to catch up with a drink in my office..."

"A port would be heavenly, brother!"

Issey was given a can of black beer he didn't know what to do with while Rohel talked about their mother's wedding. He recreated the day as if he was in a dream—and a really boring one. The turnout for the wedding was large. All of her old housekeeping staff from the Fiddlehead Inn were invited, as well as town council members both past and present—it seemed as if every red-and-black checkered coat from the Valley came to celebrate her nuptials. Into the crowd went the bouquet and then they trussed her and the guy into the car, gathering as one to offer their final kiss to this sometimes loving, sometimes disgusting woman who had a hard time staying inbounds. "We spend 100% of our lives doing things because we're alive," she had once said, and Rohel repeated it tonight. This was her fourth marriage, more or less.

Not that Issey was asking.

Instead, he was picking through Rohel's office or babe cave or whatever this room was. The room was designed in halves. In one half, there was the professional side: an architect's drafting board, a metal stool, adjustable desk lamp, wide binders, and other tools and junk poking through prominent boxes opened and unopened. Then there was the other half of the room, which was a completely different world: pristine guest chair next to drooping sofa, Telecaster in a standing rack, practice Vox amplifier, wires tangled up, fireplace with wood burned so long ago that it had no smell, fishbowl filled with wine corks, walnut pipe and bud stems, drape swag hanging unevenly. But unifying both sides was the mood, and the mood was sour. It stank. Geez, Rohel, Issey thought, light a match and move on.

But men and women, brothers and mothers, any relationships of the human variety—these were never one of Issey's old sabotages. Things, though. Things! Issey checked his watch, a lovely number from Montreal that kept time *un peu.*

Rohel, who was strangely still talking, said, "I guess you want to get set up in Mom's house."

"Indeed!" Issey was excited to open that black suitcase he had stolen from the luggage carousel. He was excited to open that mother's house and separate from it everything that didn't belong to her. Excited to be back in Bell River Valley and uncover and agitate whatever could be, should be, and needed to be his. What treasures await! Life!

CHAPTER THREE

But the black suitcase would have to wait. Issey set out to work in the valley immediately, starting with a little exploratory research, also known as Trash Day. From the boxes in the neighborhood bins, Issey was told he was living in a town of "got's:" the kid got the gaming console; the wife got the silverware set; the husband got the snowboard; the sister-in-law or some first-class moron got the camera. Issey enters various Bell River Valley homes, wipes his shoes in the mudroom, shakes out his penlight, in and out, thank you, and he's kissed each home goodnight with his new silverware set, gaming console, snowboard, camera, and a thing of coffee and bag of sugar. What dopes. The first of many.

In the late November shade, these were the easy neighborhoods, cute and stupid, the kind you don't bring home to mother. The security system warnings were decoration, the motion sensors cross-eyed, the doors easy old wood panel. Even the steel wrapped doors, locked with a deadbolt, were no match against Issey's devotional hands and lockpickers engraved with the initial of his first name—"I." The moonbeam sliced a spotlight of our man who could not be spotlit.

This wasn't high-stakes trespassing. Issey was stealing for the sake of stealing. *Until you steal something real,* Berger had said, *something with personal consequence. Then we'll bring you back.* Berger had iced him out of the *Grüppe,* from the Faneuil Hall job. It hurt. And Issey didn't really know what the Faneuil Hall job was or what it meant. Were they stealing from Quincy Market? Were they going to bomb the place? With Berger, it could be both. Or neither, whatever that meant. Issey was confused. He was always a little confused. Events, people, conversations, and facts were unimportant. Memories were debatable. Maybe not.

But the mountains were constant. Blue, green, white, silk, alpenglow— the mountains had seen him develop his craft, his *voice*. Bell River Valley had been home to his earliest trespasses.

At ten years old, Issey had mastered the mail. Thick bundles of mail wrapped in thick bundles of his fingers. Handsome Christopher Gray a hill over was in debt to the furniture store; the Whites wrote tearful letters to their son to return home and the only thing the boy returned home were their unopened letters, which little Issey intercepted, read, and threw in the trash; Shuldigen down the road ordered a lot of baseball junk; Old Man Brill kept up on his bills and dirty magazines; Susan Grant liked fishing and Bud Grant liked fishing, too, and they had a his-and-hers subscription to the same fishing magazine (Issey would steal wife's issue one month and husband's issue the following); his fifth-grade teacher enjoyed donating money to her alma mater—maybe one day she would donate some of that college learning to his class. He ripped through birthday cash and pocketed Christmas coin. Electric bills, credit card statements, weekly savers, past due notices, men's fall fashion catalogs, postcards from cruises, postcards from amusement parks, foreclosure warnings, wedding invitations, college acceptance letters, rejection slips— all into little Issey's Ski It If You Can tote bag. No one suspects the tote boy.

In the meantime, there was the clearing out job in the mother's house. These early days raiding between house and valley were crucial if he had any chance of getting restored into Berger's *Grüppe*.

And Rohel was right. Issey's vases were everywhere. But the vases were good vases. They were the memories of slippery night moves, the *belle époque* of discipline, craft, and fortune. They held the stuff of good news, all that is him, all that he knew of earth, and all that he needed to know. They reflected his preference in the shape of women (vertically), but he can't remember what they looked like or what they sounded like or how they were—if they ever *were* in the first place, and if any of it is true. Like Debussy's music: The stuff *between* the notes.

"Debussy," Issey says, aloud and alone, softly, incorrectly.

He routed the house. Dust was everywhere. The old woman was tidy but dirty and emerging quickly from this oily mess was a revelation: His mother had nothing—nothing authentic, nothing true. No interesting lost-and-found curios from her job as head housekeeper at the bed-and-breakfast. No paperwork worth reading inside her old rolltop desk. No souvenirs from travels. No art or first editions or anything that would suggest she had interests or brains. Nothing except the vases.

Spinning a glazed Methey vase in his stubby hands, Issey surveyed the living room. The Rohel shrine on the mantelpiece above an imitation hearth and *trompe l'oeil* fireplace had once been its only honest fixture. The certificates for Rohel's academic victories. The ribbons for his scale models hanging like Christmas stockings. The group photos with Rohel and the jocks, Rohel and the nerds, Rohel and the sweater boys, Rohel and the prom princesses, Rohel and valedictorian vixens, Rohel and high school sweetie Heidi Bender, the girl who made a man out of Rohel's finger. The graduation photo from the architect's college. The clippings of handshakes with men of industry and captains of furniture. The family portraits with wife and brat. All of it was gone.

In its place was a single vase, a brooding Russian lacquered folk scene.

"Surely a case of pride fatigue," Issey said. "What happened to you, brother Rohel? And whatever happened to that stinky Heidi Bender?"

Curious now that his mother had left Bell River and here she is— celebrating Issey's victories. It made him feel like an only child. It made him feel fattish.

CHAPTER FOUR

Soft entry. Tummy sucking in and feet touching down like a cat's pads. Before him, a staircase led to the prize of the master bedroom. In the distance, a true crime TV show muted his early steps. Issey liked TV. TV was for lonely people.

There was some human activity from the living room—chips or pretzels paired with light banter about the lengths of the commercials. Sharing these crisp autumn nights, TV people in the townhouse warmed him, as if they too were rubbing their palms together for a good night's steal. Of course, if they caught Issey, the charge was ramped up—breaking and entering *while* the people were in their home watching TV, *while* they were spilling their crumbs, *while at night*. But Issey never carried a weapon, so a class 6 felony did little to put him behind his plans to continue stealing forever.

The middle-class Berber invited him upstairs, but also asked him to exercise some basic guest decency. Don't bring the dirt in, friend. So Issey sat on the bottom step and removed his ankle boots and thought it over: Never once in all his enterprise has he fired a gun. Crime is great and all, until the guns show up. No, the closest he had come was a few months ago, with one of Berger's shooting boffos, who showed Issey a case full of automatics. Or were they manuals? Issey slid his hand over them. Afterwards, his fingers smelled funny and the guns felt like he had betrayed his industry. Were these the same feelings aroused within the famous bank robber, Issey's hero Albert Spaggiari?

Issey said out loud, "*Sans armes, ni haine, ni violence.*"

From the living room came a woman's voice: "Did you hear that?"

Followed by a man's: "Hear what?"

"It sounded like somebody was speaking, like somebody was speaking French. And poorly too."

"Yeah, right. Someone came into the house to speak French."

"I'm gonna to check it out."

The male: "What? Rhonda, no. Don't do that."

The female: "What's the problem? If there's somebody here, I wanna to know about it."

"But we're in the middle of a show."

"It's a repeat."

"But, Rhonda, what if —"

"What if what?"

"No, forget it. There's nobody here."

The female: "Good. Then there's no problem. I'm gonna check it out."

"But if there *is* someone here. What'll we do!" And then, in a panic, the male voice added: "Shh!"

"Some protector you are. What a bozo!" The female voice laughed and the male voice laughed too, but late and wet.

"If you're up, do you think you can bring in the peanut butter and ricecakes? And the thing of honey?"

"You said you weren't eating after nine."

"It's not—ricecakes are a healthy alternative."

"With the peanut butter? Is that like the *healthy* alternative you had earlier—the carrots with your bucket of ranch?"

"What are you—my wife?"

"You're always saying that you're fat and that your students are looking at you funny—"

"Shh! Keep your voice down."

"Why?"

"You know—the burglar. I don't want him knowing about my weight issues."

And it so continued, following Issey upstairs where he went to work. Roommates. Couples. Human people. And what was up with Rohel? What was happening to him? People were here for a reason, a season, or a lifetime. At least that's what was stenciled on the wall in this townhouse bedroom. This part of the valley sure enjoyed the wall stenciling.

They also enjoyed their sameness. He could close his eyes and lift himself to the townhouse connected to this one and there would be more of getting the same. The same linens and throw blankets, the same Erins and Kates and Rhondas overhearing French and their lads resisting ricecakes after nine. The same exercise equipment in the bedroom, the same collared shirts hanging on the exercise equipment, the cherubic angel pillows and little zip bags for makeup and that plastic cover on the razor that always wedges itself between toilet and sink. The same secret sexual lubricants and pleasure plugs in the same hideaway drawers. Don't want mother catching you with one of those rings you put around your peen— don't want to be in mother's bad books.

He poked through a linen chest at the foot of the bed: blankets, two three-ring binders, a flap of Berber carpet samples, a faded t-shirt of a Virginia Beach surf shop, a single pillow, and loose change. He pocketed the change. Cha-ching! Issey made a dollar.

But his professional instincts were bothered. Surely, there had to be something more in the chest. He kneeled and divided the items. Something was in the pillow, some blocky thing with an odd nose. Removing it from the pillow, he saw it was a tiny diary with a dervish clasp.

For his night's work, four townhouses total including this dump, his thievin' bag had been filled with nothing more than a water pitcher, two fragrant pillowcases, a framed photograph of a deer with pretty eyes and a hole in its windpipe, a diamond ring that was likely fake (both diamond and ring), and some potpourri that he wanted for the bag itself because the bag still smelled like the lobster, until finally—finally—treasure. Personal treasure.

"Not worth much," Issey *cognized*, "But not worth *nothing*, neither."

He put the diary in his bag, slipped out of the bedroom, and snatched a new box of toothpaste from the en suite bathroom. Downstairs, the television was loud. He tiptoed to the entry. He slipped on his boots and opened the door. He stole one last look.

And someone was stealing that look right back at him.

It was the female voice come alive in female form. Rhonda. She was standing in the kitchen now, where the TV's volume breached the entry. She wore a raglan shirt and tight green shorts. In her right hand was an empty bag of ricecakes. In her right mind—disorder, shock, Issey. What had she seen? Had she seen the shoeless, feet-first glide down the stairs? Had she seen the legs in black breathable active-wear? The body in a slimming black turtleneck? The hands engloved in black ibex? The face infused with pumpkin spice rouge?

She had an inoffensive little mouth, lacy masculine eyes, pork tenderloin legs. Not tall or slender or short or athletic or wide or squat, but... Maybe a little broad in the beam? Maybe wide in the balcony? He put a finger to his lips.

Closing the door one breath at a time, he waited for a shout, for a call to the man made of ricecakes. He waited for her to fumble or fall apart or forget how a scream went and make one of those irresistible pissing sounds, a slimy climax—a slimax, if you will—and she wouldn't. Slimax, that is. Instead, she held him in the candlelight of her eyes, drank in Issey's last moves. She was a woman about the right age, somewhere between twenty-five and goodnight, somewhere between twenty-five and mother's bad books. O beams! O balconies! He waited for her and she waited for his next trick. And this would be a sound that she wouldn't hear as Issey kept one eye on her and one eye on securing the door's closure. O softfoot! Click. O cattlelifter! Close.

The headache in the Bell River night was immediate and it came after working both eyes at the same. He gripped his bag. A frost-tipped branch smacked him in the face and landed him rump-first into the ground. His bag flew out of his hand and pumped behind him. Were her frosts tipped? The mountains covered him darkness. A wolf howled. Issey was somewhere in his mid-thirties but still contagious to the childhood disease of the howls coming from an imaginary wolf.

A cold snap from the glen rolled him onto his knees, then to his feet; he was made of mush; his legs did some work; and eventually he opened the door to his mother's home, where the telephone was going to town. Maybe it was Berger who wanted him back!

He coughed into the receiver. "Spadge!" He cleared his throat. "Hello? Spaggiari here."

On the other end was an atmosphere of tense silence. While he waited, Issey dropped the bag on the kitchen table. The bag, a gabardine number, was dirty and the items smashed.

"Spaggiari," Issey repeated. "Berger?"

"Issey?" The voice was a woman's and it was familiar-ish. "Right? Is this Issey?"

"More or less. And this is…"

"Shut up. Where were you tonight?"

"Home, of course. Going through memorabilia—"

"Liar. I was over there earlier tonight. Rohel said you were sorting through your things. But you weren't there."

Ah, Issey thought. *This is Anissa.*

"Ah, this is Anissa."

"We need to talk, but not on the phone," she whispered. "My stupid kid might be listening."

A third voice broke in, said, "I'm stupid?" and then there was the dial tone.

Everything was here in Bell River. He ran the water in the kitchen, splashed his face, and stepped outside to be alone with it and a cigarette.

He began scoring tonight's penalties. Issey felt un. He wanted to be non and now he was un. One measure in a quality thief's line was to ensure that no one knew where he lived or what he was doing or if he were, in fact, statistically present. There were the Rohels and their wet mouths. That's two, that's who. And now this Rhonda person and those dreamy lookers.

Rhonda and irregularities. Rhonda and her milky torso. Issey took a seat at the dining room table. He burned through another cigarette and a half-blind list:

Premierèment, her response. Of all the times Issey had been found out—and these were rare but also often—he usually invited immediate shock: Men went pip, pee, or straight into a wall; women cried "Oh my god!" and let the house fall apart. No, Issey had very little worries in the people department: They're more scared of you than you are of et cetera. But this Rhonda person wasn't scared. She wasn't anything he could put his pointer on.

Deuxièment, on his way getting lost home, there weren't police sirens. Nowhere in the pure darkness of the valley was there the report of blue or red lights.

So, she didn't call the police.

Troisièmement, in the first place, which should have been *premiere*, it was she and not the man made of ricecakes who pursued the source of those initial sounds. When they weren't pipping, peeing, or barreling into walls, men will defend any situation that might threaten some dimbulb masculinity, "No, *I'll* do it," Issey has heard, in defense of the peen. Meanwhile, that same peen is shrinking, retreating, and pooping all over itself.

He changed his clothes, hid the dirties in his mother's laundry basket.

Before saying goodnight, his eyes lit on the gabardine bag, with its junk and its more junk. Past that, he was drawn to the weird thing with the dervish clasp. The girl's diary. That was something. That was action. He'd sort out this bizarre woman. Tomorrow. Issey had already kicked his stubby legs into slumber-wear. Besides, it's bad form deboning a stranger's diary so late at night.

Enfin, legs, butt, face: she was a woman, all right.

CHAPTER FIVE

Issey waited at the doorstep of Rohel's disgusting white clapboard house. Whatever Rohel's wife wanted last night.... Who knew? He hardly knew her, had only a passing familiarity with her voice. Issey smoothed the fine, clam bisque of his hair, did some business with his shirt cuffs, and blew in his palm for a report on his breath. He didn't expect to get the bad news so quickly. As he threw a mint in the old talker, the door swung open.

"Geez, Issey! When I saw your mother's car pull up—just when we thought we had gotten rid of her!"

"Hah! And starting it up was like kicking a bag of ribs."

Anissa ushered him in, tracking behind his rump for any wandering eyes.

"Don't be embarrassed, gal. I'm something of a big shot."

"It's not that," said Missus Rohel, leading him into the entry, "I don't want Rohel and Madison coming back from Avi's horse farm while you're here."

"Rohel works at a horse farm now? And at Avi's—yuck. The guy's a pest."

"No, stupid." Anissa frowned. "You think Rohel works at a horse farm?"

Issey didn't know.

"Anyway," she said, "He takes her to do a little horse riding."

"Isn't it a school day?"

"They do a hooky day, like, every month or so."

"Isn't it a workday?"

"That's what I wanted to talk to you about. Come on. Let's go to the kitchen."

Rohel's wife was an athletic specimen of rippling altitude. Her legs went all the way up, like a pair of pants. Rohel liked 'em trim, Issey supposed. Rohel had introduced her to him at that dinner or brunch so many years ago as "a writer," but that could've meant anything.

"Coffee?" Issey asked.

"This isn't a diner."

"Then why are we in the kitchen?"

"You came over during the time I make fried chicken."

"Ah. Is this for a character in one of your stories?"

"No. I'm not that kind of writer," she said. "It's my New Year's resolution to make fried chicken right."

"It's November."

"Yeah. The year is almost over." She entered a large pantry and returned wearing an apron with a splashy botanical print. "Do you like fried chicken?"

"I suppose," Issey lied.

"Too bad—my fried chicken is terrible. That's why it's a resolution."

House dust was caught in the early afternoon light. From the fridge, she hefted a buffet-sized serving bowl brimming with buttermilk, chicken parts, and catastrophe.

"What's that smell?" Issey asked.

"Just the usual, man. Chicken, buttermilk, salt, pepper, some pickle juice, cayenne, hot sauce."

"Smells weird."

"Trust me, Issey." She put her head in the bowl and came up a little gaggy. "What do you know? Do you even make fried chicken?"

"Okay," Issey said. The woman was obviously useless and reckless—a dangerous combination. It made him uneasy.

"What can I do for you, Anissa? Your call last night sounded important."

She rested on a cutting board. "Rohel tells me you're... You know."

The straights had a hard time with it.

"Say no more." Issey winked. "Insurance. Would you care to buy some?" He winked again.

"No. He said that you steal people's stuff."

"I wouldn't put it like that."

"He said you break into people's houses and steal their stuff."

"I'm no guttersnipe, Anissa. No common celluloid thug."

"Okay," she shrugged. "He also said you're not very good at it either."

"What? He doesn't know what he's talking about." Issey uncrossed his legs. "Just right now, as we speak, I'm part of a continental crew that has authored big plans for—forget it."

"Uh-huh."

But Issey couldn't forget it.

"Rohel misses the finer point to the craft. It's cultured and rarefied and, perhaps, maybe not, as you would, Anissa, in a word: Un-exquisite."

"That's not even close to a sentence."

"I have adapted some of the code developed by the brilliant French bank robber Albert Spaggiari: *Sans armes, ni haine, ni violence.*"

Anissa waited. She asked, "Was that Chinese?"

"I'm talking about my philosophy."

"Oh, brother!" She rolled her eyes. "And what is your *philosophy*?"

"It's highly complicated, but, fundamentally, I don't believe that I should have to tailor myself to the...praxis of.... I'd just as well not, my dear, pay for anything."

"So you don't pay for things?"

"If it can't be helped."

"Hm." She spent some time with it. "Why *should* you have to pay for anything?"

"Correct."

"Some things are yours—you, the thief; and some things are theirs—them, the owner. Meanwhile, some things don't belong to them at all—the stealee's—even if they think they do; and some things belong to you, the stealer, even though you know they don't."

Her paraphrasing was, in fact, a concise version of his philosophy. It had taken him reams of nights over the goose quill to articulate the finer details.

"Ah, yes," Issey replied, "I know what I want... and I want what I know."

"Do you still smoke?" she asked.

Issey pulled two cigarettes from his interior pocket, and handed one to her across the marble counter. He lit it for her.

She took a long drag. "Bring out the pack, Issey."

She took another long drag. From a cupboard, she brought out a clay ashtray.

"Madison made this."

"Who?"

"My kid. Your niece."

Issey nodded. Anissa tapped her cigarette, and asked, "Any thoughts on what to do with this Rohel situation?"

"I've never liked the way he does his hair. It makes him look like a dweeb. And he's got a real bad habit of wearing brown shoes."

"I'm not talking about his shoes, Issey."

"Hm. He seems to be into guitar lately. At his age?"

"That's not what I'm talking about."

"Oh, I know. It's all his mother marrying and moving away again. You'd think he'd be used to it by now."

"What is wrong with your family?" She smooshed the cigarette in the clay ashtray. "You have no clue, do you?"

"Well, Anissa, this is my itinerant season. There's a lot of coming and going."

"There's no arguing that. Look," and in mid-thought, she left the room, and zipped upstairs.

Issey was left alone in the kitchen. Their coffee grinder was expensive. The tea kettle was old world modern copper. The demitasse set was heavy, gothic, and also pricey. This would be a good day's worth of work.

Anissa returned with a magazine and handed it to Issey. It was called *Gentlemen's Gentleman Magazine*.

"You'll see it."

He flipped through articles:

"Cornice or Valance: The Debate Settled!"

"Undress Him with Your Eyes. And Hands."

"The Best Beaches: The Biggest Rods!!!"

"Just the Tip: An Exploration into Gratuities"

"20 Modern Architectural Follies: Who, Why, and How, Bitch!"

And it was this article that introduced Issey to Anissa's present-day concern. Ranked number seven in the list of "follies" was the firm of Yorke Program Architects and their Middleton College Arts and Letters Tower.

The Yorke Program Architects let a lot of people down. Two hundred, in fact... In addition to his employees' comprehensive lack of faith under this arch prince of incompetence, Yorke's firm was also behind the times, using derelict computers and hack-ready software. It was an overstock junkhouse of not only architectural relics—parallel bars and rusted protractors—but of horseplay exemplifying misplaced confidence: T-squares cracked on drafting tables like a hatchet, three-sided rulers thrown as ninja stars, and, according to one former employee, a maulstick that destroyed food left in the fridge after Friday. When the Middleton College Arts and Letters Tower was nearing completion, Yorke was overheard saying, "I'm gonna make the Cathedral of Learning look like the Cathedral of Crap." Instead, it collapsed and everybody died, bitch.

"Everybody?"

She nodded and untied her apron.

"And Yorke put it all on Rohel. He was the easy face, the easy target."

After filling him in, she took the cutting board from the counter and dumped it in the sink. It made a too-loud thud and it rocked the kitchen space.

She finally said, "Rohel is an architect. It's all he's ever wanted to be."

"Is that true?"

"Well, not so much building or drafting. But he's good with clients and everyone says he looks good on a website."

"He *is* handsome. We both have the handsome gene."

"Don't make jokes," Anissa said. "Do you have any ideas?"

She gave Issey a look that asked him to share in her dilemma, her stupidity, her faith—a classic case of living between the absurdities.

"Maybe you can put it in one of your stories?"

"No. And I'm not that kind of writer."

They sat in silence for a while. Two cigarettes were burned through. The shadows moved to different corners of the house. Anissa wasn't a great smoker. She smoked through her mouth. Had probably last smoked in her twenties, at some druggy bonfire party in St. Albans.

Suddenly, Anissa was speaking. "And then the lawsuits. Everyone took him to court. Versus Minters Engineers, sued by both the structural engineer and the geotechnical engineer department. Versus Handles Contractors. Versus Middleton College. And not to feel left out, the City of Middleton got in there. They beat him up. We had to sell the house. We moved."

Issey was surprised. "You lived in Middleton?"

"You visited us." She put her hand on her hip. "I was pregnant. There was a massive brunch. It was the gender reveal. Don't you remember?"

"Hm." Issey said. "I remember *me.*"

"Whatever," she sighed. "What are you gonna do about Rohel? I'm out of ideas here."

Issey jingled his car keys. "I'll see what I can do," he said, also in a jingle. He had some plans in mind, with outfits to go with it. It was more outfits than plans, but when Issey said, "Ta!," Anissa's beak of a smile seemed hopeful. Then again, he wasn't a mind reader.

When he got back in his mother's car, it smelled cheap and the keys were drunk in the ignition. He rolled down the windows. The neighborhood's ritzy air freshened the smell of coffee and scratch-off tickets. Issey stared at Rohel's house. What went on in there? Issey pushed past the Roman shade, whooshed up the stairs, saw that there was nothing cinematic happening in the bedroom, and slid downstairs to Rohel's babe cave where he went to sit and count the hairs on his arm. Drafting board and guitar and boxes of junk from his former firm. Rohel, handsome, princely, jobless, feelings unknown, compliment deficient.

Issey turned the key in the ignition. The car made a sound a car makes when it doesn't want to be a car anymore.

So he stole Anissa's car.

CHAPTER SIX

"They said that Nixon was talking to the paintings," Rohel said. "Talking to the paintings of the former presidents. Well, no one's talking to the paintings anymore because the art is shit."

Brothers Issey and Rohel stood in the tack room of Avi's boarding stable and horse farm. The room was thick with leather. Saddles, stirrups, reins, halters, bridles, and straps hung on racks and hooks. Nearby, Madison and a stable hand—one of Avi's many, *many* grown children— refilled water buckets and spread hay in her horse's stall. Meanwhile, Rohel walked through the events of that calm, mid-semester morning when his firm's tower went down. It just collapsed right into the ground like it had been built with popsicle sticks. Collapsed like it had been designed by popsicle people. Rohel's reconstruction of what he knew was spare. The tower had been up and functional for most of the summer, when the building had its ceremonial unveiling. As far as Yorke Program Architects knew, the tower was doing its job during the fall semester, people going up, people going down, professors doing lectures, students doing notes or whatever. Most of what happened was guesswork, which eventually funneled its way into court.

"So, Anissa told you? Yeah, they all took a little piece. Yorke, Handles, Minters, the college, the city—they really let me have it. We moved.

Probably the only good thing that came out of it was being close to Mom before she married Allan and Madison getting to know her grandmother."

Issey wasn't listening. He had been pricing the many horse supplies in Avi's tack room. The leather for the various saddles was heavy, chestnut, black. There was triple stitching on the halters. The stirrups had smoky oak finishes. The saddle blankets came straight from South Texas. Another good day's worth of work right here.

Madison joined them. She came in on riding pants that were baggy and ridiculous on her stringy child's legs. "Uncle Issey!" She rushed to him and squeezed his broadsides. He patted her head.

"Do you ride horses, Uncle Issey? Do you want to see my horse?"

Issey pulled her off of him.

"Shh!" Issey said.

Behind her was the stable hand and a much older horse person, a chisel-faced humbug in a parka that Issey recognized as Avi.

"So you're visiting Bell River, Issey?"

"It's my itinerant season, sure."

The old man leaned in and whispered with a dirty smile. "I know it was you that used to steal my mail when you were a child."

"Hm," Issey put finger to his lips. "You must be thinking of someone else. Maybe it was Rohel?"

Avi laughed at the idea. Avi laughed at Rohel, laughed at Madison, laughed in the direction of her horse that looked toylike in its stall. "Your brother was never so reckless." Avi's teeth were brown and they moved like old corn when he spoke. Eventually, everyone said So Long, in the solemn Vermont way. Issey could feel Avi's eyes following them. He was a cretin.

At the dirt parking lot, Rohel's jaw tensed when he saw, parked next to his Mercedes, Anissa's car.

"Why is Anissa's car here?"

"I borrowed it."

"Does she know you borrowed it?"

Issey shrugged. "That's not really my problem, Rohel."

"She doesn't like people screwing around with her car. Dangit, Issey. Just follow me."

Unlike most cars, Anissa's was smooth and confident, and it did most of the driving for him. His eyes were off the road. His hands were off the steering wheel. There was no cell phone reception here. He held up the phone, reached left and right to the passenger side. No Signal.

No Rohel either. He was one of those fast drivers who had to make everything a race. Maybe if he hadn't raced through building that tower...

Issey took a detour, approaching the church with the slanted steeple and gliding into the slushy parking lot of the General Store.

He parked, got out, and dialed the familiar number from the outside pay phone.

"There's been a delay on the take, Berger." On the other end, Issey heard industrial noise in the background. "I'm within an ace of exacting some rather delicious family revenge."

"Doesn't mean much to me. Or for your situation. The clock is ticking."

"Is it? I thought... perhaps we were open-ended."

"Life moves on." The wind picked up and Issey shivered. "You better come up with something. Remember—something *real*."

Before Berger ended the call, Issey overheard a voice he didn't know, asking, "Who was that?"

Berger replied, "Nobody. Just some scrub."

Issey walked back to Anissa's car. The chilly reception from Berger was likely due to the distractions in the background and the high stakes of the Faneuil Hall affair. He wondered if the job could be a success without his expert lockpicking. Still, being called "just some scrub" bummed him out.

"So there's my car," said Anissa, who was standing outside. "I figured as much."

She had changed out of her housecoat and was wearing a turquoise sweater patterned with a zippy chevron print. Tight jeans showed off athletic legs and fattish cakes behind them.

"Ah, well, Anissa. Simple family lending, and I chose not to tell you. Anyhow, here is your car."

He handed her the keys.

"Just as well. You left your mother's car here. So I had it impounded."

"Why would you do that?"

"Because you stole my car, featherbrain. I had to call the Sweigarts next door for a ride and I hate the Sweigarts."

"The Sweigarts? I remember them."

"You don't. They're new. The wife's an engineer. Husband's a stay-at-home creep. I've seen him in there, watching me. I know what he's up to." Anissa mimed the universal language of jacking off (with some going in her face?). "You're lucky it was the wife who picked up the phone otherwise I would have had to deal with him and you would have had to deal with *me*."

Issey was on the verge of reminding Anissa that *she* was also a stay-at-home creep and that if she hadn't been spying on the husband, she might not know whether he was spying her. Instead, he saw himself into Rohel's babe cave.

Which was depressing. Rohel was talking in an uninterrupted string of sentences as if Issey had been sitting in there all this time. "Shoot," Rohel continued, "sometimes I think the Atlantic Ocean had it out for me. It's not a conspiracy thing, but I believe the Tower had been a telluric event."

"Telluric..."

"It's not as crazy as it sounds—I think the disaster was the ocean's fault: The soil wasn't stable; the concrete never cured right; the reinforcing bars never stood a chance; the nanotechnology used today is not the nanotechnology used then. And I told Yorke all of this. They just looked at me like I was nuts. It's the same look I get when I'm trying to find work. All interview questions are really the same question, you know what I mean?"

Issey didn't. He wasn't really listening anyway. Instead, he was following Rohel's eyes. They were fixed on those sun-stained boxes in the corner.

"What's in those boxes, Rohel?"

"Nothing. Never mind. Just some of the last of it. Let it go."

Rohel was still a handsome guy—for a guy with a kid, for a guy in his forties. If they weren't brothers, Issey would have probably had better perspective on those compassionate eyes, athletic shoulders, and listener's lips.

Issey drove away in Rohel's car. He was stealing a lot of cars from this family.

The views on the drive were familiar. Friendly houses had wreathes on the doors for the holidays. There were candles in bay windows. He passed the church with the slanted steeple. In the distance was Avi's horse farm. Some light stealing wasn't out of the question.

Three or four hours later, in his mother's house, Issey unloaded all the new items from the trunk, backseat, and passenger side of Rohel's car. It had been a thrilling, successful night—maybe one of Issey's best. Lots of skis and snowboards and machinery from well-appointed mudrooms.

Issey ran the kitchen faucet and brought cold water to his face. Like the previous night, he took his cigarette and his thoughts outside. But tonight's Bell River solitude was different. Not only was the valley warmer, but it also seemed hollow. It was like Rohel was plunging in it, and the further down he fell, the more intense were the blank spaces where friends were supposed to be. Help, the valley said. Help. What was the point of being so handsome when you didn't have any friends? Yuck. Issey mashed out the cigarette. He'd have to return Rohel's car like it went nowhere and then he'd have to walk back to his mother's home. But it was the process, and it was another night when the black suitcase from the luggage carousel would have to wait.

CHAPTER SEVEN

If Issey felt sorry for his brother last night, then he felt sorrier for himself the next day when he found out the hard way what trains offered. There was no dazzling cloche, no lacquered teacart, no *chef de train,* no sliding door. Just rows of sick people with their smelly bags, just rows of smelly seats that were stiff during the bumpy southern trip. And, Middleton, even during these late autumn days, was also sick. Middleton didn't feel like the holiday season. It was a town that was wrecked, and it was easy to see why. What was once the Arts and Letters Tower was now a Chinese buffet, surrounded by a parking lot of forty spaces—or roughly five dead people for each parking space. The Chinese buffet looked like it had already gone out of business.

After midnight, when the night shift was on the wane, Issey double-doored his way into a motel—a cottage-styled dump—and set to outfitting himself in the love: Sheridan scarf, vealskin gloves, thieving bag (still a little lobstery), ankle boots, and a new addition to the ensemble in the form of a balaclava. Outside, he sniffed the wet, neezy air for the blooming nightfall, avoided looking at the list, concentrated instead on the poetry of entering. But for all the mental tricks he tried, the air was too humid and the endgame too oppressive. Twenty minutes in and he was sweating all over.

The theft was comprehensive but rough. Stealing from Handles Contractors was easy. Stealing from Minters Engineers was easy. Stealing from the City of Middleton was easy. But stealing from Yorke Program Architects was a mess. The setup depressed him. Sad architects worked here. Their desks were nameless, their food in the fridge fearful. Yorke's office was arrogant and Issey destroyed it well enough, but little bunnies of revolt told him that something had already been stolen from the people who drifted through these spaces. By the end of the night, Issey had a sack filled with hard drives, flash drives, jump drives, papers that looked important, and all the wires to all the computers.

Back at the cottage, his clothes were drenched. In the kitchen dinette, he wrung out the balaclava like a dishrag and poured a pitcher of his night moves from his ankle boots. Little bunnies of revolt. As far as destruction went, the job was a success. He had damaged these businesses—just as they had damaged his brother. But he didn't understand why it felt so meaningless. A lot of sweat down the drain. He wondered what that little Rhonda was doing right now, safe up all the way in Bell River. There was her diary with the dervish clasp to look forward to—and maybe even some kind of romance in the sleigh-bells-are-ringing variety.

The next morning, Issey awoke to a cottage dominated by a new problem. It was his ankle boots. They reeked. Sweat must have ruined them. And his veal gloves had shrunk to the size of baby gloves. Even his nailhead Sheridan scarf—its personality had deteriorated, was shriveled and stiff. They were no longer his.

No longer his.

A criminal develops his voice by adapting his early inspirations (stealing mail from Old Man Brill, becoming familiar with the uses of official letterheads) to the various techniques of the masters before him— the Albert Spaggiaris of the plundering world—until one day a large-scale concept unifies itself to a theme, such as Spaggiari's Without Hate, Without Arms, Without Violence signature.

He stared at his stuff. His broken and sour stuff. What Issey's earlier philosophy had in execution it lacked in unity. It's like what Anissa was telling him when she was telling him about his own philosophy. "Some things are theirs and some things don't belong to them at all." And these things didn't belong to him. And now unity was developing. Life is exciting! When he shut his eyes, Rohel's sad generous face came into focus, staring at those boxes from Yorke Program Architects. Issey had stolen and destroyed in the wrong direction. It happens.

Sitting on the motel bed, he opened a phone book and set a pad in his lap. Issey made calls to contacts that specialized in death antiquities and morbid curiosities. Their enthusiasm towards his proposition was disturbing.

And now Issey's once precious items—the Sheridan scarf, ankle boots, veal gloves—they were no longer his. They no longer belonged to him. This new relationship put the mince back in his step. The motel was in the off season, and he received off-season service. He skipped the breakfast that wasn't offered, stepped over the newspaper missing outside his door, and fixed the bed, which vanished into the wall, just as he too would vanish from Middleton.

CHAPTER EIGHT

There were two sisters who worked at the Bell River Valley General Store. Pru and Tanya. They all had gone to school together. Pru was maybe three years older and the kind of person to never let you forget it. Tanya had been in a grade below. She was a grade below kind of person, whatever that meant. Because their father owned the General Store and they worked the register after school and the mornings before school and every Saturday and every Sunday, Pru and Tanya had a childhood separate from their classmates. But transitioning into adulthood, they had become essential material in Bell River Valley. The General Store was its own kind of mountain face looming, and the years behind the father's counter, years changing out the coffee pots, wiping down tables, monitoring the community bulletin board, and taking inventory, were expressed like lines cut across the benchland: there was deep knowledge carved in the eyes. The two must have known everyone, must have seen everyone, held, heard, or ignored all the conversations that folded into the valley. And Issey was one of these conversations.

Tanya was the nice one. Pru was the ugly one, the wooly-bully one. Long winters had made her skin pink. She smelled like soup from a thermos.

"Look who it is," Pru roared. "It's Mister City—Mister Boston."

"Philadelphia, darling. Mister Philadelphia is what they call me when I'm in Boston."

"And you're back?"

"Just clearing out my mother's home which I'm temporarily using as a *pied-à-terre*."

"That's not how you pronounce it," Pru jeered. "We used to love it when you'd steal from my father's store."

"You must be thinking of someone else."

"It's not like anything you stole made a difference, but it'd always get him cheesed off. All he had was this dumpy store."

"Who owns it now?"

"I do. Well, me and Tanya."

"Rough."

"I had a feeling you were back in town," Pru laughed. She had a mean laugh, and her stocky, hard body was confrontational.

"How's that?"

"The Exit-9 newspaper called it a *'slew of break-ins.'* A slew sounds like you."

Issey leaned in. "I will admit to one thing, between just us gals and the lottery tickets."

"Hm?"

He said, "When I was a child, I used to steal Old Man Brill's newspapers."

"Okay. Sure. His newspaper."

"Newspaper*s*," he emphasized, having stolen Old Man Brill's newspapers zero times. Only his mail.

Sometimes when he was a boy he'd come into The General Store with Old Man Brill's mail, letters and bills still frosty from the mailbox, and indulge in whatever new treat Pru and Tanya's father had imported from all over the world. Plantain chips and *Ritter Sport* and wasabi crunchies all exported into his sleeves and tote bag. Sometimes Eight Jeff was with him. No. Not sometimes. All the times. Eight Jeff was with him *all the time.*

Issey had one friend growing up and his name was Eight Jeff. Issey didn't like Eight Jeff, yet Issey was Eight Jeff's only friend. This had caused problems.

And this caused problems today because for Issey's scheme to work— getting in Berger's good books, getting Rohel's life assembled in some kind of order—he needed the bunchy little dolt.

Out of all combinations of human traits, Eight Jeff's was the worst. He was big-boned, thin-skinned, and soft-hearted.

"You ever notice," Eight Jeff said to Issey one day in the Bell River Valley Library, when they were around eleven, "that people read books but they only *look* at poetry?"

Issey put a pencil to his lips.

"You got some kind of nut in your tooth or what?" Eight Jeff fidgeted. They were sitting in the adult's silent corner with the adult's armless chairs, and Issey didn't want Eight Jeff sending them back to the sticky plastic chairs in the children's room.

The library had become a headquarters for young, curious Issey who spied on the patrons and the books they checked out, the books they returned. This information unbreasted individual tastes, the insides of homes, habits and hobbies, spending ceilings and money floors—and how one day he might get inside the homes of the people who checked out these types of books. Issey took notes in a spiral-bound notebook that was supposed to be for his Health Science class.

But then there was Eight Jeff rumping it up.

"Do you have a favorite element? Because I don't. What's barium? Is that real? Do you think we'll ever use our wieners?"

There was a lot of personality under Eight Jeff's rangy blond face and soapy open mouth. He tagged around Issey and had troubles with his shoelaces. Issey never wanted to hurt the boy's feelings. But he most certainly did not want to be his friend. He wanted someone else to be Eight Jeff's friend. But no one wanted to be Eight Jeff's friend. This was a problem. He had nothing to offer. He sat on the ground like a dogboy and did the knot and the bunny ears and the song that went with it. Issey stared at the dome of the boy's hair, with the hard part down the soft middle, and wondered what was floating inside it. There was a little bit of a mess embroidered in everything in Eight Jeff did.

"Your brother still goes out with that Heidi Bender?" Eight Jeff asked, trailing behind Issey who was on a trail of his own. Issey shrugged or nodded.

With his Health Sciences notebook filled with addresses, Issey discovered that the library books fit the pedigree of their temporary owners. The grown-ups who checked out books on photography lived in the nicer part of town, which was more secluded, took a full day's trek, and could be called a "hamlet." They had money and more windows to look out and take command of the rest of the world. He wanted inside these homes. Meanwhile, the grown-ups who checked out true-life mysteries occupied bottlecap patches of land in the sadder part of town, with fewer windows to shut out the world and one hundred percent more children. He wanted inside these homes too.

For misdirection, Issey carried a sled that he had no intention of using. If no one suspects tote boy, then no one *ever* suspects sled boy.

"When can we use your sled?"

Issey shook his head. "Never."

"How'd your nerdy brother get a babe like Heidi Bender anyway?"

Issey had been giving Eight Jeff the ragged ends of his day, hardly listening. Hardly talking. Hardly checking behind for the boy who hadn't been behind him for who knows how long. Days, maybe even weeks.

Christmas came and went, and eleven-year-old Issey, who was now strangely twelve, was finally a solo operation. The snow reflected Issey's glad tidings, and on the chilly mornings when the sun swept out over the mountains, it held his hand, warmed his snowsuit, and championed his thick little legs into further depths of this pickled valley town. Even when the sun was setting, casting darkened paths for losers, a glow remained on Issey's skin, piping the heart of a boy who was learning how to win. Coming home, his were cheeks blue and pink as if in a dream of silky fal-la-las. His brother Rohel was behind a closed bedroom door. Study-monger, scholarship hound. Their mother's door was open and the room empty. She was always working at the Fiddlehead Inn or getting married. The house was usually a little warm with the smell of curlers and hair spray and ironing board. Alone was Issey's happiest time.

There followed a hiatus of two weeks, during which Issey, his prop sled slicing on snowy ground, had scouted the first house he would enter. This was it. These were the people, a snobby couple who didn't have children. His notebook was filled with their habits, schedules, and books they checked out: *The Connoisseur's Guide to Fondue Parties; The Connoisseur's Guide to Dessert Wines; The Connoisseur's Guide to Murder Mystery Dinner Parties; The Connoisseur's Guide to Sun-Dried Tomatoes.* It was a house with dormer windows. Issey didn't know these were called dormer windows, but he knew he wanted to get inside a house with windows like these. What things they must have!

The day was ready for the taking, and Issey was camouflaged in a husky-sized snowsuit. He had seen the woman and the man leave the house. They left in separate cars at the same time. He shifted his hand-binoculars to the neighbor, who was taking an appallingly long time to go to work. Issey was getting cold. Finally, the neighbor opened his front door, slammed it, wrenched open the car door, and also left. His engine roared with anger and his all-weather tires spun snow and shist in the air. Soon, the only sound was Issey's breathing, and he drew a mountain-sized breath, a real twelve-year-old's huff. Winter-gray light piped life into an overcast, milky morning. He began his descent. His nose was pink. The house loomed bigger and creamier than any house he had ever seen. And suddenly in front of Issey, a frosty sun showed the boy's head, his hair newly cut *en brosse*, and then the loud rest of Eight Jeff rounded up, walking with the legs of someone important. He also had a sled.

"Hey, buddy! Didja miss me?"

Issey squinted his eyes.

"Yeah, I was real sick."

Issey dropped his sled.

"I got a lot of cool crap for Christmas. I got a sled. We can sled now."

Issey hated him.

"Hey, you ever break a bone? Because the only thing I ever broke was the mold." Eight Jeff took off his glove. Where there were once five fingers now there were only four.

"How did that happen?"

"Oh, you know."

Issey didn't know and he didn't want to know. Besides, it was the boring finger on the boring hand.

"Now that I got my war wound, what do you think my chances are with Heidi Bender? Maybe she'd wanna go out with a younger guy?"

"You?"

"Why not? I may not have all of my fingers, but I do have all of my wiener."

At that moment, the neighbor returned home. Then the woman returned home. So much for a good time. Eight Jeff had his mouth open the entire day and chewed through all of the words.

A year or so passed and Eight Jeff never took the hint. Of course, Issey never gave it to him, wearing the mask of his own dumb smile. Eight Jeff's perspective must have been that he had found a friend for life. Issey smiled his way through permission slips, field days, middle school, changing voices. He was only ever away from Eight Jeff at night and at night was when he finally entered his first house, which brought all kinds of surprises. He was in there anywhere between four hours and four seconds. He was hot. He was cold. He was smooth. He fell. He was dizzy. He was organized. He stole with fury. He stole with calm. He came out with a garlic press. He left his gloves inside. He didn't know what a garlic press was.

Whatever he did, he was absolutely buzzing—a new world had opened up—and the only thing that made sense was that he had to do it again. The biggest threat wasn't the people or the police. He was a kid with a sled! A kid with a tote bag! No, the biggest threat to entering people's homes, sorting through their things, and removing some of those things from their homes was the kid with the nine fingers and the no friends. He was dumb, loud, and fragile. Issey had to ice him out. And if you want to get rid of pest, you give 'em something to do.

Ten, fifteen, twenty years later—where does the time go? And Issey had parked at Fiddlehead Inn. There were five cars in the parking lot. The hotel had twelve rooms. Two of the cars probably belonged to night staff. Two other cars had out-of-state plates, one from Maine and one from Oklahoma. And the fifth one was Anissa's, but this was just the car he had been stealing all week.

Quartz spotlights were hooked into the garden path leading to the rickety porch. The two Adirondack chairs he knew as a kid occupied their same spot. Someone had given them a splash of paint, probably.

The place had been reliable in his memory as a rundown dump that stayed in business on New England charm alone, but what was the difference?

And he'd seen the staff come and go. The night boys, pillow boys, luggage boys, maintenance boys, key boys, manager boys—though manning the desk as Issey entered the lobby no boy was to be found.

The mistletoe mornings, hot cider burning, dusty cinnamon sticks on the plate, the wet rug in the lobby and moldy bear's head on the landing, their mother coming home smelling like Christmas and cleaning solution—Fiddlehead Inn was something like glassy sentiment but it was mostly like shit.

Behind the front desk and through the unlocked door of the manager boy's office, Issey went to work and found the same setup as when his mother called the place work and, sometimes, home.

He scored ten sheets of paper and five envelopes from the third drawer of the filing cabinet. Light from a banker's lamp showed that each was printed with the hotel's ridiculous rustic letterhead.

He folded the paper into the envelopes and tucked these into his jacket pocket. With his penknife, he then peeled open outgoing mail hoping to secure the manager's signature. Letterheads and signatures—these were essential accessories for any scheme. They were also less heavy than a thermal lance and more fashionable than a grappling hook—which he always worried made his ass look fat.

He found three letters containing the managerial signature. He threw away the rest. He found the drawer where they always kept the gift certificates. Job complete: Envelopes, stationery, manager's signature, and gift certificates. As has been said, there's more cheating behind the counter than in front of it.

Issey treated himself to a tour up the rustic staircase.

The chair railings, the scalloped runners on the second floor's sofa table, the series of fisher-cat fur pelts on the third floor, the pictures that depicted the hotel's 1977 reconstruction and renovation, the portrait of President Chester A. Arthur hanging beside the mothy Chester A. Arthur suite—gone. Modern aesthetics shaped the hotel's new vision. Lots of straight lines: silver door handles in the European mode, ski resort art in smoky silver frames, and a charcoal rendering of athletic President Calvin Coolidge replacing pork-chop Chester. Only the crisp bark of last night's burning logs from the foyer's fireplace called forth some autumnal memory of Issey's teenage no-goodery: with his tote bag, he'd say hello to his mother, and from her housekeeper's office she'd drop some soaps or shampoos into his bag.

Ah, the little soaps and the little shampoos. The little sewing kits and the little dinners, the little cloche on top of the little dinners and their regular-sized utensils. The towels, the irons, the hangers, TV remotes, pens, Bibles, menus, pillowcases, robes, hair dryers, stationery scraps, toilet paper, wastepaper basket trash linings—all of these things belonged to

Fiddlehead's. Issey was strangely protective of the place and never stole here. Not really.

The second-floor air was heavy with carpet and water running from under the ice machine. In front of him, on hands and knees, the night boy was sopping up water, ice, and piss. Issey kept his distance at end of the landing. The night boy, with his soggy rump in the air, was too old to be doing this. He had the broad rotisserie shoulders of a basement bench-presser—but that was it. The rest of him was in a shambles. He had pale thinning hair, a permanent yawn-chin, wifely thighs, and pronounced love handles.

"Eight Jeff," Issey didn't bother whispering, because Eight Jeff rounded up first. He threw down the towel and peppered Issey with hugs and hallelujahs.

CHAPTER NINE

Entering his babe cave for craft beer and solo guitar, Rohel discovers on the center of his drafting table an official Fiddlehead Inn envelope. He examines the room, wonders how it got there, turns, locks the door behind him, and then tears open the envelope like the animal that he is, with his fingers and mouth. He finds the gift certificate and note on official Fiddlehead Inn stationery. He reads:

My darling—

Tomorrow night. 7 in the P., join me for the evening. You are my book of poetry within your bosom. The idiot with nine fingers at the front desk will give you my room where I shall be twinkling and—

Yours,
A

Next is Anissa who wakes up late for a human but early for a writer. Husband has whisked daughter to school or military academy or whatever. In the kitchen, next to the French press, Anissa finds her Fiddlehead Inn letter and gift certificate. She closes the letter between her fingerlike fingers, smells the *eau de toilette* paramour-spritz on the paper, and laughs in a nasty state of ecstasy as if she's sharing a humid joke with her admirer. She reads:

My darling—

Where are all the men in a young woman's life whom she can trust in her bosom? There is only one in the world, and he would be honored if you were to join him tonight, at Fiddlehead Inn, 7pm. At the front desk, ask for the room number of a Mister R, and the useless idiot with nine fingers will give you the key. The champagne is chilled. The rose petals are plucked.

I count the minutes until we are together. Until then, I will be undressing you with my mind, hands, and penis.

With deep respect and affection,
R.S.

Here was Issey's plan, conceived and executed absolutely audience-proof. Neither Rohel nor Anissa would break the spell to the other that (s)he had received a mysterious note telling (s)him to meet (h)her at Fiddlehead's. This is renewal after all, this is operatic gestures. Anissa would lie: "I have my book club tonight." Rohel would lie: "I have my sap bucket collecting." "Maple farming in November?" "I'm seasoning the buckets. Say—what book did you read for your club?" "Um... *The Menstrual Murder Mystery Ladies Detective Agency*...?" "Sounds fun," once. "Sounds fun," twice.

Phew, the both of them think, swiping their shack-job foreheads. Phew! Then they zip off for outfits, silks, tethers, serums, and creams. The husband, with water-gelled hairdo, arrives at Fiddlehead's at 7, gift certificates in hand; the wife, all billboard skin and legs, enters Fiddlehead's at 7, gift certificate in hand. And the two of them, old dumb doves they are, are ensnared in that old coy hummer, "My Love, What Are You Doing Here?"

The day was already wet with love and destruction; the air was creamy, too cold for snow. Issey wondered if that was true—"too cold for snow." These thoughtful inner clichés joined him on the porch, where he smoked, happy to play the role of destiny-monger, holding Rohel and Anissa's in the palm of his throat.

Just then, Anissa pulled up. The kid was in the backseat. She was stretching her arms at him and must have been done with school or boot camp or whatever.

"Your brother's always been a romantic." Anissa was contemporary, dishy, rendezvous-ridden. She showed Issey the note on the Fiddlehead Inn stationery. "He's got this, like, *date* for us."

"I see," Issey nodded.

She rolled her eyes while being completely smitten. "He's so stupid and so sweet, you know? He's like a boy. He sprayed the letter with the kind of cologne that makes you want to throw up."

"It's not all that bad."

"It's dreadful," Anissa said and then added, "And how about this weird coincidence: Rohel's old architecture firm, YPA—I heard from an old Middleton pal that their offices were completely wrecked."

"Wrecked?"

"Yeah—they said it was like a wrecking crew tore through the place. Local news stuff."

"Hm," Issey whistled. "A wrecking crew, huh? Like a whole a team?"

But Anissa was onto other things. "And you'll watch Madison tomorrow while we're away."

"Watch Madison?" Issey spat. "Anissa, I have plans."

"You're lying. Now, listen, I've made a list of all the foods she can't eat, foods she won't eat, and foods she's probably allergic to."

The little girl reached out from her booster seat and yelled: "Uncle Issey! I love Uncle Issey!"

"See? Everyone loves Uncle Issey. I'll pick you up at six and you can drive me to the hotel and I will *lend* you the car." Anissa returned to her car. The car heater barked. "But, Issey, if you plan on stealing cars for a living, put the driver's seat back in its original position. God, you really *are* no good at this."

CHAPTER TEN

But he *was* good at it. A little lousy, but good at it. He was so good at it, in fact, that the questions that came later, after the night with Madison, the chain of events, the logic behind it, the cars he borrowed (three), the time he spent in Rohel's babe cave, the profound nakedness of the space, the streak of light catching from the closed door behind him, the kid meanwhile looking for a toy, and Issey sneaking through Rohel's desk drawers, bureau, drafting table, and boxes at the casement windows—all of it would remain in gestures between dream and dust, ceiling and floorboard. But this was where it was at. Those boxes from Yorke Program Architects. Stealing is great and all, but family is different. With family, you want to strive for excellence.

"I got the book I want you to read to me."

"Book? I told you to grab a toy. We have places to go," and he scooted her into a car that was not her mother's.

Madison asked, "Is this your car?"

"Yes."

"But this is Mister Sweigart's car. He gave me a ride in it from school the other day."

"If you knew the answer, why'd you ask the question?"

Issey sat in the new car, did some hotwiring, then stopped as a scene unfolded in front of him: a porch light came on and then a handsome-ish neighbor type stepped onto the stage and he just can't believe his eyes.

"That's Mister Sweigart," Madison said and waved from the backseat. "Hi, Mister Sweigart!"

Issey thrust the car in reverse and twisted some complicated gearbos. The car spun forward. From the rearview mirror, the Sweigart dummy stood gaping, like so many other suckers, who just watched their cars driving away from their homes, surely not being stolen, surely. Not. My. Car. Stolen. Surely. For as much fear is sold to the gapeholes, no one ever believes it'll one day be them. They'd rather think the car was taking off on its own, lashing out for a dance partner with other restless sedans.

"Uncle Issey, where are we going?"

"Out. For hot chocolate."

"I love hot chocolate! Uncle Issey, do you have a wife?"

"No."

"Why don't you have a wife? Do you want a wife?"

"Shh." Issey raised his eyebrow in the rearview mirror. "I can't drive and answer your questions at the same time."

The coffee shop next to the post office and bike repair shop was called the Post and Bean. The valley was changing. The years during his absence had been confusing ones. New people arrived from New York and Boston and Philadelphia. They filled the spaces surrounding four-way intersections with coffee shops, beardy microbreweries, and workshop studios. But it was all junk. In the coffee shop, on shelves and running along the hardwood floor were retrofitted Vermont whatnots. Pewter Snowflake Bentley reproductions and spooky scarecrow bookends and ski-pole tong-and-spatula sets and the endless series of empty baskets, mason jars, maple syrup bottles.

Issey chose a table by the window. He checked his watch. The dealer from the death antiquities and morbid curiosities was late. Madison was bored.

"Uncle Issey, I'm going to wash my hands."

"Whatever."

In the parking lot, a flabby maroon hatchback came and went. Otherwise, there was no activity. The Post and Bean coffee boy called out their order of apple pie with melted cheddar on top, this disgusting regional thing that Madison wanted.

"And the hot chocolate?" Issey asked.

The coffee boy was so thin and pale that his skin appeared blue-ish. His reactions were underwater.

"You *wanted* that. I thought you were just humoring her."

"I was humoring her. That's why I got her the hot chocolate."

The boy snapped his fingers *gotcha* and set to making the drink.

When Madison returned, hands pink from overwashing, the hot chocolate was waiting for her at the table. She guzzled it like an animal and then she tore down on her apple pie. Still no new cars.

"Who are you waiting for, Uncle Issey? Is it your wife?"

Issey stood. His chair scraped on the hardwood and echoed in the coffee shop. "I'll be right back."

"Where are you going, Uncle Issey?"

"These questions—are you a cop?"

"No?"

"I need to make a call. Stay here. I'll see you from the window."

She had whipped cream and cheddar cheese on her nose, mouth, chin, cheeks, hands, and clothes.

Outside, reception continued to be hopeless, but the payphone was better anyway. He dialed the contact's number. The guy answered and his voice wasn't pleasant. "I said I'm coming."

Then Issey dialed Berger's number. The phone rang a dozen or so times. Madison waved at him and he stared into the sound of the ringing. During the last phone call, Berger had seemed distracted by an abounding industrial noise in the background. The phone continued ringing. Issey felt abandoned, forgotten. Madison continued waving. And still no one was answering. She came to him outside before he came to her. "You look sad," she said and took his free hand. With the other, Issey replaced the receiver to the hook. The death antiquities and morbid curiosities dealer was suddenly there, and Issey pulled everything from the trunk that he had taken from Rohel's babe cave, and Madison was a surprising set of hands and big girl energy. The dealer's face, thick and clean, was a menace of delight, and he bought all of it, way over Issey's projections and Madison helped some more—she never got tired! It was a lot of stuff to unload and the stars looking down at them were extra radiant.

Flushed with cash, Issey let Madison convince him she could have a creemee for dinner instead of dinner for dinner. They set off for the General Store and drove with the windows down. Cool autumn night filled the car. Madison's hair was blowing, and she watched out of the backseat window as they passed the Misfit Farm, Denton's Art Supply, the Bell River Barn, Icebreakers Café, and the church with the slanted steeple.

At the General Store, Issey nodded at Pru behind the counter. The little girl was putting her fingers on the ice cream display case.

"Rohel's kid," he said.

"I know whose kid it is. I know Rohel. I know his kid. She takes after you."

Madison looked up at Issey. "They don't have creemees."

"They have ice cream. What's the difference?"

"A creemee is a creemee and ice cream is ice cream—*that's* the difference!"

Issey pointed at his watch, shrugged at Pru, and said, "Time to go."

It was a lot of driving that night. They were going back and forth from the valley to stores that stayed open past six. He had to dump off stuff to

Rohel's and switch cars a few more times. The night was settling in. When Issey returned Sweigart's car, the thing was fogged with vapor and ice whiskers. Anissa's car wasn't much better. He turned on the wipers and the leaves collected on the windshield scattered.

"I'm cold, Uncle Issey," Madison whined from the backseat. "I'm hungry. I wanted ice cream," she said.

"You said you wanted a creemee."

"Ice cream—creemee. It's the same thing, Uncle Issey."

"Here. This'll hold you over." From the wrist of his coat, he tossed her a tube of sunflower seeds from the General Store. "I don't suppose you like wasabi peas."

"I *do* like wasabi peas!" the girl lied.

From the same wrist of his coat, there magically appeared a packet of wasabi peas. She tossed a handful in her mouth. Immediately, her cheeks caught on fire, but she held it in like a big little girl liar.

"Maybe you can read to me now?" She pushed the picture book onto the front seat center console.

"I *am* driving, stupid."

When they parked in the furniture store in Burlington, she asked if now was a good time and then asked a few more times when they finally rolled the operation back home.

"No. There's work to do."

Issey tasked the team with bringing Rohel's stinky botch-hole back to life. The walls were first, overrun with witch-grass and scapegoat weather. He opened his palms, cast them at a distance and clapped Huzzah! In an instant, the walls were an exhilarating array of celery, lime, lettuce, kale, canary, buttercup, butterscotch, butter rum, and butter-butter. It had been a pioneering night, and it was still going. Issey told her to make some of those flatbread pizzas he had seen in their freezer.

"You know how to use the stove?"

"No." Madison's clothes were covered in all the paint.

"You're big enough to figure it out."

Venetian blinds replaced Roman shades. There were new pillows and shams for the couch. There were the rabbit fur throws, clamp spotlights, wrought iron bookends, a pastoral tapestry, winter nights candle, Jazz Age playing cards, World's Fair sketchbooks, and two stainless steel growlers for all those beers Rohel seemed to like so much. When Madison eventually burned the flatbread pizzas and set off the fire alarm, Issey lifted her by her armpits to push the ignore button. His back was singing—the work had been heavy for a single night. The little stringbean had been heavy for a single night! Her eyes had tears in them from the smoke coming from the stove. He wiped them with his monogrammed "I" handkerchief. The house reeked of burned farm-to-freezer pizza, but the winter nights candle was a success. Madison blew her nose in the handkerchief and Issey told her to keep it. She hugged his leg. Then Madison was put on vacuum duty. When that was done, Madison was put on window duty. When that was done, Issey told her to put on her jammies and he'd read some of the picture book to her. She whisked off. Sad, eager-to-please Madison, future Hall of Famer in the Dummy League.

The room was coming together. It was nearly midnight. Stuff that no longer belonged here or there or anywhere, just drifting material goods. And the money—the money!

Issey's cell phone buzzed.

The screen read, "UNKNOWN CALLER."

"I've been... getting your calls... not safe."

The voice sounded like it was coming from the other end of world, but Issey knew the voice immediately. Berger. The reception was, of course, unreliable at best, and Issey searched in panic for any area of the house that might get some kind of signal. At any moment, Berger could ice him out again.

"Berger! I can call you from the home phone here."

"Are you listening ... shut up and... We're now short one... And what do...on now?"

Issey replied fast, maybe recklessly fast.

"I did what you said and stole for real. Something real, you said. Something with real consequence."

Issey sped through the list of items—the blueprints, the sketchbooks, Yorke Program Architect contracts, the flash drives, the tools, even the stupid guitar and amplifier.

"Well? How's that for a successful take?"

"What?...some loser architect... you paying attention?"

Issey recreated the deal he made with death antiquities and morbid curiosities dealer, ran down the prices that each item had brokered, low to high for dramatic effect. Madison entered the room. Her jammies were purple and printed with umbrellas.

"Still...dumb. You can fork over the...when you get here."

"You want me?"

"...just told you...flaked out on... slow-witted. You know the type... Faneuil Hall is still a... Get here at two... rolling in at three, three-thirty, while it's still...but we need a fourth... Can you get here? Sooner is ... to later."

Madison carried her *Graham the Mole* picture book under her arm. Her feet were in the kind of socks that made the toes look like dog paws. Her golden hair was dog hair and filthy from the night's work. She pushed out her book. It was twelve-thirty.

Issey was driving again, upwards on Schröder's Gap, which was as unpredictable as his thoughts and also closed for the season. His legs were shaking. It was another car or maybe the same one he had been stealing all night. Dense meadows that had been open when he and Madison were out hours earlier were now terrific walls of black. Fog covered huge patches of road. On his right, trees obscured an Olympian drop-off from the road to the valley floor. The steering wheel floated left and right. If he could get this hump up to 70 or 85 miles per hour, then that would get him in Boston just in time for Faneuil Hall. But these mountain roads weren't making it easy. The car shimmied. The car straightened. The car shimmied again. There was no one else on the road at this time of night—no one this stupid—and the only thing in the distance was black night. The night was so unforgiving, so deeply black, that he wondered if the car was moving at all. In the backseat, Madison smiled in her umbrella jammies. Her cocker spaniel eyes were glazed. She waved at him. Issey groaned. He turned the car around.

"Graham's burrowing hut was visited by a powerful gust of wind. WHOOOSH! His hickory nuts, clover hay, acorns, and berries were turned this way and that. Graham the Mole was very confused. And just like that, his bucket was empty."

Soon, the only sound in Rohel's house was Madison's snoozy toots. It was almost two in the morning. Berger and the *Grüppe* were probably doing one last run-through in their Winter Hill base. Berger, smooth in evening grain, waits for Issey. The other guys are ready to go. Their nightwear is synthetic. Various mechanisms click and snap. They're ready. Madison asleep on her father's sofa, on its new Miami Nights sofa cover. Issey covers her with a blanket. Berger looks at the door. He values dependability. He's one guy short. "Who we waitin' for?" "No one. Just some scrub."

Issey sat at the kitchen table, drummed his fingers for a bit. His thoughts turned to lockpicking, small intricate details done again and again, sometimes taking up entire days—endless days. Lockpicking took patience for wasting time, and even when one of the pickers lined up, there was another to insert and maneuver and balance. Like any art, the endeavor was rarely successful—so it was romanticized and every Johnny Hobby-Hard thinks he can do it.

The first time the lockpicking worked, Issey was just out of high school, which he may or may not have graduated. He was alone in an abandoned industrial site near Barre and he had been at it for hours. The knees of his pants were filthy. His back was singing. Every time one thing worked, something else went wrong. But then something turned in him, like a separation between door and entry, apprentice and artist, earth and Issey. The pins turned slightly within the chamber, but where one lockpicker had interfered with the other an hour ago, Issey could *feel* the right combination moving in the right direction now. He didn't know exactly what he was doing right, but he knew everything he had been doing *wrong*. The mechanism finally turned. The door opened. Any other success he may have blundered as a child and teen into was banana-first kid's stuff. But this was the real deal. It was so thrilling that it made him weak, too exhausted for the entering part of the breaking. He even threw up some. But eventually you get inside. Eventually all the tricks were learned. And in the distance, new problems whose outline he couldn't see were taking on greater character and hunger.

"You've got a lot of nerve, fatso!"

CHAPTER ELEVEN

Walking was a problem. The problem was that he sounded like he was walking. He should have sounded like nothing. Instead, he sounded like he was walking. Untrained squeakers chirped on hardwood, pant legs whooshed in rumpled runner rugs, soles chirped on kitchen tile. When he looked at his watch, he had finished six houses and the night had hardly started. The heather gray gym bag he had stolen was heavy. He was switching between handle and shoulder strap every few rooms. His hands were cramping. His neck hurt. The floors were sticky and walls sodden. The couches were baggy. The kitchens reeked of lentils and brownie mix and rat spray. He had walked into a poor neighborhood.

Outside in the still air, the valley was dialed in for a big storm. Clouds the texture of fish scales had been following him all day. Several hours earlier in the afternoon when he was with Rohel, that fish scale sky was already in full effect. The three pm clouds brightened the valley rather than darken it. Alpenglow reflected streaks of silver and pink off the mountains. The pale mass in the horizon said that a big one was coming. And Rohel was still complaining.

"That was a lot of nerve, fatso!"

They were back at Avi's horse farm, and back at this old conversation. It was another hooky day for Madison. It was another hooky day for

Rohel, though Issey was figuring out that Rohel no longer had any kind of job.

"So you just sold... everything?"

"Everything."

"My blueprints?"

"Sold."

"My notebooks?"

"Sold."

"And my drawings and photos?"

"Gone. Everything. Out with the old—in with the new!"

"The whole room, Issey. Even my Telecaster?"

"That Telecaster was the least of your worries. Or maybe the most. Were you going to become some sequined rocker man?"

"It's a hobby."

"Grow up, Rohel. Look, all of it had to go. Anything connected to the Yorke Program Architects—it was taking you into some dark and lazy places. And now that you've rid yourself of all that YPA failure, you've got a fresh start." Issey smiled. "You can be anything you want to be!"

They were strolling in the farm. Madison waved from atop her horse. The horse trainer, another of Avi's well-built teens, told her to keep both hands as a pair. "Heels down! Roll the thighs in!"

"And you worked out the whole room with the Fiddlehead manager? He was that dweeby friend of yours growing up, right?"

"Of course!" Issey lied.

"And you painted the walls? Why? How late were you up?" He was full of crisscrossed questions. "Madison was in bed before ten, right? She's on a strict sleep schedule."

"Of course!" Issey lied some more.

The choice of Rohel as the scapegoat for the Yorke Program Architects was starting to make sense. He filled out a suit nicely, enviably. He was slender and long, six feet tall soaking wet. And his handsome face didn't put people off. It was a sedate handsomeness. When Rohel smiled at a stranger, which he did often, it made their day better. They might even say,

"A cute guy noticed me today." People enjoyed him. He was a bright moment, a reassuring fragrance.

But this connected itself to the other possible reason Rohel was the perfect face for the collapse of the Middleton College Arts and Letters Tower: maybe Rohel wasn't all that smart. Sure, he had he studied a lot, had bought all the right books and graph paper, but Issey wondered if Rohel was just *looking* at the books he was supposed to be understanding. His eyes were more compassionate than smart. Issey worried. Was it just a box up there where brains were supposed to go?

Or maybe he had just lost his mind. It was the trend these days. Anissa had lost her mind. Well. At least she lost her earrings and necklace and the bracelets. A lot of the stuff she had been wearing when she went to meet Rohel for their Fiddlehead Inn rendezvous did not return with her when she and the husband returned home the next morning, all blushing and moon candy. Her hair was blown out and it was also matted. The gap in her front teeth had gotten gappier. Anissa and her runway cheekbones; Rohel with his leading man body—Issey saw them for what they were. *Sphinxes without riddles.*

And maybe Issey had also lost his mind a little? What was the line of thinking—get Rohel and Anissa out of the house, clean the place blind, score big with the lead architect responsible for the collapse of a college building, get in Berger's good books, return to a life of soaring success and bespoke tailoring? Maybe Issey wasn't very good at this? Maybe it was the maple syrup. Maybe it was the oncoming snowstorm. Maybe it was the poor neighborhood, the lentils, the rat spray. Maybe it was the sound of his walking and coming up short. Maybe it was all the leather in Avi's tack room. Maybe it was the idea to steal all the leather in Avi's tack room.

It wasn't a bad idea. It was a horrible idea. But it wasn't a *bad* idea either. Sometimes they're just hiding in plain sight.

CHAPTER TWELVE

When Issey closed the door behind him, the condo wept, as it should. All condos should cry a little after midnight.

The snowstorm had come and gone, and it left the valley in a sheet of white. The snowstorm had been to Issey's benefit. That night at Avi's horse farm, it had covered his activity completely. Issey had so thoroughly deboned the horse man's tack room and potting shed and a little of the main house that Rohel's car was bellyaching the entire way back home. Cars are always a hassle. They're a big mouth and fat chassis. It's why he did most of his work on foot. And that car might have been Issey's only mistake. Because he knew he'd be taking the lot from Avi's farm, he had parked Rohel's car maybe a little too close to the entrance gate of the horse farm. As he had approached, Issey thought he'd seen a surveillance camera hidden in the woods—or was it just the woods? It was too dark to do the math.

In the following days, Issey offloaded most of the leather goods in Lebanon and Manchester, and he was back in business, doing light work in condos and some of the newer developments. If only Berger could have been there!

And tonight he was feeling good, maybe a little hot. The Bell River air was as blistering and pure as his night's good steal. However hot he was, he was also shivering, and a pre-dawn line of baking took him to the General Store.

Baking?

But when he saw the baker, it made sense.

There was Pru and there was Tanya, the other sister from the grade below. He remembered Tanya's ponderous straw hair, her wet crackerjack nose, her spring semester battle with head lice. She never seemed contagious, though, because when she wasn't itching her head, face, hair, legs, and the shadowy areas under her sweatshirts, she was winning with her deranged smile. Everyone liked Tanya.

And here she was years later, the same bright gal, arranging the General Store's deck furniture and straightening the long bench for the winter coffee drinkers and cigarette smokers. He waved at her, and she itched her back.

"Morning, Issey! I heard you were back from Boston!"

"What is that delicious smell?"

"I do the baking!"

Her hands, sturdy and machine-like, finally got good use from all the itching.

"Come inside and warm your cockles. We don't open for another coupla hours."

Tanya walked him in, bolting the door behind them. A hothouse of treats greeted Issey—furious gusts of chocolate, sugar, and buttered bread on silver trays.

"Oh, my word! What time do you wake up to do all this, Tanya?"

"I'm on an Aussie's timetable. I swirl in reverse."

In the dawn half-light, she gave him a lively tour. Muffins were robust and manly. Cookies were romantic hybrids of Snickers, M&M's, brownies, and other cookies. Danishes were celebrations garlanded with silky drizzles, pink curlicues, and chunky granola. This was a totally different place from the one under Pru's command.

"I'm so happy you came!" she said. "How about some whoopie?"

"Whoopie pie?"

"Oh, I don't make that."

He dropped his bag onto a table and his bottom onto a booth. Tanya returned to her workstation, organizing treats and placards inside the bake case.

"It wasn't like this when your father ran the place."

"The old days was just morning coffee and mud. We needed a little bakery, a little nook for rituals and gossip..." Tanya winked. "It's a lot of gossip these days."

Tanya winked some more. Or maybe it was flour in her eyes. With Tanya, it was probably both and dirt.

"Muffin?"

"No thanks. I'm watching my chin."

"Good choice. Kinda lookin' like you're made of muffins."

"Nevertheless... You were talking about gossip."

"You know Pru."

"Not really."

"You know, she's talking all this trash about you coming back. I try to tell her it's not you. We grew up with Issey. Issey's one of the good ones. His mother was a local landmark. I try to tell her it's not you. But you know Pru. She's kind of a dickhead."

"Not me? What do you mean, 'Not me?'"

"Well, all this stuff in town and then when I heard about that big robbery in Boston, it got me worried."

Issey sat up. "What are you talking about?"

"It was this big thing in Boston about a week ago. I thought you were one of the guys. It was so weird, like a little school play or something—but..."

While she was talking, Issey took out his phone and searched for headlines. There was no reception.

"Do you have Wi-Fi?"

"Issey, don't be insane. Here, I saved the article."

She brought him a newspaper. *Boston Globe*. Whatever had happened at Faneuil Hall made the *Globe*. You never want to make the paper, let alone one of the major ones. The headline read:

"Fumbling Faneuil Hall Heist Ends in Hilarity, One Dead."

Issey read the article with one eye open.

At 3 am on Thursday, three men entered Faneuil Hall ... wearing three-piece suits, sunglasses, and fanny packs... State troopers rushed to the scene...One suspect... the initials B.B.B., taken into custody... J. McCauley, 42, lifelong Chelsea resident, fatally wounded by security guard at Quincy Market.... Manhunt underway for the third suspect... last seen wearing white three-piece suit, sunglasses, fanny pack.

The news was disturbing. If only Berger had just trusted Issey and his lockpickers. And who's to say what would have happened if he didn't have Rohel's kid in the backseat?

"What do you think about that?" Tanya asked. She had been reading over his shoulder.

"It sounds thoroughly misguided."

Issey's condo loot had spread all over the General Store table. Even if the steal was good, condos always depressed Issey afterward. And now on top of the Berger news, the stuff looked especially worthless.

"And I tell Pru that you had nothing to do with Avi."

"Avi?"

"Avi. You know. Avi."

"No."

"Owns the horse farm."

"Never heard of him."

"Anyway, turns out, he got *cleaned* out. It was when they were asleep because they woke up and found the place empty. House and stable. Avi's wife—I can't remember her name, something Israeli, like the Israeli lady name for Avi. She had some kind of breakdown."

Issey checked the time on his watch, the one that he had stolen from Avi's. It was late. The watch was ugly. He collected his bag and slid out from the bench.

"But now you've upgraded to horses."

Issey was confused. "What are you talking about?"

"Three of Avi's horses were stolen."

"Avi's horses?"

"And Pru—you know Pru. You can only guess what's she's saying."

"No. What is she saying?"

"She saying, 'Issey stole Avi's horses.'"

Issey shook his head then patted his hair. He smiled. He frowned. He put one hand on his hip and the other hand in his pocket. He leaned on the counter. He picked up his bag. He leaned over.

"Tell Pru... Please tell her to please stop saying that."

"When she gets something in her head. You know how she is."

"I don't."

"Still," Tanya pursued a new line of thinking, "I can't say I'm proud of you, pal. I can't say it because as a business owner with Pru, and a member of the Chamber of Commerce... You know what I'm saying."

"No."

"Then we're sprecken zee same Deutsche."

"Horses? Why would someone take horses? How would that work?" Issey's words felt chunky. He didn't even know if he was saying things. Horses!

In the middle of a yawn, Tanya ran her fingers through her crispy hair. "But what would you do with horses, right, Issey?"

Issey pleaded. "And I don't even eat meat!"

"There you go."

"Tanya, if it comes down to it, you'll have to be my material witness!"

"Oh, no." She shook her head and closed her eyes. "I'm known to be something of a liar."

All the placards were set, the cases gleaming with silver rows. The morning was ready for business. Here, there was perfect order. In the valley frosted in white, there was perfect order. But for Issey, the world was starting to turn upside down.

"Have something—a coffee, a treat. You earned it." Tanya smiled at him. "But do it quick. If people see you in here, it'll put me outta business. Love ya, pal. Now get out!"

CHAPTER THIRTEEN

It does happen, though it's rare, but Issey hits the bottle for ideas. There was a lot of weird alcohol in the house. There was a lot of weird everything in the house.

Issey went from lime spritzer in the morning to shandy in the afternoon to sherry in the late afternoon to Evitas in the later afternoon to spiced Negus in the evening. This intense and casual drinking, inspired from the childhood pages of *The Connoisseur's Guide to Casual Drinking*, brought him closer to nature and further away from reality. Out the window, both forearms on the top rail, a sugary snowfall had started. His glass was dry. The house was dry.

Issey untwisted a bottle of Brennivín schnapps. Caraway seed cleared the living room of so much sap. He poured himself a sipper. He downed the Brennivín schnapps and then he poured another and downed it faster the second time to avoid the taste of Brennivín schnapps. No new ideas.

He paced and needed time to think and that was challenging because he did most of his thinking when he was sliding in and out of people's homes.

Horses. Horses!

He tried to distract himself. In the corner, there was the black suitcase he had stolen from the airport luggage carousel weeks ago. That should have been a fun diversion. There was that girl's diary with the dervish clasp.

Rhonda or something. That should have been a fun diversion—even a delicious one. But he was drinking for ideas, getting to the other side of the river, and after two in the morning, some of the girl's features were fading. Was her hair short or long, curly or straight, crimped or marcelled? Was she fat or fat-faced? Dry or wet or on fire? He was in love with her. Probably not. Was this how love worked? Something about forcing a square peg into a round hole, but why be crass? Maybe just a peek in the diary? He gave it up, slopped some booze in his mouth, invited better ideas for a drink, monitored his weight in his mother's standing bedroom mirror, posed in different outfits, thought about those horses, did some more slopping, remembered the time when he slummed in the North End, remembered a neighbor, Jake DeRosa, who was fooling around with an Irish girl who was a dry drink of red while also fooling around with a brassy Italian broad who found out about Jake's drinking problem. This was one of those moments when Issey learned something: the beginning instructs the ending, and the Italian woman sent the message to old Jake that it was over when she deposited four jars of Jake's homemade tomato sauce on his doorstep, which Issey stole. Did Rhonda's jars have a slope? A spoonful? He gulped. Life: entering unknown vessels in which to crank one's sauce. He took notes, just as the non-violent Spaggiari must have done—Issey wasn't some minor league flimflammer. He knew things and the flash hadn't forgotten him. He was hopelessly drunk.

On the gong of the third day, Issey got rid of all the alcohol by drinking it the night before and the notes he took were illegible. It was those horses. How? Horse thieves—why? That trade, from his understanding as an "unbiased observer," had gone out of style exactly in 1904. But how did they do it? Horses! And three—three horses! How could it be done?

Somewhere on the fourth day, between pressing his outfits for the week and curing the hangover bloat with chin exercises, the outside world came calling and split his head in two. The doorbell rang.

It was Anissa, and she was loud and in love with herself. The self-satisfaction dripping off her Burberry winter coat and crossbody writer's bag sank into his bones. The morning beams and cold air she brought in from the outside pulverized whatever was left of his brains.

She was thanking him—in an arrogant way—for the night at Fiddlehead Inn, for getting rid of all of Rohel's "toxic attachments," for rejuvenating her guy, for whatever he had done for Madison. "And that room! What a makeover!" Issey's hangover was so intense that his minced brains couldn't take in any new information from her. In the middle of a compliment that was leading towards an insult, she entered the front room and stopped talking.

"What in the hell?"

He saw it from her eyes and where to start? The twenty boxes of shoes, stacks of video games and their consoles, snowboards, skis, ski poles, ski boots, ski wear, walking sticks, various bottles of alcohol, various Vermont memorabilia, various cameras, watches, necklaces, rings, cuff links, bracelets, brooches, scarves, colognes, perfumes, moisturizers, eye creams, pillow sprays.

"Issey, it's like a warehouse in here."

"I'm clearing things out of our mother's." His voice was hoarse.

"This is seriously all your mother's?"

"I'm acting as lares and penates, darling."

"That doesn't mean anything." She toured the room. "Why do you have so many walking sticks?"

"It was our mother's game. She'd buy them for Michael Metcalf in Connecticut when she was on the hunt. Metcalf didn't bite. Do you want some?"

She turned to another section. "And all these boxes of shoes?"

"Yes."

"There must be half-a-dozen different sizes."

"She was a bloater."

"Did she also play video games—on four different consoles?"

"These are obviously for Madison and her friends."

"She doesn't have any."

"Exactly," Issey said. "Gifts might sweeten the deal."

It was a little too rapid-fire for Issey's head. But once Anissa settled down, Issey pieced together that she might have some word on what, if anything, was happening in town.

"So... what's new?"

But Anissa couldn't take her eyes off the piles and piles.

"Anissa."

"I heard you," she said, irritated. "What do you mean?"

"Oh, you know," Issey lied. "Hollywood gossip. The presidential election. Anything else in the local variety you might have heard at the butcher's."

"What are you talking about? Look, you've got to clean this up. It's a disaster. And if Rohel finds out—"

She put her hand on her hip.

So, there was no news.

She asked, "Does Rohel know about this?"

"What is there to know?"

She found a place that wasn't jammed up with stuff and put her bag down.

"We can fix this."

Anissa had a lot of plans, she told him. She knew how to move these things, how to organize them so they'd be out of sight but functionally within reach. "You're not the only one who can redesign a room." She told him to get a coffee going. She took out a designer's pen from her bag and some scraps of paper, cleared space from a coffee table that obviously did not belong to Issey, and began sketching ideas.

"I thought you were a writer," Issey said.

"That's right," Anissa said, less irritated now and more impatient. "Is that coffee ready or what?"

Issey went into the kitchen, poured her coffee, and returned. Maybe the horses thing hadn't gotten out. After all. Something. This head thing wasn't going anywhere.

Fragments. Maybe *Anissa* hadn't gotten out. After all, she was a stay-at-home writer creep. Rohel certainly didn't know about any horses. He would have been over first thing, in a state of tousled handsome panic.

"Do you get out much?" Issey said, spilling some of the coffee. "I mean to say, do you have a full social calendar?"

"What?" Anissa looked up from her design-work and nodded towards the coffee. "Just put that down. I'm in the zone."

Issey put the coffee down and then just stood there. Here was the concern. With what he had stolen so far in Bell River—all that Anissa had seen plus the dry goods in the pantry, frozen dinners in freezer, sundries shelved in the medicine cabinet, wrinkle creams crammed in the night table—with all that added together, it came to an admirable sum, a *professional* sum. But each individual item on its own wasn't going to have a hundred cops rolling out to find a ski pole and a Stouffers mac 'n' cheese. And nothing crossed over the threshold into grand larceny. He kept the loads small and respectful. Issey knew the limit of what he could leave with. Besides, those people probably didn't know the stuff was gone in the first place. They probably didn't even know the stuff had been *there* in the first place. People are greedy and people are stupid.

But he went overboard at Avi's. He could argue that he was lured in by the intoxicating cured leather, the craftsmanship of the saddles and girths, the Texas-ness of the saddle blankets. Each saddle was thousands, and he accepted lowball offers from those cheats in Manchester and Lebanon as a way to stay under the asportation threshold. But that was just lying to himself. He stole out of joy for the craft. Lie. He stole out of greed. Another lie. No, he stole because he just didn't like Avi. Avi was a bully. He was rude. For all he had, he never seemed happy, he never smiled with generosity, and he never lost.

But three horses? That's jail time. That's crossing the threshold. That's putting Issey out of business. That's three horses. Horses! He had nothing to do with any horses. Issey didn't like horses. Issey didn't like animals. That's why he didn't eat 'em.

"You can probably guess from my accent that I'm not from here."

Issey had forgotten Anissa was in the house. She had moved from the living room to the kitchen.

"It's really different from where I grew up in the Eastern Shore."

"What's that now?"

"It was so humid. Like unbearable. And when I met your brother at a conference in D.C., he sold me on Vermont. He painted a real scene, a magical wreathy wonderland."

"And?"

Anissa looked at the kitchen counter and into the living room with all the stuff.

"It's lonely here."

"Hm."

"There's not a lot of people to talk to. But the snow's beautiful, I guess. It gives the landscape some curves."

Issey nodded. "Is that from one of your stories?"

"Yes." Anissa sighed. "From one of my stories."

They said nothing to each other. Issey was very worried and very hungover. Anissa drank her coffee and set it down. Every sound she made was awful, chiseling. Every action she made was days ahead of his brain.

"Issey, did you really steal all of this? Are you actually good at this?"

Issey replied, "Anissa, darling, I'm just a guy who—"

"Whatever. Just shut up and get us some sandwiches."

CHAPTER FOURTEEN

Twenty minutes later, and in the opposite direction of where the sandwiches were sold, Issey was in the lobby of Fiddlehead Inn. He stopped to read a framed newspaper clipping, with his hands crossed behind his back, in the pose of an intelligent person.

"What ought to be done with the old state is to turn it into a National Park of a new kind—keep it just as it is with Vermonters managing just as they do."

Yuck. The Dorothy Canfield Fisher quote and newspaper clipping were relic enough to keep framed behind glass, unlike the revamped Fiddlehead Inn. The place had been so thoroughly modernized that it resembled the old place in geography only. His last visit, about week ago, was a good visit. Before this complication with the horses. He had watched childhood person Eight Jeff, with dripping chin of Protestant extraction, on his hands and knees sopping up ice machine matters—matter of water, matter of boys, matter of piss.

Today's Eight Jeff was part of an altogether different culture. He was out of uniform, in thigh-hugging jeans, but his eyes still had an electric concern for hotel duty—as if, at any moment, he might have to zip up an emergency exfoliator to the Dorset Room.

"Issey! What a surprise!"

Eight Jeff had a face that was made of lips, and it brought back childhood memories. None of them were good, especially any that featured Eight Jeff.

"Let's go to the downstairs bar."

"There's a bar?"

"And a wine cellar! Can ya believe it?"

As they descended to the bar, Eight Jeff went through some of its history. Town council shooting the proposal down, year in, year out, old guys worrying about drunk driving and traffic lights and flatlanders and deforestation and development. Samuel Cutts and Robert Jaffee and Henry Hatch. Old men, old ideas.

"Hm."

"And your mother really stood 'em down!"

"My mother?"

"She was pride of the valley," he said. "She gave a funny presentation about hotels in small towns that had bars and their drunk driving incidents. She showed how there was little connection between hotel bar drunk driving compared to drunk driving in towns that did not have hotel bars, and she used the famous Batchelder Study to prove her point. She also said that she was drunk, and everyone laughed. I thought Henry Hatch's heart was going to explode!"

Issey didn't know a lot about his mother, only that he was a good son. And even that was a little thin. Didn't matter. The only thing on his mind were the horses and if the news had spread.

"For her endeavors, we have the Sugar House. Get it? The out-of-towners love it, and we get 'em *sugared* up!"

Issey stared at him.

"Pretty far out, right, buddy?"

"I suppose." To Issey, this was a lot of saloon pantomiming. Even so, he was feeling less sick. The more Eight Jeff spoke about this addition, the more likely it was that news of Avi's horses hadn't reached him.

And the Sugar House bar was a fine piece of fly-in-amber staging with its fieldstone fireplace, cordwood bundles, Calvin Coolidge portrait, Morris chairs, maplewood tables and bartop, and a massive moose's head centered above the backlit railing of whiskey, vodka, rum, and gin. The bartender was young and tattooed, with a complex mustache and waxed canvas apron. He was probably from Austin.

A well-manicured man built like a derrick occupied one of the six barstools. He was enjoying a cognac and his grim time alone. Everyone was starting to look like they were from Texas. Texas saddlemen coming to get him.

"Can I get you a drink, Issey? On the house. After all, I owe you one!"

"Of course," replied Issey, having no idea what Eight Jeff was talking about. "But let's save that drink for later."

Eight Jeff walked his big butt to the bar. The bartender, who had previously reeked of self-righteousness and mustache oil, broke character and smiled with genuine warmth. "Eight Jeff, is this *the* Issey you were telling me about?"

"In real life!"

The bartender flung a bar rag over his shoulder and offered a too-serious hand at Issey. Issey shook it, but he didn't like it.

In the ensuing camaraderie, the Texas derrick man stood to leave, "Well, fellas, I better get back to it."

Before he left, he said to the trio, as if he was continuing an earlier conversation:

"Here's one for ya: The student asks the master chef, 'Sir, how do I know when the chicken is done?' The master chef responds, 'When it stops fighting.'"

Eigh Jeff hollered, "That's one for the books!"

"Any news on that Wi-Fi?"

Eight Jeff replied, "They're working on it."

"They were working on it last time I was here."

"But don't you come to get away from all that?"

"Still..."

"Still is right, Clint. You've got the trails, the brewery tour, the charcuterie workshop, the getting-away-of-it-all."

Issey's voice made its debut, "It's a wreathy wonderland!"

Why was he shouting?

"Is that so? A *wreathy* wonderland?" This Clint person evaluated Issey up and down—hungover, heavy, a little crowded in his clothes—and decided he had had enough of it. His body was imposing and broad. It knew to command space. He was the tallest person Issey had ever seen. But this was the hangover talking. Clint had another look at Issey.

"I know you from somewhere."

"Wonderful! I'm in the ingredients industry!"

"Anyway, folks..." Clint, the Texas oil man millionaire giant, had enough and finally left.

But before Issey could ask Eight Jeff questions about this Avi horse thing and rumors regarding Issey, a new set of guests appeared from under the shadows of the staircase. This was a youngish couple fresh and pink from a hike. They were happy to see the manager and even asked him to join them for a round. They also evaluated Issey, and took a seat at a table far, *far* away from him. Issey's hangover made his skin feel creepy. He was still a little drunk. And then another guest came, a young Korean guy with expensive clothes, distracted face, and topiary hair. He asked about the Wi-Fi. Eight Jeff bowed slightly and gave his little speech. "...the getting-away-of-it-all." The couple waved over Eight Jeff. Eight Jeff put his hand on the Korean guy's shoulder and said it was going to be all right. "You don't come all the way from Los Angeles for the Wi-Fi! Let's have a drink with the Courtneys over there."

And one after another, guest after guest. They ignored Issey and joined a growing corner that had become a dreamlike hotel community fostered by Eight Jeff and his weirdo face, body and nine fingers.

"It's like this all the time." The bartender was speaking to Issey who had forgotten where he was. "Everyone likes Eight Jeff!"

Despite this, apparently no one knew anything about any stupid horses.

CHAPTER FIFTEEN

But Pru did. Pru had been running her big mouth from her linoleum throne at the General Store ever since this horse thing had happened, maybe even *before* the horse thing had happened, and she was sitting up there like a mean old hog when she rang him up for the sandwiches.

"Pru, your pumice stones—these would be shelved where?"

"What's a pumice stone?"

"I see," Issey said. "Well, it'll just be the sandwiches then."

"Is it a crystal?"

"No, at least. Hm. It's a stone maybe? I use it for my calluses." Issey rubbed his palms together, as if he were talking to someone who didn't speak the same language as him.

"But you have such silky skin—like you never worked a day in your life!"

"That's the pumice stone, darling."

"We don't have that."

Issey smoothed his hair. Other customers were waiting behind him. Here was his chance.

"And what kind of *work* have you been telling people I do?"

"What?"

"I hear that you've been spreading gossip. Gossip, Prudence. Gossip of the fishwife variety."

"What are you talking about?"

"Spare me. Tanya tells me you've got lots of theories into things regarding my activities about which you know nothing."

He let her have it—this hangover was really taking him places!

But Pru just frowned at him. "Oh, Issey. You can't trust anything Tanya says." She began taking the other customers, two-handing the conversation. "You of all people should know that."

"Me of all people," Issey repeated.

"You remember how it was when we grew up. Tanya's not ..." Pru breathed heavily, sadly. "All the letters of the alphabet aren't all lined up. I don't know what's she's been saying, but it's probably severed from reality."

"But she..." Issey didn't know what to say. He looked at the guy standing next to him whose order Pru was ringing up. All of his stuff looked normal, uncomplicated. Shaving cream, microwave burritos, zip ties. "She makes the pastries."

Now Pru was looking at him the same way she had discussed her alphabet soup sister. "Anyway, about those pumice stones, you'll want to hit up Bell River Naturals—you've seen it. They have the flag with the honeybee on it."

"I guess I had it all wrong." Issey picked up the sandwiches for Anissa. They were wrapped in deli wax paper with a strong fold held together with a GS sticker for "General Store."

"Thanks for the recommendation."

"All goes in the same pot." Pru smiled. "And listen, next time you see her, be nice to Tanya."

Bell River Naturals was the centerpiece of a series of shops in need of a facelift—there was the photography studio, the lamp repair shop, the Chinese food place, and The Béarnaise King. He slid Anissa's car into several parking spaces.

Inside he found all the lifestyle choices his booze-bowl of a body needed. The place was coriander, chimes, incense sticks, talisman flowerbed tools, mandala coloring books. His oversized figure rumped down tight aisles. Under the shelf with the prickly bars of soap was his pumice stone. But when he finally had the bar in his mitts, the whole thing was a bust: the price was outrageous, and no amount of Moroccan lavender and bird music would massage the bills from his wallet and into this store's purse. He pulled himself up, haunch over breadbasket, and carried the pumice stone to the counter.

"Pardon me." Issey drummed his fingers on the counter like a real paying customer, like a real pinhead. Some of the gluten-free lip balm shook in their display boxes. "Surely, this is an error."

He handed the girl at the register the pumice stone. "People don't pay for this. Not at this price."

The girl smiled vaguely, examined the price sticker, and then scanned the item on her computer.

"About the price. To your question—is this the right price?—the short answer is No. The long answer is Nooooooooooooooooo."

He stood there. His mouth was probably open. He had come down with a turbulent case of the all over's. The fever was quick. He was dizzy, cross-brained, guts up.

Behind the counter was Rhonda. The girl with the dervish clasp.

"Yikes. Tough crowd." She returned to the business of her computer screen and pointed at a line he couldn't see. "But you're right: the price on this pumice stone is mislabeled. It should be five dollars more."

"Then I'll take five of them!"

"How about that?" She was just as surprised at his response as he was, and it flattened her face. She already sort of had a pancake face. "I'll get them."

When she tailed it from the checkout counter to wherever the pumice stones were, some of his brains returned. He could think. Kind of, mostly, rhetorically. And here was that thought. Everything about Rhonda was better in person. She was delicious, the way her legs were just above sea level, the way her yams went all the way up to her duchess potatoes, the way she hoisted her khakis with a kick before she bent over, the way her tummy dripped out from under her cable-knit sweater. Here was the living human being woman person, where for these last few weeks he had only known her as a kind of thinning image, a kind of fat face. But with so much activity getting in the way—the Rohels and the horses and long conversations with Berger's unanswered phone and maintaining his chin and drinking endlessly for ideas—her character had become misty. But she was here. She was here. And he was here too.

Of course: he had been *there*. She had seen him in her home when he was stealing her stuff. Right? Or was it a dream she had? But why think about things?

She returned with two pumice stones. Her hair was brown and curly and smelled like the store. But this could have been the store.

"Turns out, there's only two remaining, but I can order the other two and call you when they arrive."

Her voice was hoarse, the same pepper from the night he had entered. She had been criticizing her roommate for eating after dark.

She held a pen above an opened spiral-bound notebook.

"What's your name and number?"

"My name is...Iss..." He hesitated for some reason. "...ey."

"Zee?" She asked. "Your name is Zee?"

"Issey."

"Ah. That's with two Zs?"

"No—there's no Zs. It's Issey—Iss-*see*."

"*Je vous comprends.* I-S-S-I-E?"

"Just give me the notebook. I'll write it for you."

He took her pen and wrote his name and number in the notebook.

"I see. E-*Y*," she said, stretching the Y so that it sounded like "WHYYYY." Some line of thought crossed her mind and she pursued it, examining the name and number with his face.

"I know you from somewhere."

"I hear that a lot."

His skin, once smooth and age-defied, had new predatorial skin walking all over it. It was baggy, alcoholic, carpet-sour skin. Did she remember him? Anyway, whatever thought she had was dropped and she said she had his number and would call him.

"And look—about those pumice stones. They might take a while to get here. This store's not really made of promises, if you know what I mean."

He didn't, but he liked the way she said it. The sap was rising!

CHAPTER SIXTEEN

Anissa's work led Issey to spaces in the house he didn't know were available. In the attic, the stuff had been organized and labeled in bins. Empty bedroom closets were now packed with the boxes of game consoles and silverware sets. Irregularly sized items were used as tasteful accouterments or eccentric design. The walking sticks were integrated in the umbrella stand. The ski poles were hung on the living room wall as an artsy star cluster.

He fought his way through bad ideas—how would he remember everything? why did she put this thing that way? who did she think she was?—but the results were clean and maybe even a little purifying. The hangover was certainly heading south.

Apparently, that feeling was contagious. It was the first time he had a conversation with Anissa without a lot of remarks and stingers. She seemed softer, more Rohel-like. She talked about transitioning from the Eastern Shore to Bell River Valley, about getting used to four-way intersection rules, irregular store hours, decoding certain Vermont gestures. "There's like different ways of waving when you're driving, apparently." This conversation was a nice change of pace. Normally with her it had been a lot of reading between the lines. He wondered if she knew what was between those lines. Writers. What a pain.

Anissa took the sandwiches, said, "Thanks, pal," collected her purse, pen, and notebook. In the ensuing silence, there was a series of awkward brother-and-sister-in-law gestures that ended in a pat on the shoulder. Even if Issey's body was shaped like a hug, he wasn't a natural for it.

"We'll see you next Thursday?" she asked, and Issey nodded. Issey didn't know what Thursday was.

She opened the door to dusk. On her way out, she turned and took a final look at her work. She was happy. "So you stole all of Rohel's stuff just to make him feel better?"

"I guess so," Issey said.

Anissa gave him a look. "You're really doing something weird here, aren't ya?"

CHAPTER SEVENTEEN

A day of rain—thick, solid bars of rain—was followed by a day of unseasonable warmth and then a wild temperature drop where everything suddenly became frozen. Even those solid bars of rain froze up. The Bell River seasons were all out of order. Issey hoped Rhonda was thinking about him.

Rohel drifted in and out—after dropping off Madison at school, after picking up Madison from school, on his way to the new craft beer club he had joined, on his way home to sober up from the new craft beer club he had joined. Apparently, Rohel had been such an instant hit at his new club—the nose, the low body fat, those eyes filled with compliments—that one of these microbrewing bozos, with a connection at a prominent Bell River architecture firm, squeezed Rohel into a job interview after Thanksgiving.

"Perfect timing, too."

"Why's that?"

"It means there's less urgency selling Mom's house."

Issey was bothered. "You're selling her house?"

"Well, yeah. why'd you think I had you come up here and clear everything out?"

Issey said nothing.

"She and Allan are all set up, and she wanted us to split the money."

"Two ways!"

"*Three* ways," Rohel reassured him. "Me, you, and her. Meanwhile, I'm still paying for everything. Did you ever stop and ask why the electricity was still on and the water still running? *And* the landline? You think all of this was just running on its own for no reason?"

As a matter of fact, Issey had chewed through ideas that their mother was paid up with the water collector and the heat collector and the telephone collector. He thought it must have been on account of their mother's age and community standing, a standing nourished by the virtue of her age, not on virtue itself, so back again to age. She was always old. Logical conclusion: she got lifetime water, lifetime heat, lifetime telephone. Case closed, matter munched.

"Of course!" Issey said.

"You say that when you're not paying attention."

"I'm always paying attention."

"And it's a little nervy of you getting so handsy with the house sale. You're never here. Why should you get *anything*?"

Issey shrugged. Rohel was getting whiny.

"And you never applied yourself. I was begging you to go to college."

All this bored Issey. And he did go to college. Once, for research. During a summer in Burlington when he discovered that Vermont—both the state and the University of—does not lock its doors. Unfortunate for Issey, but fortunate for Vermont: this was the period of young Issey's lockpicking internship which had suddenly become too easy. If all the doors were unlocked, where was the learning? Palming for a new plan, he stole a bottle of gin and some face's bus ticket to Montreal. There, he found not only leg-crossers and cigarette smokers who were confident in their abilities of speaking two languages poorly instead of one language averagely, but also that their lock mechanisms were completely inverted—a little of this up there and a little of that down there. What a bust! In the mornings at a St. Sulpice café, he drafted in his notebook different lock cylinders, and ordered coffee and eggs but was instead given a finger of port and an ashtray. In the afternoons, he toured Montreal, drifted, window shopped. Facing the other side of a swooning fainting couch was this woodchuck in brown pants and oversized green winter coat. Issey the Treeboy. That was no good. He needed aesthetics and sweetness. Throughout the day, he took slimming zip-ups, graphite chinos, paisley scarves, and a stunning pair of ankle boots. He was young. He had sway. He had swish. The owner of *Galerie Vincente* invited him to a rooftop party overlooking Notre-Dame *Basilica*. He was shown around, with a flute of champagne and a developing smoker's wrist. It put him in touch with the Gwenni Von Maxies of the scene, and maybe even Gwenni Von Maxi herself, if Issey could remember her name. A collector named Claudia Bünd was an early admirer. She spoke highly of the Curvo-Linear Stylists, but worried about "devolving movements in Prague." Issey laughed at the parts that were probably the punchline and said, "Ah, so," at the parts ringing with significant cultural designation. These might have been a punchline too. Issey didn't know. He was too busy getting whisked from place to place with this Claudia Bünd woman, who was teaching him the difference between *étagère* and *boulangerie*, *éclair* and *décolleté*, *dejeuner* and *petit dejeuner*. "I thought '*croissant*' was the French word for breakfast," Issey said. Nothing in the volumes of the *Connoisseur's Guide* had prepared him for her, not unless he wanted to show her how to host a murder mystery fondue party. One morning in the bedroom of her triplex walk-up, Claudia Bünd announced it was time to have his hair styled. They entered the salon as a pair. To the front desk person, she spoke wild French and pointed at her inamorato, protégé, nephew, son—whatever Issey was. The hairdresser was pushy and maybe offended by the quality of Issey's head. He swore and smoked and sometimes breathed husky and hateful curses at the back of at Issey's neck. Regardless, Issey slid from the lunatic's chair thirty minutes later, reporting to Claudia Bünd a real agile look. Claudia Bünd, who was also going for something new, head segmented in foils, told Issey to wait for her at a café. And it was at the same St. Sulpice café he had stumbled into weeks ago, outfits ago, *coifs* ago, where Issey crossed his kind-of slender legs, smoked cigarettes, and drank port like an after-hours pro.

Things were moving fast. He didn't understand what anyone was saying. They didn't understand what he was saying. And he often had the impression that they didn't understand what they were saying either. He was eating—and stealing—a lot of probiotics. She never called him by his name. The port and cigarettes went to his head. Eventually, new-look Claudia Bünd joined him at the café. She was hardly recognizable. Her hair was platinum, short, edgy. Even her eyes seemed different. "I told them I needed to pay the parking meter. I pointed to my purse—'I'm leaving it behind and will come back for it.'" Issey asked if she needed to return. "Haha! The only thing in that purse was an old sweater. And they can keep it! *Allons-y!*"

So that was it. She was deranged. But she was also brilliant. She was a lot of everything that wasn't really there. She was Hollywood Regency, but she had no money. She wore a different scarf and pair of sunglasses every day, but some of her other clothes were junk. She talked about foods like they were overflowing from a musical fantasy—blue hubbard, roast pheasant, saffron oxtail, hazelnut *millefeuille*—but most of her meals came from the Couche-Tard. Skincare serums and designer eyeshadows and glistening creams took up all the real estate on the bathroom sink, but she smelled sweaty. There was no comparing her to other women her age because at that point in his early adult life he didn't really know any other women of *any* age. Most were teachers or the woman at the Bell River Public Library or his mother. The only similarity was that their relationship, like those others, was—thankfully—transactional.

"The *Galerie Vincente* people are having a Murano glass exhibition in two weeks," she said, in a different apartment, with all different furniture. "I want to take all the Murano glass. And I need your help."

So this was it.

"But you need more training."

"Training? *Moi?*"

"Issey. All the clothes you're wearing—I watched you take them. All day I watched you. Because I was doing the same. But you didn't see me, no?"

"No?"

"No. That's because I was dressed like it was a Tuesday. That's because I was the older woman in the back. No one looks at the older woman in the back." She laughed, with her platinum cut, looking nothing like Tuesday's older woman. "I followed you all day. I watched everything you were doing. I saw bad technique. At one point, when you were in the shoe store, I wondered if it wasn't bad technique, but *lazy* technique. Or insanity."

"I guess I just thought—"

No, she insisted. It was just bad. Okay, she conceded, his instincts were better than adequate, said as a kind of half-compliment, but the rest needed work, and she was willing to show him what her husband Erik had shown her. Measuring twice and cutting once. Identifying the opportunities and recognizing the challenges. Cataloging information. Using crowds. Looking for entrances. Looking for exits. Looking for cameras, blindspots, false mirrors, out-of-place characters. On his end, he impressed her with his lockpicking, but annoyed her whenever he brought up Albert Spaggiari, the famous bank thief who never used guns or violence, who drank wine and ate pâte in the vaults. Bünd accused Issey's hero of "high art," and because Issey had no other real-life mentors, he took her word in blind faith. She had authority. She was "age-y." And she had pulled that trick with her purse at the beauty salon. But was this right? She mentioned her husband Erik often, and eventually Issey started wondering if the instruction she was giving Issey was part of Erik's masterclass or if they were all the things Erik couldn't do right himself. For as much she revered her Erik, he was—apparently—in jail *a lot*. Issey had initially thought, with the way she pronounced his name—*Eh-riq, Eh-riiiq, Eh-riiiiiiq*—that he had died. But this was just the phoniest way to pronounce his name. No, Erik wasn't dead. He just serving his latest round of jail.

"Do you listen to music?" she asked him and knew the answer already by the absolutely disgusted way she asked it. "You must. If you want to engage in your biorhythms. If you want to be an artist." She exposed him to Satie, Chopin, Poulenc, Debussy. "It's not what's there. It's what isn't there. The shadows between the notes. That's us."

For all the talk of training, the night at *Galerie Vincente* was easy. Everyone was smoking and drinking prosecco on the rooftop with Issey. They had forgotten about the older woman. "They always forget about the older woman," she smirked. Claudia Bünd had a handtruck and a pickup waiting for her in the alley. They didn't even need to use the large bag of tacks she had brought as misdirection. Later, when they were miles away, they unloaded the cases of Murano glass, and Issey gasped. "They're beautiful."

"They're vulgar. Those *Galerie Vincente* people are vulgar."

Issey figured they would keep it, and it was another lesson. Instead, they were going to offload the stuff to her fence. They drove who-knows-where for who-knows-how-long. Issey had a vision of robust Bünd supply lines, from Montreal to Detroit to Toronto. Instead, it was just an old guy in St. Andrews wearing a cable-knit sweater. But what he still didn't know! Lesson upon lesson. On the very long drive back to Montreal, there were demanding explanations about how this one wooly bully fisherman was part of a long chain of fences who took the art, tunneled the art, and transformed the art into cash. She explained these relationships, how they were cultivated through a love of money and art, but Issey wondered if this was true. He began questioning the foundations on which all of it was built. Because when the cash came, it was disproportionate for all the work, let alone the endless talk *about* the work, about technique, and then the long digressions showcasing Erik. She and Erik dancing at Funky Claude's Bar in Montreux. She and Erik conning balneo-therapeutic treatments in Karlovy-Vary. She and Erik double-dooring in Garmisch. She and Erik making shadows on Venetian *fondamenta*. For all these breathless travelogues, Issey wondered if Claudia Bünd's enterprise had reached its summit, and was now operating on an *indifference* to money and art and time itself. Issey was internalizing a lot of questions. He was young. Everything made him little over-excited, afraid, annoyed, and bored. The drive was long. Issey had time to think. This was always trouble. His talents lay elsewhere. He was unable to explain most things, events, and feelings. But on the unending driving back to Montreal, he knew exactly what he did not like. And this was it.

When Issey returned to Bell River Valley, everything had changed. Experience had snuck up on him, and where his experiences had become enlarged, the valley had suddenly shrunk. It was miniscule, backwards, dumb. He walked through the familiar mountain curves and domestic raids, through the orchards and the potting sheds, the leaves drifting in a brook, the money in the purse. In the wind, he thought he heard the *Galerie Vincente* crowd or sniffed espresso creamy in the night. He even listened for *Eh-riq, Eh-riiiq, Eh-riiiiiiq*. But there was nothing except lonely Bell River Valley.

And then one day in the valley when he was walking up one hill just to find his way down another, all the things he didn't like about Claudia Bünd he suddenly missed. After a month of empty wandering, he returned to Montreal—for the steal, the pursuit, the art, and the contradictions. Eventually, he found her at the Couche-Tard. She wore a green t-shirt and draftsperson's jeans, a tote bag slung over her arm, with a classy silkscreen logo of some literary symposium. She looked like a visiting McGill professor who was also perfectly toned. The t-shirt was tight and put on a display of sculpted triceps and runner's shoulders. At the moment he saw her from across the street, she was putting microwave food in her bag. She was putting tuna packets in her bag. She was putting water bottles and tea bags and little creamers in her bag. Issey would have been stunned at her recklessness if not for a sudden disaster at the hot dog station where a young guy—in his early twenties, not necessarily thin—was blowing chunks into the condiments. The young guy also was crying—crying and blowing chunks. The diversion was obvious but also thrilling, and when he returned to tracking Claudia, she was out of the store.

Allons-y was right. Issey flattened himself into the dark creases of his pursuits. In and out. Philadelphia. Boston. New Haven. Manchester. Always in search of the stuff inside boxes. People really kept around a lot of their lies. Years passed. Mothers coming and going. Vases coming and going. Did Erik ever exist? Time was served. Issey fought to keep on his arrest weight. Claudia Bünd certainly existed, but only in the background.

And while she may have been out of sight for Issey, Issey was never out of reach for her. She knew of an enterprise in Cambridge headed by a fashionable maniac named Berger and was a shadow connection for Issey's (brief) inclusion into Berger's *Grüppe*. They had big plans! They just didn't include Issey. And now here he was, back in Bell River, where the police came knocking.

CHAPTER EIGHTEEN

Issey opened the door and gestured for the officer to come in. Too cold to be outside. They had met before, under different circumstances, at the Sugar House bar, when he was less of a police officer and more of a Texas oil man millionaire.

The officer smiled. Issey smiled back. It's always a little awkward. Sometimes, they'll shake hands; other times, they just spin you around and throw you facefirst into the dirt.

He wasn't one of those. This police brought manners with him. He also brought in some of the cold weather. Its sweetness reminded Issey of night adventures.

"It dropped again," Issey said. "The temperature, I mean."

"Sure did." The officer looked outside. He was a giant. "We might have a big one over the weekend. You can kinda smell it, right? When a big storm is on the way?"

Issey nodded, looked at the coffee machine. "You're a police officer?"

"Sergeant." Despite a rancher's smile, he was puffed-up and hound-dogged in his uniform, more manly than in the Sugar House bar. "Sergeant in the sheriff's office."

"Clint, right?"

"Clint Davenport."

"Of *the* Davenports?"

The officer laughed, but too much. It wasn't that funny.

"I thought you were a guest at Fiddlehead's."

"No, I was just in to see Eight Jeff." He paused. "He's the first friend I made when I moved here. I've never met anyone so generous."

Issey wanted to throw up.

"Anyway, what brings you over, officer?"

"Just call me Clint. They call me Sergeant Davenport at the station. But Clint's fine."

Issey was skeptical. He sat at the kitchen table, offering a chair to Sergeant Davenport. The officer sat and removed his sheriff's hat. He had matted rancher's hair.

Sergeant Davenport said, "So here's the thing, Issey, and keep in mind I'm not here under any official police stuff. We're just talking."

"Okay."

Davenport looked uncomfortable. "For about the past month, there's been stealing. There's been breaking and entering. It's been a lot of stealing and a lot of breaking and entering."

"Okay."

"Which is weird because this town don't get a lot of stealing and a lot of breaking and entering. This is a pretty tight community."

"Okay."

"And it's all happened in the past month."

"Mmhmm."

"Like these clusters of houses getting broken into. All within this past month."

"Okay."

"Turns out you came here—."

"This past month."

Sergeant Davenport's voice remained calm when he switched topics. "What brings you back?"

"Family stuff. My mother remarried and—"

"Congratulations."

"I didn't marry her," Issey said. "Anyway, my mother remarried and moved out of state, and I'm helping my brother clear out her house." Issey smiled at the empty house. Anissa had done a great job.

"Your brother does real estate?"

"No, architect. Why?"

"Just curious. Eight Jeff told me your brother did real estate."

"No. Eight Jeff is always wrong. What else did he say?"

"Not much. He just thinks you're the greatest." Davenport exhaled as if all this time he had been holding in his gut. "*Are* you the greatest?"

"I don't know. Probably not." Issey's voice also remained calm when he switched topics. "Where are you from? Texas?"

Sergeant Davenport laughed—again, a little too loudly. "Texas? My wife'll drop dead when I tell her!"

"I thought you were from Texas. You seem like a guy from Texas."

"No." he shook his head like a real hound dog. "Oklahoma."

"Isn't that the same thing?"

Davenport shook his head some more with eyes enlarged. "And you want to never say that to someone from Oklahoma."

"Anyway..."

"Anyway, you want to get on with your day, and I want to lay all my cards on the table. First, I should let you know that I'm recording this conversation."

"You can do that?"

"Sure." Sergeant Davenport looked at Issey. "Right?"

"I don't know. Why would I know?"

"It's fine."

"But I thought you said you weren't here under any official capacity."

"I'm not," Sergeant Davenport frowned, "But it's better for you if I record our conversation. Anyway, I'm probably more on your side than my own."

"And that's on the recording?"

"Oh, shit."

Davenport murmured something else, then gathered his composure.

"Anyway, I'm new here and I like it here. And I want to lay all my cards on the table."

"You said that already."

"You know why I moved here, why I made the lateral transfer from my old department in Oklahoma to this one? I transferred because I thought Vermont would be a better culture fit. At the Sugar House, you said Bell River is a 'wreathy wonderland.' I never heard that before. And it's true. The valley is like right out of a calendar book."

Issey nodded.

"But you know what happens when a police officer transfers from one department to the other? You keep your seniority, but you lose all the good stuff. You're back to basic patrol. Speeding tickets. Skateboarding complaints. Vandalism reports. It's not good. You're kinda starting all over again."

Issey nodded, was maybe drifting off a little. He wondered when this rambling Davenport person would find his point. Normally, Issey admired the police. He liked the uniforms, the belts, the polish. He had clipped articles about the famous Lieutenant Bread in Boston and, during his early initiatives with Claudia Bünd, followed cases of the Sûreté du Québec's Inspector Dutilleul. But this Davenport was a boob.

"And I don't want to be shipped out of here in a box, if you know what I mean."

"What?"

Shipped out in a box? What had Issey missed? How long had he been asleep?

"Appreciate my position. I'm doing this as a courtesy for Eight Jeff. And he painted a picture of two best friends—"

"Not best friends—"

"Two best friends growing up in the valley, one going one way and the other going another. He's forever grateful you got him the job at the hotel. You saw him up the ladder. He loves you. You're his best friend. But casually he said he was worried about your habits. So, I looked you up."

Issey nodded.

"You got yourself a bit of 'rap sheet.'" Davenport put it in quotes. "You do small. You like intimate areas. Even in some of the larger cities, you stick to small. You're not violent. From your record, you don't terrorize or carry weapons, which I appreciate. Which I think everyone appreciates."

"That was years ago," Issey replied, "Another story for a never time. Besides, I'm in the scouting business now."

"I thought you said you were in the 'ingredients industry.'"

"That too."

"That's good, Issey. But the thing is, everything that's been happening here—the breaking and entering, the stealing—that's all you. And your return to Bell River coincides with what's happening." Davenport added, "This past month."

"Uh-huh. I guess."

Issey was skeptical. If Sergeant Clint Davenport had anything more than a weird feeling, they'd be having the conversation "downtown." There was no evidence, no probable cause. Issey lit a cigarette. He offered one to Sergeant Clint.

"I don't smoke."

"Neither do I." Issey lit his cigarette.

Sergeant Davenport shook his head. "And now I come upon a situation with these horses."

Issey nearly swallowed the cigarette.

His instincts told him to take it with professional pride. After all, Sergeant Clint Davenport was a big deal. He was huge. He was from Oklahoma. He was from Texas. If Issey was a horse thief, he'd be the great criminal mastermind. Animals and night moves and all that. But Issey's other instincts—all of them—were damaged. Someone was doing a really good job, a job that was beyond his scope and skill. Meanwhile, hidden in the house were the fruits of his artistic product. But was it art? Day old stuff, snap-on plastic, bag salad dreams, wads and wads of production-line vases and faux fur flummery. This was junk fantasia. What was he going to do with all these shoes?

"Wouldn't it stand to reason that I'd have the horses now? Where would I keep them? In my mother's bedroom?"

"You tell me."

"I wouldn't even know where to begin."

Sergeant Davenport continued. "Those horses are microchipped, so if they happen to turn up in an auction, I'll know. And I'll be there—because I am tired of writing vandalism reports and being on taillight duty. You know how many years I got in Oklahoma?"

"Is it a lot?"

"It's a lot. And it sucked there and it's nice here. Everyone is nice. And none of these nice people wants a horse thief in their town. If they find out it's you, they'll be doing back rolls just to get rid of you."

"Back rolls?"

"Back rolls. Back flips. You know what I'm saying."

"So what's the solution? I didn't steal any horses. Do you want me to just leave town?"

"Yes." Davenport nodded. "Yes."

"You're asking me to leave?"

"I'm *begging* you to leave. Go somewhere else. Develop new skills."

A line of ash drooped on Issey's cigarette. Issey thought it over.

"I thought you were trying to make a big arrest. Why ask me to leave?"

"Eight Jeff."

"Eight Jeff?"

"I'm telling you. He's a great man and I owe him a debt of humanity. And today, he's your free pass."

Issey took a drag of the cigarette and got nothing but filter. He set it in the ashtray, leaned back in the chair, and folded his arms.

"And you recorded all of this?"

"Gotdammit. When I get home, I'll have to delete some of those parts. Thanks for letting me know."

Issey finally said, "Give me a couple days."

"Okay." The sergeant had more to say, but the sound of car door closing outside interrupted him. Rohel.

"Is that your brother?"

"Mmhmm."

"It's funny—him being the architect. He's the one that builds the homes; you're the one who ruins them."

"I guess you're not familiar with his work."

Sergeant Davenport didn't get the joke.

"Two days," Sergeant Clint Davenport said firmly. "And then you're gone on Monday."

"Two *business* days. It's Friday afternoon. Give me two business days and I'll be gone by Wednesday."

"You'll really leave?"

"You have my word."

"You leave on Wednesday."

"Do you want to shake on it?"

"No." Sergeant Davenport replied. Issey could sense that he had tested the cattleman's patience. "Just keep your word."

Rohel opened the front door with wide astonished eyes.

"What's this?"

"Brother Rohel! Sergeant Clint Davenport of *the* Davenports is here to arrest me. Hahaha!"

"What—Jesus!"

"No one's being arrested, Rohel." Issey rolled his eyes and rose from the chair. His smile felt as big as his appetite for a good steal. "It's nothing what you think. We were discussing the area. He's new in town from Oklahoma. It's called a 'lateral transfer.'"

"*What* is called a 'lateral transfer?'"

Issey looked at Clint Davenport, shrugged. "He'd never get it."

Sergeant Davenport also stood. "Wednesday, Issey."

A deal was struck. Issey grabbed the officer's hand finally and gave it a good palming, reaffirming his connection to life, community, and the law. The officer took it back.

"Of course!" Issey proclaimed.

Then Rohel and Issey were alone.

"Well, brother?" Issey said, smiling, a new day ahead of him—all worries. He smiled. All worries.

"Should I even ask?"

"No." Issey lit another cigarette. He was smoking too much these days.

CHAPTER NINETEEN

He stole as if someone was ahead of him—and someone was: the horse thief. Who was this master who had gotten away with it? Who was this guy on the tips of everyone's lips? This guy threatening Issey's stability? People loved this guy and people hated this guy. Issey stole with passionate meaningful naked polite rude abandon. He stole to brighten his lazy senses and tighten his chin. He stole with reputation and *technique*. Come inside, these night homes said, please, and Issey entered this disgusting scrap that had puffed up its eaves by calling itself a "converted farmhouse with *cathedral* ceilings." He was on top of *that* gourmet marble kitchen countertop, on top of *that* gas-stove fireplace, on top of *that* Art Deco sideboard. He was curving and soaking and disappearing like so many items in this dump. He hid in the mudroom with the ski gear, boots, and pants. He slid on a railing. He coached his body to fit in a transom. He slid into a shadow cast by the peacocking fanlight. Footsteps that weren't his approached at the head of the staircase. Someone turned on *that* upstairs Bohemian chandelier and someone cried *those* pissy things and Issey was mounting *that* chandelier. You frightened boob. You owning cow. He ripped the guts out of the chandelier and ripped out of the house.

Similar to his early years, he camped out at the library at two in the morning. He unzipped the gym bag and felt inside. Not much feel-recognition. Some cracked figurines, a pack of tea candles, a cache of pens, markers, and wooden rulers. Expensive-ish bracelet. Diamond-esque earrings. Jewelry-like jewelry. And a chandelier. Sergeant Clint Davenport didn't have a clue!

And that big mouth Eight Jeff. Big fat big mouth blabbing to the police. Issey wanted to go over to Eight Jeff's house right now and punch him in the face. He wanted to go over there and smack him around, kick him in the stomach, take off another finger. But Issey didn't know where Eight Jeff lived.

And that big mouth Oklahoma oaf Clint Davenport. For a police person, he gave away a lot of information. It was like he was on the first day of the job, or the last. They don't make 'em too good anymore on the ranch, Issey supposed.

A whining snow squall announced the breaking of the storm. The library's walls shook. Books shivered. Tables wobbled. The goldfish panicked. But the goldfish had been dead for years. He collected his belongings, and now that he was warmed up, it was time to pursue greatness. Issey was going to find those stupid horses.

Outside, to his right was a bleak turnoff towards Clifford. To his left was a field covered in an unspoilt sheet of ice and snow. He searched for what they saw, or would have seen, those horse thieves. He searched for horse tracks. He searched for areas of opportunity. It would have to be someone who had access, someone who knew their way around—probably a customer, someone who had dealt with Avi and his teeth.

But downslope winds dropped quick accumulations. He pressed the edge of the icy field. Left and right, gusts of wind and nasty pelts of ice stabbed at him, and he trudged those stubby legs and widening torso, warm and slimming in shapewear, but a little hopeless in weather, all the way to Avi's horse farm. It was all unbroken, uninterrupted white. Not one hoof or gallop, not one shoe print or tire tread.

The walk was uphill. This was the other side of the mountain and there were no shortcuts. He followed the wild roar of the babbling brook, the line of foaming ice, and so many rocks. Issey continued and peeked and pressed until the brook fell out of view. The dirt path pitched to a weird gradient and Issey walked on, sweating hot, sweating cold. He was nervous, as he should be: finding those horses might get him Berger's approval. He knew he had fallen off the trail. The road flattened. Daybreak was a few hours off, but bright clouds were surrounding him. Issey entered the white mass.

Behind him, Issey heard an engine roaring up the mountain. Soon, beams from headlights began curving in his direction.

Issey skittered off the road—against the mountain's rising-face.

It was a brown pickup with a hitch on its tail. It burned into the mountains, the hitch snagging left and right. Issey waited until it was out of sight then coaxed some bravery from the mounds of his body, molded in layers of shapewear. There was no feeling in his face except courage. He tracked the truck's red lights in the distance. He saw it make a right turn, the only right turn carved into the landscape. Avi's horse farm.

The storm advanced. There had been signs. The dark sky that wasn't dark. The marbling in the dense clouds. The retreating wildlife. Issey lit a cigarette. It went out immediately. The wind took it out of his mouth and snapped it in half. Issey reached for it, but the split cigarette was flying away, into the clearing. In the distance, a faint snow squall could be heard. It intensified, the wind grasping trees like a belt. Issey was in the middle of an all-out weather attack. He pushed against it. His face, earlier so wild with greed, was now cleaved in two. Stupid courage face. He couldn't see. May have slipped. Protecting his face from tiger ice. Cheated his way through. Icy pelts of snow. So cold on your ears you go deaf. Sudden pushback from all sides. The howl of the squall. Beware the end of the road.

The light from the moon flickered on and off. Some animal lunged forward. Treasures from his bag spilled into a white mass he could not see. Issey reached for his bag. "My chandelier!" The animal whined. Another arrived, hissed. The animal turned on hind legs and roared for other animals to attack. He could only make out large eyes. A bear made an appearance. Berger's disappointment. Confirmed. Issey closed his eyes. Rhonda, watching him steal her diary with the dervish clasp, waiting for him to come again. "Give me that old time religion." Claudia Bünd appeared, her face a landscape of continental Europe. He made a fist. The snow squall, a kind of arena holding madness, was at full capacity. The animals came for throat and legs. Issey's fist connected so hard that one animal's teeth met another animal's eyes. The first bear went down, then the second, then the third, the fourth, the fifth, the sixth, the ninth, the tenth. Issey was punching everything in sight until there was nothing left but the white of their bones and the screen of snow and the pumping of his heart.

"Hey, pal. What are you doing?"

CHAPTER TWENTY

Anissa.

"Anissa!" Issey was wedged in snow and dirt. He swept pieces of dead animal under him, bones and teeth and guts.

"I'm not a—I was attacked."

He pushed his hands in the snow and found only snow.

"It's time to go home, Issey."

Anissa bent and wedged her hands underneath him. She was shoveling him off the ground.

"I'm surprised you didn't freeze to death. It's a good thing you wear, like, ten girdles."

"It's not a girdle, Anissa," Issey shouted. "It's *shapewear*."

"And your nose all bloody. I'd say let's take you to a doctor, but you'll probably refuse..."

"Absolutely not! Take me to the hospital."

She took a folded tissue from her pocket, a tissue that looked like it had a history, and held it to his bleeding nose. He must have battered the animals into a snow-fine powder because the ground was completely clean, spared of bone, teeth, and guts. It was just a stupid dirty ground.

"I was attacked by—some kind of wild cast of animals," he said through the tissue. "I had to protect myself."

"Did you kill some animals, Issey?"

He looked for carcasses.

"Did you snap their necks and throw them into the river?"

"I'm not a monster. I fought... I mean, I think I fought them..."

"And there's not a single scratch on your face?"

He looked for signs of battle in the snow.

"There were so many. I—Where's my bag?"

"Don't worry about it."

"There were so many of them."

He looked for some gnarl on his knuckles.

"Let's go home."

He was confused. The babbling brook's drop was much closer than he had remembered—but this was just minutes ago. Maybe he had been pawed into the crevasse. Maybe he had blanked out. It felt like a different day—because it was. Bright morning lights from the north reached them where there was formerly no light.

"Did the animals punch you in the nose?"

"Probably. There were so many of them. At least ten."

She held the tissue clipped to his nose, staunching the blood and waiting.

"So is this worth it?"

"What?"

"You break dinner plans, break your brother's heart."

"Dinner plans? When did we have dinner plans?"

"You said you were coming over on Thursday. I told you when I left, see you on Thursday and you said yes."

"Good grief, Anissa! What's the big deal?"

"It's Thanksgiving, stupid."

"Oh," Issey said. "That was *this* Thursday?"

Anissa clenched her fist. "Look at you: passed out, got leaves and a bunch of shit all over you. Rohel's not your enemy, Issey. *We're not your enemy.*"

She had him by the nose.

Issey pushed her off. "It's not bleeding, Anissa."

"Well, third place prize goes to the guy who says his nose isn't—."

"Shut up. We need to go to Avi's horse farm *right now*."

"What?"

"Don't be Rohel, Claudia."

"Who's Claudia?"

"Don't be Rohel, Rhonda."

"Anissa." She threw the blotty tissue onto his chest.

"*Anissa*. Don't be Rohel—*Anissa*. We need to go to the horse farm right now and track and see the site. There was a brown pickup truck with a hitch. I saw it. The hitch big enough to hide Avi's horses. Somebody sent at least a dozen animals after me when I—when *I got too close*. Sergeant Davenport will never make inroads unless I do the driving for him."

"Jesus, you talk a lot when you talk a lot."

Anissa picked up the tissue from the ground and then she tucked the bloody thing in her front pocket, like a mother or a sister or a pal. All the signals were a little starry-eyed.

"Come on, Anissa—we need to go. Now!"

"Why don't we go home? Haven't you had enough of Avi's horse farm for one night?"

Issey's mushed brains and face were made up, and he charged ahead, wobbled ahead. She steered him into her car and there was nothing she could say or do except drive them to Avi's horse farm. The car went up and up and up. Issey could have sworn he was on level road when those fifteen animals attacked him. Avi's horse farm dropped into view. She took the same right turn the brown pickup truck with the hitch had taken. Except it was a left. And the truck wasn't brown. It was green.

Issey spilled out of the car.

"Issey—wait!"

Fifty yards away from him, he could see Avi's wife resting her damp head on one horse. Avi was hugging a bag of grains and feeding the other horse. A third horse was getting its muzzle stroked by two policemen.

Sergeant Clint Davenport, in full uniform and belt, stood in the fields, flanked by a half-dozen other police with notepads, cameras, and plastic baggies. Davenport wore a shark-face of grim professional intensity that had been absent during his informal interview with Issey. Anissa joined

Issey and waved at Eight Jeff. What was Eight Jeff doing there? He waved back and shouted as loud as he could:

"Tell Issey to go home! We'll see him later!"

"Maybe!" she shouted back. "He's a little brain damaged and more than usual!"

She put her arm around him and led him back to her car.

"You really are the worst at this, aren't you?"

Issey slumped in the car while Anissa clicked on her crossbody seat belt like it was an aerobic exercise. She cut the car in reverse.

"Rohel and I—we can't figure it out."

Issey stared.

"You didn't show up to Thanksgiving and that hurt him, but then he worried he upset you when he told you about selling your mom's house, and when you weren't home and nowhere to be found, we called your buddy Eight Jeff—"

"He's not my buddy."

"And he said he'd call his friend in the police. We all came out looking for you. And then I had a feeling where you'd be."

They had reached paved road.

"Where are we going, Anissa?"

"To your house. I've taken care of everything—secured everything safely away."

"You were touching my things? Why are you always touching my things?"

"For your party. Issey—don't you get it? Everyone wants to see you. You rescued the horses!"

PART II

CHAPTER TWENTY-ONE

With the news of Issey's daring midnight rescue of Avi's horses still steamy like morning snow, life was glorious. Everyone who attended the party at his mother's house had a hucklebuck of a good time. Issey had never heard so many nice words said about him, and he believed each and every one. Rohel cracked jokes and cried some. Anissa guzzled champagne and whispered: "Look at you—hero. You own everything." Some guy called Sweezy high-fived him. Tanya and Pru from the General Store mingled with a fella named Derek. Some crusty in a lover's overcoat declared, "I knew he had it in 'im! Find a horse—he can find two! For he's a jolly good fellow! For he's a jolly good fellow! Which no one can leave behind! Which no one can leave behind!" Voices joined in, voices he didn't know, faces he was unsure of, hands that gave him drinks and slaps on the back. Sure, Issey was confused and still dethawing, but he was always confused, always dethawing, and he never met a mask he couldn't wear. Sergeant Clint Davenport, the last to arrive, as a duo with Eight Jeff, congratulated Issey's industry.

"See, Sergeant? Dinnit I rest assured I'd get 'em?"

"You've been drinking."

Issey pointed to Eight Jeff. "Your buddy's a man of his word, young boy." Issey raised a glass. "I take what I want and I want what I take. *Prosit!*"

And that was the party.

The morning after a big snowstorm is always a whooshing door to the white chiffon, to the light catching a curling snowdrift. The air tastes like vanilla. The kids hoot on the saucers to see who can make it down the steepest inclines with the most broken bones. The town hall makes an announcement. Issey had no hangover because he only pretended to get drunk, and he replaced one mask for another since news in the valley traveled so fast that it smacked him in the face as soon as he opened the morning door.

Issey was the hero of Bell River Valley.

Newspaper articles focused on his bravery and selflessness. The Vermont Public Radio show *Every Hamlet a Wonder* interviewed him for a ten-minute segment. During Career Day at Madison's school, he spoke with eloquence and charm—his job title was Hero. There was a truffle burger created in his name at a newish gastropub. At the General Store, his portrait was drawn, framed, and hung. The owner of the Post & Bean gave him a lifetime of free coffee. Madison declared the Post & Bean coffee to be the best coffee in *the world*.

"But you don't drink coffee."

"I do, Uncle Issey! I do and I love it!"

For a while, Issey enjoyed the spoils of his good deed. The horse rescue was the pinnacle of his philosophy, and the recognition for a lifetime's work was a long time coming. He had a passing interest in reflection; he was hardly at home with his thoughts or in his home. Simply, he was celebrated. Playing into the hands of some greater power—some hive mind of the valley—that was out of the question. Nothing was fishy. Everything was pure. As pure as his set of diamond cutters. As pure as his rescue of the horses, which...

He looked forward to the town hero thing drifting into a pleasant memory. Eventually, the event would be forgotten. *He* would be forgotten. And then he'd be free to roam into the houses of the suckers who slapped praise upon him. Then he'd leave. Then he'd set off towards the city, towards a better set of suckers who had better things to steal and sell.

Maybe he would reconnect with Claudia Bünd and see what kind of work she had available.

But things took an odd turn.

The event looked innocent enough. Issey was waiting in line at the coffee shop and Madison was sitting at their corner table, using Issey's Mont Blanc to practice her psychotic cursive on napkins, when a man in his mid-fifties wearing an orange down vest and needy lips introduced himself as Brooks Bosworth. He shook Issey's hand even though a hand hadn't been offered and kicked off an uninterrupted story about a set of nesting dolls decorated with the faces of Soviet Union prime ministers, from Lenin to Yeltsin. He loved his nesting dolls. They were part of a trip he had taken with his wife and his wife's best friend to Moscow, and he was proud of his haggling—particularly in front of that "lousy bitch she brought with her"—bartering a ballpoint Bic, two packs of Wrigleys, and ten American dollars for the *matryoshka*. These were good memories and now they were all gone. He didn't say if the memories were gone or the wife was gone, but it was likely both and more—he had the eyes of a man without age or sex, the broad whites washed daily with tears, sadness that he probably deserved a kicking for. Most of his story came out as deranged.

And now his nesting dolls were gone too.

Would Issey, perhaps, be capable of doing what he had done for Avi's horses to his nesting dolls? Somewhere in there, he used the expression: "I must apply to you for help."

Holding his espresso and Madison's hot chocolate, Issey saw Madison sitting at the table and she waved, with a big fat smile on her thin weedy face. Bosworth was blessed with a lack of awareness, a lack of sympathy for others' hatred towards him. On the other end of innocence, Madison had ruined Issey's Mont Blanc, shredded the napkins, given up on her cursive, and had ink on her lips. He'd never get rid of this pest.

"I'll pay you."

"Then I shall start my investigation tomorrow, Cogsworth!"

"Oh! Oh, wow! Thank you!"

Of course, Issey had called him the wrong name on purpose—the pest was more Cog than Boz—just as weeks earlier when he first returned to the valley and had stolen the lacquered nesting dolls on purpose. It was junk now, junk taking up space in his house.

The following day at the coffee shop, Issey presented the item bundled in newspaper, and Boswurst, with his hair licked by mother, gushed and lapped Issey with hugs. Issey handled it well enough, knowing that money was coming out of the squeeze.

"How did you find it?—Who had it –"

Issey tossed "professional discretion" his way, and Bosworth fetched it and his wallet. After paying him, the advancement of Issey's new status continued to strike: Bosworth recommended Issey's services to a pair of friends, Heather Baldwin and Cheryl Xu, two football *femmes* whose autographed crapola had also gone missing, and would he "be willing to do what you've done with Avi's horses and my beautiful nesting dolls with their..."? Of course! Of course! And Issey did so the next day. They were funny, those two, single-minded, literate, unforgiving, and strong—not at all the company he imagined that would suffer a drip like the Boz.

"We were friends with his wife," Heather Baldwin said, like it was part of an argument.

"Ah—was it one of you that joined them on their trip to Moscow?"

"God no," Cheryl Xu said, "That was that lousy bitch Sarah Beanbag or something."

"Bennett," Baldwin corrected, "Sarah Bennett."

"Yuck," Xu said.

"Yuck is right," Baldwin agreed. "We liked his wife well enough but after she drowned herself, we felt a moral obligation to keeping him upright."

"Anyway, enough of yesterday's news. About our stuff..."

And that's how Issey's hero status transitioned into the next natural stage he was corrupting. He had suddenly become the finder of lost things, with a client book and a Madison folded into the program, which went something like this: People would meet him and his niece at the Post & Bean. They would share their stories about their missing stuff, the value and memories it had, where it might have gone, where they might have misplaced it, and who might have been responsible for its theft (though most victims correctly blamed themselves). In turn, he wrote every detail in his notebook as if he wasn't pretending, as if it all wasn't piled, blanketed, boxed, or floorboarded within his home. As if it wasn't all just junk to fill their days and his pockets.

The huzzahs continued. His clients were spellbound by his ability to survey the setting, identify irregularities, and secure what was no longer there, using his hunter's sensibilities that led him to *finding* these lost things. Sometimes he would locate the item onsite and sometimes he sought counsel from his anonymous "contacts" who tracked underworld routes, whose identities he had to keep secure—for all parties involved. These uncanny gifts and resources, on top of his ability to listen without comment, on top of the adorable shuttle-witted niece who accompanied him during meetings and walk-throughs, *on top* of the lifelong goodwill the town offered him after the recovery of Avi's horses—all these toppings said Move Over, Saint Anthony, you egghead loser—and Hello! to the new head of the lost crap committee. Issey brought them results. He was the straight line between them and their things—no weepy prayer or faith assembly required. His clients paid him in hugs, cries, laughter, and money. Always money. Most importantly money. They were suckers—suckers who didn't deserve their stuff, suckers who didn't deserve to hold onto their money when they paid Issey to recover the stuff he had stolen from them. He felt robust and delighted. The season had finally changed in his favor.

Of course, giving back provided unfamiliar customs and rules. He began using jargon for a job that never existed: "walkthrough," "Blue Thursday," "detagging," "unpicked" vs "handpicked." Twice, he even used "lateral transfer." The suckers were convinced. The suckers were confused. And interacting with so many of them sometimes wore him out, and their fleshy happiness over junk confused him about stuff and the value of relationships, questions that he wasn't smart enough to straighten.

But the money!

At the Post & Bean, Issey cautioned new client Ms. Pinhas: "I can't make any promises."

"But you'll try? It's the most beautiful gold leaf necklace. And I've looked everywhere!"

"It's probably in the most obvious place." Issey sipped his espresso, pinky up. "Like a second pocket first situation."

"What?"

"It's like how you never find your car keys in the first pocket you look."

"Yeah?"

"That's why you always want to look in the second pocket first."

"What does that even mean?"

Issey beamed. "It means whatever you want it to mean and it means whatever *I* want it to mean."

Ms. Pinhas looked at him like he was an idiot.

Madison was agreeable, unlike most brats, and this won her a job. If he was retrieving the irretrievable 100% of the time, his skills might come off as suspicious or, worse, lucky, so he used her as a front for smaller items—cufflinks, earrings, cigarette cases, necklaces, bracelets, baubles, baseball cards, Beanie Babies. A child, he reassured a skeptical client, particularly *this* child, has a limitless imagination and her success was testimony to the dense field of her brains. Still, Madison's eagerness to please and the happiness it put on her face after a successful find annoyed him. Wasn't it just October that the child was a mute and depressed bum?

"Was she with you when you reunited Avi with his horses?" asked new client Chuck Reed, whose face was oily with curiosity. He was simply *dying* to know more.

"She played a part."

"Pull open the kimono and tell me more!"

"She may be on the stupid side, but she's invaluable. The girl's good at finding things that shouldn't be lost."

"Did she help find the horses? The story barely made the Regionals in *The Free Press*. And *The Valley Pointer* was just bad prose." But Chuck Reed stopped. "You're not going to reveal your secrets, are you?"

"Professional discretion, Mr. Reed, is the better part of valor."

The less that was said or asked or *answered* about those stupid horses, the better.

"The kid and I can be at your home at noon tomorrow for the walkthrough."

Issey's influence on Madison was positive. She exhibited patience with her school projects and her fine motor skills improved. As a reward, Rohel bought Issey a used car for after-school pickups and weekend activities, which seemed more like a reward for Rohel and Anissa than for Issey.

But life was moving too fast to take them seriously or understand the inevitable change within their family dynamic since he had become the town's most prominent citizen. Even with the car, Anissa still interfered. She entered without knocking, leading with her nose and filling out the room in a coal gray coat with a confident loop around the waist. She looked like a beautiful Venetian scene painted on the side of a van.

"How's our little girl today?"

"Madison's fine."

"I wasn't talking about Madison."

She was back to that kind of Anissa. Either way, Issey had been organizing his inventory and wasn't interested in Anissa's day-old wisecracks. He didn't like Anissa coming to his house—not after the night of the party. She had moved everything, touched everything. Sure, she had done an adequate job of storing and hiding, and, sure, he was rolling the town and giving it all back, but he didn't like people touching his things while he still possessed them. He didn't even like her looking at it—or the *way* she was looking at it.

"So you're just undoing all the work I did in your house?"

"These aren't your things, Anissa."

"They're also not yours."

"Hm."

"And what's your plan with all this? I'm sure it's stupid."

"Anissa, there are no stupid plans."

"You're thinking of questions, Issey. And there *are* stupid questions."

"I don't think so. Or do I?"

The "walkthrough."

After the first meeting with the client, Issey returned to his house, going through the stock shoehorned in plastic containers in the attic, preparing for the walkthrough the following day at the sucker's home, all part of the process leading to the item's eventual recovery. If the item was large, he would have to wait until "Blue Thursday" for "detagging." If the item was small, he would entrust the recovery to Madison. If the client was a slob, Issey would "find" the item in the client's house.

Caddy was the mechanic and there wasn't anything messy about him. He kept a clean garage and a clean bungalow where, weeks ago, Issey had stolen nothing more than the big man's Ronson lighter.

He put it in Madison's hands: "Where do you think would be a good finding place for this?"

"Under the bed!"

"Idiot. Never under the bed. We've covered this. That's where everyone looks when they've lost something—if that was the case, there'd be no need to hire me. Do you think I found those horses by searching the most obvious spot? Avi could have found the horses himself."

Madison ooh'd. "How *did* you find them, Uncle Issey?"

"Um—just never mind."

"You were so brave!"

"Mhm. And you were lucky that Mrs. Pinhas was a slob when you *found* her gold leaf necklace in her couch cushions, but get it together."

Madison pouted, her lips crusading like her father's when he got pissy, and then he felt bad for her and bad for Rohel who had entered the house unannounced.

"I thought I was dropping her off."

"Yeah, no. I had a client meeting today, but they can wait."

"This is at your new firm?"

"Something." Rohel shrugged. "Speaking of new... you really are changing Mom's house."

"Heaven forfend, Rohel, if I clear out some of the slimy olla podrida!"

Particularly glaring after Issey's jolly-good-fellow party was how little control he had over the things that were not his. Rohel had rearranged chairs from their mother's dining room table and when Issey tried to make them right, they never sat right. The drapery hung instead of swept. The guy named Sweezy spilled his Cape Cod and Issey's house shoes continued to stick to a dime-sized circle on the hardwood. Sergeant Clint Davenport moved the coffee table when he and his stocky idiot friend Eight Jeff sat on the floor and drank beers. The coffee table wouldn't re-center and their big butts stretched the rug. It was chaos. So he junked all of it.

Rohel pulled up a chair—again with the pulling—and sank into it. "Is this coffee table new? Is this maple?"

"Curly maple." Issey read his skepticism. "It was a gift."

"How about a cigarette, Issey?"

"I don't smoke anymore, Rohel."

"Geez—you've *always* smoked."

"Have I?"

"Always."

"Hmm. Now that you mention it, I suppose I have." Issey shrugged. "And now I don't."

They didn't know each other. At a certain age, siblings share their childhood stories of breaking the rules or breaking a bunch of things in the home or yard or neighborhood. They had none of this.

"Forget it. Look, I'm paying for the heat and the gas and the landline because, you know, you're getting on your feet and doing *something* like honest work."

Issey missed cigarettes.

"Tax season's coming and all I ask is that you pay the property tax on the house."

"That's it?"

"That's it."

"Then I'm your man." Issey whirled his finger.

Rohel smiled. "Seems like everything is changing."

"Like?"

"Like everything. Like you—you're settling in. Anissa is happy—mostly. She can get in her moods. You know how it is with her work."

"What does she do again?"

"She's a writer, Issey. How many times do I have to tell you? She's a writer."

"But she never does any writing."

"That's her process."

Issey nodded and Rohel continued. "And Madison—Madison is flourishing. She's reading at a third-grade level."

"She's in the third grade."

"Yeah," Rohel whistled, "things are really clearing out." He stood over items in the living room. "Well, at least Mom's things. There seem to be quite a few new additions..."

"These are gifts from clients. Everything else is inventory."

"It's a lot, Issey."

"Mm."

"You're not worried about police?"

"Once those items are gone, Rohel, they're gone. They're not going to have a hundred guys fall out for a pair of missing skis. Besides, I'm finding it all for them anyway."

"What about your clients figuring out this... *enterprise?*"

"It's fine."

Issey explained how his scheme was audience-proof. He was managing perceptions and offering his services at a price. Anything beyond his self-interest would appear off key.

"You still have to make up for Thanksgiving."

"These days, my dance card is completely full."

"It's Anissa, right?"

Issey hesitated.

"I get it, Issey—if it smells like chicken shit and it tastes like chicken shit, you're probably eating my wife's chicken salad. She cooks like she hates food."

Madison and her golden head skipped into the room with her backpack and *Graham the Mole* lunchbox.

"I thought of a really good spot!"

"Bad news, chum." Issey patted her on the head. "I'm going to find it on my own tomorrow. You can use your hiding spot next time. Practice at home."

"I will!"

She took the Ronson lighter out of her lunchbox.

"Was the hiding spot your lunchbox?"

"It was!"

"Use some common sense. How did Mister Caddy lose the item in your lunchbox?"

He took it from her and buried it in his pocket.

"I love you, Uncle Issey!"

And that's when Issey decided to get rid of Madison. He threw in Rohel as part of the deal, too.

CHAPTER TWENTY-TWO

Tax bill? What was Rohel thinking? As soon as he had gotten enough from this absolutely delicious situation and squeezed the last drop from the suckers he had stolen from, he'd be out of this town forever. But the rewards! They just kept coming. Brina Marque, a printmaker from Oregon, gifted him with 200 business cards printed on expensive stock, designed with a luxe font: "Issey. Bell River Valley Finder." One woman knitted him a sweater. Another couple gave him jars of maple tapped directly from their sugarhouse. There were microbrews and maple fudge, Abenaki copper beads and Vermont copper coins. Necklaces, amulets, bracelets, and rings. One man passed on his grandfather's black walnut cane because Issey "stood for something." A divorced couple parted with four Sabra Field prints. So many new items were crowding the old stolen ones that he had to separate them in piles.

Meanwhile, Berger's case was slippery. After the Faneuil Hall killing of McCauley and arrest of B.B.B., there wasn't so much as a blurb in the newspapers about "the manhunt." At the General Store payphone, he tried Berger again and again. Issey knew it was too early for anyone to answer, but if he didn't give it a few tries, his day would have felt incomplete—or irresponsible, maybe. He was propped up by his elbow on the payphone's housing, completely unprepared for the low shoulders and weak jawline staring back at him in the reflection from the store window. A boob on the payphone, a boob in the middle of some see-through grift, chained to the dirty leash of a payphone. It belied the role of town hero. Not good for business. So he took his business home and parked himself on his charcoal sofa, a new *MCM* number he had recently purchased with his earnings. A man, his phone, and his *MCM* sofa. He got to dialing. No answer. He tried Berger some more. He dragged the phone and his dialing finger to the bathroom and worked on his face and chin in the bathroom mirror. He dragged the phone and dialing finger to the bedroom, which had also gotten a good facelift with modernist clean lines taking the place of his mother's old crusty arrangements. He went full on Scandinavian, a set up that was as clean and disinterested as the ringing tones on the other end of the phone that eventually put him to sleep.

The following morning, refreshed in a slimming turtleneck and Henry Hatch's lost bangle bracelet in his blazer pocket, Issey saw that an overnight sleet had iced much of his street. The cold was brutal, in the controversial range, with a wind chill pushing the temperature well into the negatives. It froze the car door. Ten minutes later, he poured boiling water from the kettle onto the car door's frozen lock and handle. The glass shattered instantly.

Back in the house, searching for a heavier coat, an unexpected visitor strolled inside.

"Anissa," he sighed.

"Why the sighing, man?"

"What can I do for you?"

"Hmm. I wonder." While she wore her coal gray coat with the confident loop around the waist, her mood was somewhere between *-esque* and *-ish*. She potted around the living room.

"I was thinking of catching a movie."

"Terrific." He motioned her towards the front door. "What's showing?"

"Whatever, Issey. Your *life* is a movie."

"Of course!"

"So, you're, like, everyone's favorite," she burped, "but I think you're *bogus*."

"Maybe. Unfortunately, a very tedious client is waiting—"

"You think life's just a big movie and it's gonna be merrily merrily ever after. But what would you know? Why do you get to have all the fun?"

He ushered her outside and locked the door behind them. In the cold air, her breath was extra tangy.

"Are you drunk?"

"Maybe a little. Maybe not. Maybe a lot."

Issey loaded her into her car.

"I get it," she slurred. "You don't want to deal with the kid anymore. But others of us gotta eat too." Anissa placed her right hand over the body of her breast. "I know your tricks, juicebox. You gotta include me some day. I *organized* all that. I put everything away."

Issey paused. "Is this what's upsetting you?"

She leaned into the ignition, cut the engine on, and leaned back.

"What-errver," she said. Her chin folded into her neck.

"Don't fall asleep, please."

"Shut up. I'm going to a movie." She seemed surprised when the car yanked her from the driveway, in the opposite direction of the movie theater.

Henry Hatch was in his mid-sixties, mostly obese, with the sharp happy intensity of a Valley rustic who filled his retired days attending harvest fair committees and League of Women's Voters meetings. He had a reputation as a real chore, always running for some public office or some council seat to park his big lonely behind. He never won. He didn't inspire confidence or affection from others. He was a crusty know-it-all and his suit jackets were always too loose, like he was wearing his much fatter father's clothing as a pathetic old son. When Hatch opened the door of his bungalow, with those overlong sleeves that touched his knuckles, Issey was greeted by the memory of his night adventure there: the smell of pine spray, shepherd's cheese, cigarette smoke, and newspapers in bundles. Henry Hatch's compact home was a stagey mess of magazines in wicker baskets, wood carved carousels, a small organ with red, green, and yellow buttons, boxes of puzzles, unhung picture frames leaning against overcrowded walls, and books—lots and lots of books and crap.

In the dining room, Hatch must have been halfway through a mutilated frozen dinner. Surrounding the dining room table was a new Austrian hutch loaded with *Sound of Music* memorabilia. No wonder he was so unpopular. The house was disgusting. Issey was ashamed to have ever been inside it.

Hatch pulled out a long cigarette.

"Care for one?"

Issey mirrored the client's behavior even if he had lost the taste. The first drag was painful.

"You don't smoke, do you?"

"I quit," Issey said.

"Me, too. But I still smoke every day."

Issey coughed.

"Where would you like to start?"

Issey's next drag had more burn than the first. He set the cigarette in an ashtray and Henry Hatch carried it and his big body alongside him. He was a suspicious old woolgatherer who owned too much stuff, and it wasn't unreasonable that a slim piece of jewelry would lose itself in the dark creases. Issey couldn't decide if he wanted to "find" the bangle bracelet here or wait a few days and rely on his phantom contact who, through various backchannel sources, would reveal to Issey that the bracelet had been sourced from Hatch's place to another place, usually a pawnshop in New Hampshire. This was custom with large or unusual items. And it was believable that anything large or unusual or terrible was in a New Hampshire pawnshop.

"I'm glad that things have gotten better for you," Hatch said, bending where Issey was bending, holding the ashtray for both of them.

"What does that mean—since when, what?"

"From your childhood."

Issey met Hatch's eyes. He had possum's eyes. He had possum's teeth and a possum's swinging broadside.

"I suppose," Hatch continued, "that finding two horses in the open is much easier than finding a single bracelet in this Aladdin's cave."

"Three horses," Issey corrected him.

"Right." Hatch took an ugly drag. "It was *three* horses you found."

The winter sun had been weak and the house grew dark. Issey started preliminary canvassing from room to room—this just to breathe and plot the quickest way out. But even when he entered a new room, Hatch was close behind, tapping an infinite cigarette against the ashtray's rim. Soon, his wide shadow consumed the entire space.

"Mr. Hatch, if you please!" Issey protested, "I do my work alone. It gives me an ear for introspection."

"Certainly!"

Henry Hatch remained in the doorway.

"But you don't expect unrestricted access to my home. I don't mind you searching, but these are my *belongings*."

Henry Hatch rested on the door handle. The gesture came with a sailing line of cigarette smoke.

"Try under the bed. I would have done this myself, but the bad hip and so on. You do it. Under the bed." He tapped the cigarette. "I'll watch."

Never under the bed, he had warned Madison. Now those same words had a different meaning, and Hatch waited and watched, his head gesturing him onto the pine floor. The leaves of a tree scraped against the bungalow.

Issey got on his hands and knees like some catalog boy. His bottom was facing the ceiling. A dog barked outside. The pine floor was cold. He heard a short rasp of the long cigarette and rustling of the pleated maroon bed skirt. Issey was a little nervous. Hatch made him nervous. His intensity, his body, his stuff. More of it had traveled underneath his bed, but it was too dark to identify much more than bolts of yarn, a few books, wire hangers, a brush for a dog. If he could just reach into the inside pocket of his jacket and remove the bangle bracelet without Hatch's seeing. Getting away from his doorway eyes, getting to the other side of the bed—that was the idea.

And he had to do it now. Issey pushed himself off the floor, and Hatch, anticipating Issey's move, straightened in the doorway. Issey leapt onto the bed—"I think I saw it!"—and rolled to the opposite side and fell on the floor with a plop. This swift and brilliant move allowed him a clip and he plucked the bracelet out of his pocket, reached his arm under the bed, played with various objects for effect, and dropped the bracelet in what felt like a crispy old hand towel.

The cigarette smoke had crossed the room and, along with it came Henry Hatch hovering over him. Issey was on his stomach. "Maybe this is it..." "Yes?" "Yes!" "Bring it to me!" With one hand, Issey folded the bracelet in the hand towel. He pulled it closer to him, against the furry skin of dust and hair. His heart was beating fast.

Issey had stars in his eyes when he got to his feet. Hatch faced him, his cigarette still smoldering in the ashtray that he held.

"Mr. Hatch—I believe this is your sister's bangle bracelet. I felt the curve in the towel."

Issey opened the towel, and Hatch said nothing. It wasn't the reaction Issey had expected.

"Hm."

Henry Hatch took the bracelet from the towel and left the room. Issey followed him to the dining room. His legs were mushy. When he reached the dining room, Hatch was tearing off a check with several zeroes in the right places.

"It's made out to CASH. I didn't feel like writing out your full name."

"Perfectly fine." A rehearsed smile gathered across Issey's lips.

"Things are really landing right for you."

Reading Hatch's face was difficult. He seemed more miserable with the bangle back in his life than when it was out of it. The meeting had too many varieties of mood, burdened by the Bell River freeze, a politeness to leave things unsaid. Issey dropped the check in his inner pocket, joining other folded checks.

Then Henry Hatch asked, "You said it was three horses?"

Issey nodded.

"Three horses in the middle of the night. That must've been..." Hatch looked past Issey, into his living room. "Well, I don't know how it must have been. How *did* you manage three horses without getting crushed?"

"I can't begin to describe the horror, sir."

"But there was plenty described in the *Valley Pointer*. A stormy night and all that."

"You can't trust the media."

"And you led the horses to Avi's horse farm?"

"Uh-huh."

"Were all three were dressed in their bridle?"

"Yes."

"Each horse that had been missing was wearing its bridle?" he asked again.

"Yes," Issey repeated.

"And you led all three by the reins?"

Issey nodded.

"All three? All at once?"

"But there was more to it, Mr. Hatch."

"Oh?"

"So much more. And if I could only put that night into words. But, words, Mr. Hatch—nature hasn't been as generous to me in the 'words' things of talking."

Phew. Issey sat in his car, going "Phew," staring at Henry Hatch's lonely, dirty bungalow. The house stank. The man stank. "Phew." A biting wind came in through the massive hole that was his driver's side window. Hatch knew more than what he was saying. This put Issey at the disadvantage of saying more than he knew.

Issey wondered, Why had Anissa come over? He was looking at Hatch's bungalow, but not really *looking* at it. What was she doing there? She had said, *Why do you get to have all the fun?* What fun did she mean? She was action ready, but ready for what?

More wind came in through the window and images of Anissa went away. Issey couldn't drive through town with a missing window. He'd look like an idiot! Still, something about Anissa's behavior bothered him. But like any charming sociopath, Issey ignored the conventional signs of trouble, and exclaimed, "To the lubritorium!"

Caddy lit a cigarillo with his reunited Ronson lighter. "Explain to me why you'd pour boiling water on a car door."

"I thought the ice would thaw faster?"

"Or you thought it would fuck it up faster." The big man shook his head. "And you're from here?"

"More or less."

But Caddy wasn't—wasn't from Bell River Valley, Vermont, or even upstate New York. He had relocated from Portsmouth, Virginia, where he had been a mechanic on the naval shipyard. He brought with him a hot Southern accent and a well-fed face that always seemed to be in the middle of smoking a cigarillo and cussin' you out. His customers were loyal because they were scared of him.

"Surprised you didn't fuck up the lock cylinder."

"Oh, *I'd* know better than that," Issey winked. "Locks, you might hazard, are my specialty."

But Caddy was only paying attention to the car, and good thing too since Issey was talking too much and didn't know why.

Caddy said, "This ain't a auto body shop."

"This ain't?"

"Man, shut up." The smoke poured from his cigarillo. "And it ain't gonna kill you to get snow tires."

"I think these tires are all-season. That should work for the year."

"You *need* snow tires."

"Then it looks like I'm getting snow tires!"

"Gonna be a few days."

Of course, Issey reasoned, a few days. Parts and labor and snow tires and whatever else Caddy needed because whatever Caddy said went. To the east, the beginning lights of Fiddlehead Inn dipped into view, smoke piping from its chimney.

"Mind if I use your phone?"

Caddy nodded towards the shop window. "Might as well get the paperwork started. You have arrangements or you need to borrow a car?"

Issey was thrilled. "I guess I'll borrow one of yours!"

In the office, he stood behind Caddy's service counter and tried Berger again. Ringing only. Caddy had a good view of the covered and boarded bridge. More ringing. The brook in front of the shop was in full throat. Still nothing.

The fact was—Issey didn't know how the horses happened or what he did or why they were back at Avi's. All he knew is that he saved them. At least that's what they said.

Why was Anissa there? Not there at his house. But why was Anissa there, that night? How did she know where to find Issey? How did she know the horses were back at Avi's and that Issey had saved them? She was involved with something.

Caddy dropped paperwork and keys for the loaner on a battered desk calendar. Issey put a flourish to his signature, with the phone's receiver crooked between his ear and shoulder.

"Why dontcha give that up?" Caddy said. "Ain't nobody home."

CHAPTER TWENTY-THREE

Issey missed the preparation: polishing his lockpickers, testing the batteries for his penlight and tactical flashlight, scrubbing his thieving bag, steaming his outfits, and flexing his fingers in a new glove. He missed the walks and the watching, the powdery evening when suckers were settling in, the adrenaline of toeing past the threshold, being inside, the last step on staircases—the phantom step—undressing dressers, cabinets, credenzas, etageres. He missed the cool rush of the sparkling sky at three in the morning, the mid-afternoon wake-up tickle the following day because last night was forever and the dream was in the living.

Now he was morning guy, daytime guy, reliable, town-centric, open air, both hero and ordinary citizen who did his shopping at the General Store and dropped things in a plastic basket like a sucker. Toilet paper and paper towels. Dish soap and bread and deli meat and toothpaste.

He missed his shopping bags and urban totes as props, camouflage into the mainstream. The bags now just held the things he'll eventually throw away. His fear of becoming statistically now-ish was coming true.

It bothered him most at bedtime.

Bedtime was his work hours. He had been looking for opportunity, yet none materialized. Going back to work was too risky. There was a truffle burger with his name on it. There were everyone's lips with his name on 'em.

He missed the water bottle that he disliked. He hadn't used it in weeks because his mouth hadn't been dry and he didn't realize how much his work gave him dry mouth. He sometimes generated saliva when he had the small flashlight in his mouth. Now he was practically dripping with the stuff.

He missed knowing that the burden of proof was on the accuser—what a challenge, what a thrill! He missed listening to the police radio—the lonely 10-4s and midnight static, a connection between Issey's world and their world, isolated globes orbiting people's snowglobes, which he had snagged out of principle. But now those worlds were lost and he had returned the snowglobes.

He missed darkness, his evening companion. He missed his night silhouette, the Issey who used to be as smooth and distant as ambient light, who could fade into brush, who could transform his coat into an ermine's.

Issey sat up in bed. Henry Hatch's questions kept him up. Unlike Issey's other client Chuck Reed, who just wanted Issey to "open the kimono," Hatch was aggressive, angry even.

He picked up his client book on his bedside table. Next to the client book was the stack of those luxury business cards from Brina Marque.

Henry Hatch. Bangle bracelet. Sister's
Bill Beading. Pearl earrings
Mrs. Robertson-Redeux. Two snowboards
The Kimberley Family. Video game console
Dr. and Mr. Rangel. Three stretched canvases
Bryan Fulcher. Women's shoes (four pairs of different sizes)
Thom Bethnail. Original estate blueprints.
Sandy Corwin. Bavarian Walking Stick
Dan Vanetta. Czechoslovakian chandelier
"Caddy." Ronson lighter
Susan Gilmont. Missisquoi Abenaki golden shears
Chuck Reed. Reuben Harmon copper coins Vermont collection
Mr. Helmholz. Skating rink snowglobe
Donya Clark. One pair of skis and one snowboard

~~Emma R. Pinhas. Gold Leaf Chain Necklace~~
~~Felicia Fitzgerald. *Mastering the Art of French Cooking* original~~
~~printing~~
~~Miss Sigrist. Dead husband's Central Park snowglobe~~
~~Dotty Boudreaux. Video game console~~
~~Bobby Erbe. Monterey snowglobe; Ithaca is Gorges snowglobe~~
~~Brina Marque. Entertainment center~~
~~Heather Baldwin. Autographed football helmet from (team?)~~
~~Cheryl Xu. Autographed football from (player?)~~
~~Brooks Bosworth. Nesting Eggs~~
~~Avi. Horses~~

Each had its own story, of cherishing last night forever, but as each item left so too did the memories of himself.

Dan Vanetta's chandelier. The chandelier was Issey's last great steal, on the night of the horses. Vanetta, owner of the valley's mandolin repair shop, a youthful husband and father—younger than Issey—with a boyish face, thin brown hair, and friendly mouth, had hired him about a week ago, but told him there was no great rush since the family was traveling to San Diego and would be gone for two weeks. In the meantime, the mandolin shop had "gone fishin'."

But Issey had no idea where the chandelier had gone. In bed, he retraced his steps on that heroic night, toes cozy in a pair of hand-stitched wool socks, gifted to him from Miss Sigrist, or whoever. What happened that night? What did he do with the chandelier?

Tomorrow's priority was Dan Vanetta and his chandelier. And a chandelier is a lot of money. But the money was getting on his nerves, as if all the people who paid him were now expecting him to give away all the money he had earned. The local economy. Yuck. People can be real creeps.

CHAPTER TWENTY-FOUR

Distinct sounds came from upstairs. Wheels from luggage, light stamping of snowboots, the staff coffee machine beeping off, "Good evening" said in front desk tones and a reply of "Bon soir!" with two sets of footsteps crossing east, leaving Fiddlehead Inn. Issey drank the finger of port the bartender had given him. It was amaretto.

He had been looking for it in the house all day. Looked in the bins where Anissa had previously stored his things. Looked in the attic where Anissa had *also* stored his things. Even looked at every ceiling in the house and discovered that there were more ceilings in his house than he had thought. But still no chandelier. He needed a break. Might as well give the Sugar House another chance.

Eight Jeff loved him up. He was wearing a blousy button-up shirt with a tropical print, and his rubbery neck was perfumed.

"It's dance party night, Issey."

"Yuck. No."

"Don't bring all that cold from outside in here," Eight Jeff hollered. He had become someone who hollered. "Get into the groove. We call it, 'The Winter of Our Disco Tent.'"

"Does everything have to have a theme?"

Issey was looking around. Something, anything.

"You good?" Eight Jeff asked.

The Sugar House had filled with faces that were new to him. They were young. Some of them looked like servers getting off their shift. Some were maybe computer wizards—technical and conservative and athletic— while others smelled fresh off the slopes, with one guy showing off goggles around his neck and neon yellow sunscreen on the bridge of his nose. One guy dressed up like an old timey pilot. There was the nouveau farm owner, the history professor-turned-yoga instructor, the whole line from the cider mill, the juggling team and their glow-in-the-dark juggling pins. The local community theater was represented. And there were dudes in ball caps as part of the brewery crewery. Their clothes were fresh, their faces were fresh, but there was experience from somewhere else—an anxious pause, a premature "Um," a too-loud laugh. They knew each other, leaning on tables and walls in the limited cellar space. But something was off.

Eight Jeff was still standing there, smiling, serving. "Looking for anyone in particular?"

Tropical dance music came through the walls and ceiling at a cool volume. Fiddlehead must have swapped out the occasional quaint cooking class and snowshoe tour for a tricked out sound system.

"We even got a DJ from Los Angeles who comes in *just* for these parties," Eight Jeff boasted. "Well, that and the free ski passes."

Eight Jeff pointed out the guy in the DJ booth, a tiny and fashionable music man with flared Gucci pants and a flared Gucci beard.

This crowd. These people. They were as staged and unreal as the Sugar House itself. Issey was unreal. Something about being in the middle of nowhere, with his victims who were folded in the same nowhere. It was like the backwards bridge in Grover Gap. You moved a little differently— the wrong way, but whose wrong way? Once you adjusted, the whole system was another gem of the valley. All these people were a lot like Anissa. They were "new" Vermont. And there's no middle of nowhere when new people make their own inroads, spreading around their memories and arms, and getting all amused at the backwards bridges.

Someone in the Sugar House claimed, "Ideas are fun, but they don't really solve the problem."

"Hey, Issey!" one of the new people said.

"Issey! Hey!" another new person called.

Issey waved. Eight Jeff was smiling in the DJ booth with the tiny Los Angeles Gucci man, handing him drinks and records.

Issey was leaving without paying and that's when he saw her in the crowd. The girl with the diary with the dervish clasp. The girl from the new age store. Rhonda. Rhonda or something. And she was dancing, just slightly, just moving her fattish legs and frothy torso to the phrasing of this tropical dance music in the middle of the valley. And she was the deepest part of the valley. She was dark and she was cool. She was part of the crowd and she was distant from it. Her hair was a tangle of curls and Friday nights. She wasn't looking at anyone. Those pretty watercress eyes weren't those kinds of eyes.

Upstairs, the lobby fireplace crackled. Issey stared at the embers. Go downstairs and see her again? The embers sounded like static from an old record.

The front desk was empty. He toured behind the counter, clicked on the banker's lamp, ran down the names in the guestbook. There was the cashbox. There was the supply of pens and sewing kits and toilet paper. Conditioning, breathing, eying the clock. Sugar House sounds from the cellar traveled upstairs, those new voices and bass pulses and Eight Jeff's thick hips creaming the floor and walls. Rhonda was there. Some pens fell off the desk. Some cash fell out of the cashbox. The cash was on the floor. The pens were on the floor. Everyone knew him now. He'd have to leave all that junk where he found it. But Rhonda was there and that was good enough for tonight.

A floating mountain face watched as Issey swerved Caddy's rental car on his way home. He wiped his joyful plummy face. The roads were unpaved. They weren't meant to balance both steering wheel and romantic thoughts.

He was home somehow. Home and in the dining room. On the couch. Issey took off his jacket and laid it across his lap. Who was Rhonda? Didn't she know it was him? How could she not? He had a bagful of her stuff. She had been in the kitchen. She had watched him coming from down the stairs. She had watched him leaving, closing the door. Right? Didn't he steal her stuff?

He slapped his legs and stood with decision-making resolve, his jacket falling to the floor. It was time to break the dervish clasp of her diary. "Just a few pages and then we'll call it a day!" It was probably in the attic, when Anissa had touched everything that wasn't hers and hid everything away. It wouldn't be in the downstairs pile where he had reorganized client items. And it wouldn't be part of this growing pile that was spilling into the kitchen.

But on his way, he was distracted by the glint of something he had recently seen. Something he had recently *held*. And it was on the kitchen counter, in front of the toaster oven. And it shouldn't have been there or anywhere in the house. It was Henry Hatch's bangle bracelet.

CHAPTER TWENTY-FIVE

The precise order and superior standing that was vital to his hero's maintenance since the horse rescue was now feeling thin. How had the bangle bracelet climbed out of Henry Hatch's home and climbed into his? Issey was pulled in every which way and direction. He picked up the receiver to call Anissa. Even if it was around midnight, she would be up. Writers are up at midnight. She would know about the bangle bracelet. She had made a mess of all his things.

But the phone was already ringing.

"Hello...? Albert Spaggiari residence." He said it like a creep, dropping the T in Albert and turning Spaggiari into soup.

"Al-bear? Maybe I got the wrong number. Is this 802—" He recognized the scratchy voice. Rhonda.

"You have the right number."

"Is this Issey?"

"It is."

"Not Al-bear?"

"It's complicated."

"Thank God for that. If you were answering the phone with a phony name and it *wasn't* complicated, then I might think you were some kind of moron."

He ran his fingers across the smooth metal twine of the bangle bracelet. The only explanation was that the bracelet was a message. From who, he didn't know yet.

They had been walking along field rows deeply pleated with snow. Dawn light stretched to the abandoned gristmill, and they followed a split-rail fence that seemed to extend the length of the valley. It was three in the morning.

"When I read about those horses and heard about it from customers, I knew it was you. I was hoping you'd remember me," she was saying, "I was hoping you would come back to the store, but you never did."

They stopped walking. A colorful dawn was greeting them. She took his hand. He could feel in her palms some of her thrill on the night he had robbed her.

"And then there was your stupid face at the bar tonight."

She wrapped her arms around his neck.

"And I really like *a stupid* face, mister."

And now she kissed him, for the fourth time.

Still—what was the bangle bracelet doing back?

Sunlight poured into the bedroom. Rhonda smiled then snored some and then she woke up again and then she kissed Issey again and again and again until he was finally awake.

Issey walked into the living room wearing a silk robe. Rhonda had opened every curtain and blind and shade in the house. The way some people were greedy about career advancement, she was greedy for sunlight.

It was too early for sun, but honesty had never been one of Issey's problems. Life! Applause! Take what you like, darling!

The last woman he had known was Gwenni Von Maxi. Or was it Mary Anne Loggia? Or Bianka Fröhlicher? Whoever it was, she seemed to only understand five words and two of them were "me" and "I." Those relationships always began with some revulsion.

Rhonda joined him, holding two full cups of coffee.

"And you're just giving all of this away?"

"Some things belong to no one." Issey drank his coffee. "Some things should only belong to me. And some things go back home." This was an old version of his philosophy, the one he had explained to Anissa, but the philosophy had a different color now. "Of course, there's a massive charge for my services."

Her hemp body wash floated through the inventory. He named every house, every night, every unlocked window and gumwood door. "And what about this one?" Rhonda spied an unopened Crown Royal box, and he told a story of entry and escape. "And this?" Taffeta linens still in plastic, of daring and delight. "And these?" Two hose trolleys, a probing inkblot adventure that needed a vice jimmy for the owner's toolshed. "And all these vases—so many vases!" An endless disrobing of a town's collection of things. Every so often, he put his hand in the pocket of his silk robe and rubbed his thumb across the twine of Henry Hatch's bangle bracelet.

Despite the mystery of the bangle bracelet and despite the blooming romance, he had to return to work. He pulled up a chair by the phone and sat. The spine of his client book got a good cracking and the long-postponed messages on his answering machine got a good listening-to. He was sensitive to their yearning, to their need for his business, and he wrote the names LaVoyce Van Recklinghausen, Craig Kilby, Johnny Brin, and the Russets. He made appointments with each, tried on different outfits, waited for the report from the bathroom mirror—and the mirror had good things to say. The book on him would be that he had blended in so well with valley society that he was almost milky.

"Smells good," he winked at the slimming mirror, "if you like smells."

Their smiles were creative, Rhonda laughed all the time, and they were undressing through dawn to dusk. The imagination was an expensive place—to put on a tuxedo and dance the Vermont sonata, to jet to the mountains and belt the Mount Mansfield Rhapsody. Rhonda was fresh and young and then their whiskies sours arrived.

But for as much as he was enjoying this romance, the case of Hatch's returned bangle bracelet was still a problem. He needed information. Issey received most of his news from the sisters at the General Store. There was none. The crime section in *The Valley Pointer* reported on the occasional vandalism, but no recent theft or B 'n' E. And the Classifieds were just as slim—free firewood, at-home yoga classes, missed hook-ups, lost gundog, lentil workshops.

As Issey combed through *The Valley Pointer,* Tanya brought him a coffee and an *éclair.* Her long straw hair was less crispy these days since she had shaved half of it off. "You still seeing that new age girl?"

"Indeed."

"Don't judge the quality of the horse based on the farmer's smile, Issey."

"Meaning?"

"Meaning, the only time that store gets spiritual is when the cash register rings."

"She doesn't own the store, Tanya."

"Where is she from?"

"I don't know. I didn't ask."

"She didn't say."

"I assume that she's from here." Issey closed the newspaper and folded it in half. "And if she's not from here, then she's from someplace else."

There were holes in Rhonda's bio, for sure. He didn't know where she was born, her education, her interests, or anything else about her life. These were boring things and he lacked the training to be interested.

"I just don't trust what she's sellin'. From one liar to another."

"I'm no liar."

"I wasn't talking about you, fatso."

Later that afternoon, Rhonda came home from the new age store smelling like camphor oil.

Issey asked, "Any word on those pumice stones, Rhonda?"

She wrapped her arms around his neck and kissed him, again and again. "Oh, Issey, give that up. We don't do orders." She had lips as fresh and as biting as the early December sun.

The Russets got their snowboards and goggles, Johnny Brin his aluminum walking stick and silver Braille watch, Craig Kilby his cheap video equipment, and Van Recklinghausen her midnight velvet capelet with the golden chain. He was awarded in smiles, hugs, handshakes, and money. Cool, fanning luscious-lips money. There were also gifts, heavy and ribboned, tossed and junked at home, in the separate gift pile. Business was robust, with new names appearing in his client book, some as far as the Northeast Kingdom, and there was no shortage of inventory—it just continued flourishing, which was curious since his last night on the job was the night he rescued Avi's horses.

And then one morning, on the kitchen counter, Henry Hatch's bangle bracelet was joined by Caddy's Ronson lighter. He sat with it, thickheaded and eye-eyed. He ran his dumb thick fingers along its bronze edges. He returned to bed.

CHAPTER TWENTY-SIX

"This is going to be a watershed moment, Issey."

"What does that mean?"

They were lying in bed, she on her stomach, looking up at him; he on his back, eyes on the ceiling.

"But my name isn't Rhonda."

He faced her. "What?"

"It's Molly."

"It's not Rhonda?" He sat up in bed and pulled the bedsheets close to his chest. "*Molly?*"

She nodded.

"Why do I know you as Rhonda?"

"Beats me. You're the only person who's ever called me that." She shrugged. "I just went along with it."

"Molly?"

"When we go out to the Sugar House, everyone calls me 'Molly.' That or 'Mols.' Didn't you ever notice people calling me by a completely different name?"

"I thought they got it wrong."

Her hair was a silky mess. Why had he ignored this?

"Molly." Issey tried out syllables for weight and emphasis.

"Is this gonna be weird?"

"Mohll-lee."

"You have heard of the name before, right?"

"Molly…"

She punched him in the tummy. "Soft!"

He stood and threw on a robe.

"Molly! I adore it!"

He sailed downstairs and got the coffee going. While he waited, he picked up the toaster and looked at his chin in the toaster's mirror. The day was for the taking—*life* was for the taking. Rhonda. Molly. All the same.

More like: least of his worries. The kitchen counter had been getting crowded and he had to clear it to make room for new items that had come in over the past week. Pinhas's gold leaf necklace and the Julia Childs book were reunited with Henry Hatch's bangle bracelet and Caddy's Ronson lighter. He had no idea how they were coming in. They were just coming in. They were just advancing. With this pile, he had created a third pile, separate from old inventory and new gifts, a third pile lacking any real order. He'd deal with the third pile later. This advancing pile. He put the toaster down. His chin was fine. It needed work. It was fine.

From the living room there were rustling sounds—it was all sounds wooden, clinking, stacking. It was the sound of the piles. He hurried into the living room, his robe winging out, and found her at the front door, holding a snowboard. Two other snowboards were at her slippered feet along with a set of juggling pins.

"Rhonda, what are you doing?"

"*Molly*, Issey. We went over this."

"Molly, yes, Molly."

"Thank you." She huffed sarcastically. Everything was kind of a joke. She returned to the snowboard, oohing and ahhing.

"*Molly*."

"Hm?" She wasn't looking at him.

"What are you doing?"

"Can I have these?" She pointed to the juggling pins. "I've been wanting to take classes with the juggling crew."

"Molly—that's..."

"And these new snowboards are *rad*. Did you get 'em for me?"

He wrenched the snowboard from her fingers and kneeled to collect the other two.

"Don't *touch* the items," he snapped.

"Oh—whoops. I didn't know—"

"It's all business."

His back was to her. Three was a lot of snowboards to carry, so he carried them one at a time away from the front door. He passed her several times as she watched him in silence. What was she thinking? He'd have to put these in a different pile since he couldn't place the owner or owners at the moment. There had been a lot of snow-sport junk in the inventory and their owners all had the same face. Over a cup of coffee, he began adjusting the piles. She may have stayed in the house or she may have left, whatshername. Issey didn't see her for the rest of the day.

Issey was sitting on the sofa with his legs crossed. He sipped a piña colada Molly had made the night before, prepared in large batches.

Rohel had left a lot of messages. His voice was unhinged. "That police officer who was at your party was here. He was asking questions. Everything's okay, right—isn't it?" Madison interrupted twice. She missed her Uncle Issey and had thought of a bunch of really good hiding places. Anissa called. She left Anissa-type messages, three to five seconds of silence. The whole family was unhinged.

Every morning, Molly used to tell him her dream from the night before and every morning he pretended to be interested—these stories without consequence, these stories without a center. It was a lot of haggling for his attention. Her winter coat was hanging on the coat hanger in the entrance. She was out for a December hike. The last time he had seen her wearing her winter coat, he had known her as Rhonda. This was around the time she had stopped telling him her dreams.

She was a lot different than he had imagined when he had raided her house. She just was... not how he had thought she'd be. And now that she was a Molly, everything had changed. Molly took juggling lessons. Molly made piña coladas in December.

He sucked on the piña colada, trying to ignore the ever-growing piles behind him, in front of him. The piles were all over him. They were getting furry.

Refreshed after Sunday morning's farmer's market, Issey and Molly carried tote bags loaded with cheese, crackers, geraniums, and a lot of beer. Molly's beer was headache beer, and it was a load to carry. And he couldn't complain. A lot of the stuff he got for free—as a gesture of thanks or goodwill or something. Molly enjoyed being on the arm of a bigshot.

And the town center was dressed in full holiday cheer. Holly, pine, and balsam were fragrant in the air. Loudspeakers played light Christmas classical. Someone was even roasting chestnuts.

At a park bench near a dog park, Molly opened one of her beers. She used a bottle opener that she kept on her keychain. The young people recognized Molly, said, "Hey, Mols." They saw Issey as a figurehead and nodded, "Sir." The older ones also nodded at Issey and didn't like that the young woman was drinking beer in the park. Still, the beer was from the local brewery so they couldn't complain.

There weren't many people at the dog park. It was too cold. Some of the smaller dogs had on doggy vests. Issey wondered how much those would fetch.

"Every time we hold hands," Molly leaned into Issey's arms, "I become a dog walker."

Everything was kind of a joke.

"We should go on that hot air balloon ride I was talking to you about."

Issey didn't remember this conversation. "But isn't it thirty degrees— on land?"

"It's never too cold for a hot air balloon ride," Molly smiled. "Besides, Keith owes me."

Issey didn't know what that meant, but he rarely pursued answers for questions he wasn't interested in asking.

She drew in closer to him. "Ever think about going back?"

"Huh?"

"You know—back. To your old work."

Issey shook his head.

"Why?"

"No—it's..." She was almost swaddled in Issey's arms and he could only see a daydreaming head and cool flowing eyelashes. "I just like the image. Shadow man. Night man. Molly's man."

He followed her eyelashes. It was like watching the curls of smoke from a cigarette someone else was smoking. "In people's homes. Sliding in, sliding out. It's almost unbelievable." She drank more beer. The sound of Molly's voice was getting on his nerves.

At 2,000 feet and rising, Bell River Valley in December poured open to Issey and Molly. Mountain torrents swept through rock and vegetation. Trees were naked and gray, and most of the good birds had left for the winter. Snowmobile trails ripped through the pastures. The community center's tennis courts needed new line painting. Issey drew their bright white lines from this great height. As he did, the town shrunk to the constellation of his activity, and he continued tracing for Molly's benefit, lighting each roof with his star. There was Caddy's auto repair shop and the mechanic's weatherbeaten bungalow. Issey had lifted his jewelry and Ronson lighter from the man's bedstand as he snoozed. Caddy was a big man, but he slept tiny. Nearby, he traced a line to Mrs. Robertston-Redeux's. He had been tired that night and snagged easy leftfield junk from a screened-in back porch. Chuck Reed was her across-the-street neighbor. The take at Reed's had worn him out since the choices were vast, and a simple rootle through the theater director's armoire alone gave him a headache. Eventually, he settled on the Abenaki coins and they were probably the least valuable thing in his home. There was Old Man Brill's house with its crooked stone chimney. There was Henry Hatch's cheerless hutch with its dirty bangle bracelet. There was Emma Pinhas's mousey cottage and her gold leaf necklace. There was Brooks Bosworth's empty nesting dolls.

In the quiet moments, Issey stayed quiet. Then, when the pilot opened the blast valve and the burners erupted, with the calm broken and wicker basket rattling, Issey pulled Molly close and continued calling out various houses. She shouted, "So many! That's amazing!" The image of him thrilled her. "I know those people! They're greedy people!" And then the burners shut up and thankfully she shut up. The nylon balloon was blue and white—the colors of winter. Issey recognized the pilot from somewhere, a young man, about Molly's age, with an Oldsmobile mustache.

"There's our house!" she squeezed his hand and smiled, bundled up in a massive faux-fur overcoat and pom-pom hat.

A nod to the east brought him to Rohel's white clapboard house. From this high up, it was larger than he would have thought, and the roof looked chest-out, as if it was holding back tears. While the answering machine messages from Rohel had drifted off, the silent ones from Anissa did not.

A couple of clicks north was Avi's horse farm.

Occupying an elegant western arm was Fiddlehead's.

"The elevation isn't making you nauseous, is it?"

Her mothering annoyed him. Of course he was nauseous. But he just shook his head and gave her a thumb's up. And then the descent began and it was trouble. The bottom of the basket snagged several treetops. With curving hips, the pilot sprayed propane to straighten the balloon's course. It didn't work. The three of them swooped as one. Issey gripped the basket's edge. Molly took his arm and put a protective hand on her winter hat. They rocked against hardwood, tipped onto flatland, and eventually the basket coughed out its passengers. Issey rolled into a naked thicket,

Molly spilling gently behind him. The ground was hard and cold, but all they lost was their lunch.

"My goddamn eggy salad sandwiches—they're piss!"

The pilot was mopey as he went over the damage. "Sorry, sir," he said to Issey. "Sorry, Mols. You okay?"

"Who taught you how to pilot—Johnny Brin?"

Molly was shaking. She had dirt and leaves on her pom-pom hat.

"I meant to graze that first tree. The rest... You okay, sir?"

Issey nodded. The guy was treating him like he was Molly's father. Issey wasn't *that* much older than her.

The pilot put his fists on his hips, like a real stuntman. Issey remembered where he had seen him—during a night out with Molly, at the Sugar House bar. He was one of her pals who called Rhonda "Molly." He was the guy who dressed up like an old timey pilot.

"We probably did some damage to something. Just so long as my passengers aren't hurt."

Then the pilot joined his hands with theirs and recited what felt like a poem he had recited hundreds of times before, half-memorized, half-made-up.

"...You have flown so high and so well
That God has joined us, my two friends, my two bros,
And set you down gently back again
Onto, into the loving arms of earth, Mother Earth."

Molly took her hand back and smoothed her huge faux-fur coat. "What is that?"

"It's custom after every flight to recite the Balloonist's Prayer."

"We should have said a prayer before the flight."

The pilot leaned into the basket. "I guess we'll probably hold off on the champagne. She'll probably be a sprayer. How about we all get a drink at the Sugar House?" He pushed his thumbs toward his aviator's scarf. "First round's on me."

"You *do* owe us," Molly said.

"Don't you need to get your stuff?" Issey pointed to the hot air balloon basket and massive nylon material stretched across the field.

"Nah." Keith waved it off. "She's not going anywhere."

But Issey wanted to walk alone and see the valley. He promised to meet Molly at the house later. She kissed him goodbye. It was a too-long kiss and a little loud, and Issey didn't enjoy it in front of Keith. Eventually, he had his face back, and all three waved until Molly and Keith finally fell out of sight.

Oh, Molly. In all of his romances, it was only a matter of time before one party figured it out. Nothing about the women was ever normal. Nothing about Issey was ever normal. And finding out who was *really* out of this world took about this far into the relationship. Sometimes, the woman got there before Issey. Sometimes, Issey got there before the woman. Or did he? Probably not.

Someone said Hello to him with a smile. Issey smiled and moved on. He just wished that Molly was different, that she could return to being Rhonda. His walk took him to an upscale neighborhood with cement driveways and duo carports and white shale porch. A guy was organizing grocery totes from his trunk. Issey tracked the cloth bags, a bouquet of tulips, the camping gear, the baby seat, the car's make and model. He recognized the home's French windows, peacocking fanlight, and its witch window. He had been here before. He had been *inside* before. It gave him a rush, a heady kick on his topper, knowing that he had been inside this man's house—this trunk boy, this tote slave in his weekend jeans... but then he recognized the front door. There was intimate knowledge of the door. There was intimate knowledge of the windows. *Both* had been points of entry: Issey had been here twice—why had he been here twice? Did he rob the place twice? The house wasn't that beautiful.

The man turned.

"Hi, Issey!"

"Afternoon, neighbor!"

Issey smiled and moved on. The guy probably had a normal wife with only the one name.

An aggressive hillside would have taken him to Garnett's woodlot. He traveled south instead, towards sparkling water.

Young people, Friends of the Tributary Conservation, waded in the steam, collecting samples to monitor.

"Hi, Issey!" called one of the conservationists.

Issey waved. The sun was too bright to see who it was. The voice was female.

She called back. "You and Molly had a picnic?"

"No—our hot air balloon capsized!"

"Oh no! Was it Keith?"

"Yeah!"

"He's not very good!"

"Our eggy salad sandwiches were ruined!"

"Gross!"

"Very!"

"Maybe we'll see you two at the Sugar House soon!"

"Maybe! Maybe not!"

Issey walked on.

He found himself where it all started: Old Man Brill's house with the crumbling chimney and the choo-choo mailbox. He gave the tiny boiler a few taps and listened. Full of mail. The sound he loved, even if he had outgrown it. The front door kicked open.

"Get away from my mailbox, punk!"

"Hi, Mr. Brill!"

"I'll kill you!"

"Spring has sprung and the bird is on the wing!"

"I'll kill everyone you know!"

The grassy aroma from the rolling farmland brought back memories of his early years. Old Man Brill's mailbox was *his* place, where his fingers did all the work in the man's rusty old box. This town and its suckers— Vermont's lights were brilliant during the holidays.

And when he got home, Sergeant Davenport was waiting for him.

CHAPTER TWENTY-SEVEN

Sergeant Clint Davenport looked as if he had been stationed in his police cruiser for hours. The driver side door was open, his long leg was stretched out of it, and a circle of peanut shells was swirling around his boot.

"Hello, Sergeant!" Issey waved. "What do you want?"

"Issey, hello!" Sergeant Davenport slapped his hands clean of peanut dust. He was in a friendly mood. "Let's go to the station. You can follow me or we can drive together."

"That bad, huh?"

Issey got in the backseat of the police cruiser. It smelled police cruiser, all right. No joking about that. It smelled like gun polish, heavy leather, and sandwich meats, but the peppermint tea was new.

At the rear door, Davenport popped his head in. "You don't have to sit in the back, man. You can sit in the front."

"Oh," Issey said, surprised. "Normally, they have you sit in the back."

Davenport laughed at Issey and closed the door on him. In the front seat, saddled in behind the wheel, Davenport said, "*Normally*, huh? You're in the back of a lot of police cars?"

So it was like that. They drove in silence for about ten minutes through the valley's maple groves. For some reason, he remembered being in bedrooms and he remembered the putrid heat coming from other people's laundry hampers. He never got used to that smell. And he was glad he didn't have to deal with it anymore.

To Issey's surprise, Davenport was a nervous driver. He wasn't used to Bell River roads yet, the ice winches that slip up the tires, the frost heaves that wreck suspensions. You wouldn't think someone so tall, so built-right, so *manly*, would have road insecurity. Issey wondered if Davenport had the same problems on his cattle ranch.

It was Issey's experience that being in the backseat of a police cruiser changed the outside society to a completely foreign place. Look at them, walking around. Shopping and driving and living carefree.

But today, there was nothing that separated him from the backseat of a police cruiser and the mainstream of society. Maybe it was Davenport—this huge outsider that Issey felt a little sorry for. Maybe it was just getting away from the house and Molly.

"I told my wife about you thinking I was from Texas. She didn't think it was that funny." Davenport laughed. "But, you know, she's having a hard time fitting in. We didn't think it would be this... chilly."

"I have a sister-in-law who's been dealing with that for years." Issey said from the backseat. "She's not from here either. She's from Virginia."

"Oh, yeah?" Davenport's eyes perked up in the rearview mirror and they met Issey's. "Maybe we can put 'em in touch."

"Maybe," Issey said, drifting off from the conversation. "Maybe not. She's a writer, so don't expect a lot."

They drove for another five minutes saying nothing. Davenport's driving picked up some confidence as they were getting closer to the town square.

He asked, "Is it common here for people to just, like, walk with ski poles and cleats? Even for just regular walking?"

Issey nodded, thinking of something else. Every so often, a voice from a walkie-talkie broke in with numbers and locations. It was official static in the cruiser.

Why was he here, in the backseat of a police cruiser? Why couldn't they just have the conversation at home? It was finally catching up to Issey that something wasn't right.

Davenport's face was rugged, yet serene. It didn't appear official. He looked like he was back at the homestead, up there whittlin' a duck caller.

Issey couldn't picture anything he had done wrong. He had actually been... good. Right?

They walked into the police station side by side, like buds coming in for coffee and paperwork. For all his years in Bell River, Issey had never been inside the police station. This one was mostly empty. Davenport had gone somewhere else. There was a glowing fish tank with exotic yellow fish moving from one end of the tank to the other end of the tank. Davenport reappeared and then led Issey into Interview Room 1.

"Just give me another minute," Davenport said. "I gotta get a bunch stuff, so hang tight."

It was the old move and Issey was a little disappointed in Davenport for having to pull it. And then just as soon as that thought came, it went away and Issey had it. He knew why Davenport brought him in and he couldn't believe he had been this short-sighted. It was that stupid bangle bracelet and that stupid lonely old fishwife Henry Hatch. The whole thing had been a massive set up. Hatch had come into Issey's home. Hatch had placed it on his kitchen counter, where it would be easy to find. And just when life was cozy for Issey, Hatch would twist the tin.

But how did he do it? How did he get his big butt moving swiftly from entry to exit? No, that wasn't possible. Issey was the shadow man. Hatch— forget it. Hatch could hardly walk.

It was Rhonda. Or Molly or whatever her name was. Henry Hatch had... what? He knew her. He hired her. Gave her the bracelet to deposit at Issey's house. Molly was a sneak. Everything was a joke and nowhere for her were there any boundaries.

He saw it all. The moment he met her at the new age store, there was something off, something very different from the young woman he had met on the night when he had broken into her home and had stolen some of her belongings. He just couldn't trust her anymore.

But the timeline was off. The bangle bracelet was on the kitchen counter *before* he saw Molly that night at the Sugar House. Wasn't it that night? Or was it the following morning?

The door crashed open. Davenport came in, pushing a cart with a TV on top of it.

"There's no Wi-Fi in the valley, so we had to download the footage and then burn it to disc. It takes forever."

Davenport rolled the TV cart in the middle of the room, on the wall opposite the false mirror. He grabbed a yellow legal pad from the cart and held it up. "I can't always keep my thoughts together. It helps to write everything out."

Issey finally asked, "So why are we here, Sergeant?"

"Oh, geez!" Davenport shook his head. "I didn't say?"

"No."

"See? That's why I always write my thoughts down. I mean, you're not a mindreader. You don't know why you're here. Geez, Clint."

"So why am I here?"

"Issey, you have no clue?"

"No."

"Gosh, I'm sorry," Davenport said, sadly, "but we have a bunch of evidence showing you stealing from Avi's horse farm."

CHAPTER TWENTY-EIGHT

The video showed Issey in the tack room. It showed him cobbling together saddles and stirrups. It showed him smelling the smoky finish on the stirrups. It showed him leaving. It showed him coming back. It showed him hefting saddle blankets and then leaving again. It showed him coming back again. It showed him looking around. It showed him touching things. It showed him taking small things that fit inside his black gloves and pockets. It showed him picking up another saddle and then leaving. It showed him coming back with the saddle and returning it to the rack. It showed him walking around, picking up more small things that fit inside his pockets and then finally resolving the issue with the saddle and taking it with him. It did not show him coming back. The video ended.

And the entire time Issey was thinking, "That's what I look like in those pants?"

Davenport had his enormous legs crossed, sitting all the way across the room. He looked at his legal pad with his lists of questions. He made a face at the questions and set the legal pad on the floor.

"So what do you think, Issey? It doesn't look good."

"Hm."

"There's a lot we know and... Well, as far as information goes, you're sittin' in the nosebleeds."

"I don't understand, sir."

Davenport was confused. "Did we not just watch the same video?" He looked at the television. "Did you miss something? Did *I* miss something?"

"Sir, I'd like to help you with this, but I don't know what I'm seeing."

"Issey," Davenport laughed, "that was you."

"Me?"

"That was you."

"Me? How could you think that was me?"

Davenport was puzzled. He played the video again. It showed the saddles, the stirrups, the leaving, the returning, the touching, the blankets, the stuff that could fit in a glove, in pockets, leaving, returning, debating the saddle, settling the debate, leaving.

"I mean, Issey—"

"I'm sorry, sir, but I don't get it."

A lot of activity had indeed been captured in the video. But it did *not* necessarily capture Issey. It showed a dark blob of a human being. More blob than being... Issey stretched his chin a few times... The lessons in Montreal from Claudia Bünd were always fresh in his mouth—and one of the most basic was to spot the camera. Always know where the camera is pointing. Issey knew there was a camera in the tack room. Of course he did. He wasn't a maniac. It's why he wore a mask. It's why he wore layers. It's why he hugged that juicebox of a body into the blind spots and dark creases of the tack room.

"Issey, that's you. There's no denying that's you. That's not even a question."

Issey caught Davenport in a lie. He didn't have "a bunch of evidence" on him. All they had was this video. They're all the same, even the ranchers from Oklahoma.

"I'm sorry, sir." Issey said. "But I don't see any face. It's just some creep. You know me better than that."

"I *do* know you. I know you have a history of residential burglary. I know you appear reasonable but also," he cleared his throat apologetically and said, without raising his voice, "but also not reasonable. The walking opposite of reasonable. And I know that after you were done in the tack room, you then moved on to the horses."

Issey said nothing. Davenport waited, but nothing was going to come. So Davenport picked up his yellow legal pad, removed a pen from his breast pocket, and scanned his questions.

"Now, did you take the horses *after* you raided the tack room?"

Issey waited for the next question.

"I figure you took 'em after, that you unloaded the stuff back wherever you hid it, and then returned to the horse farm. That's why I think you were debating about that last saddle. But I might be wrong, so you'll have to clear that up. But we can do that later."

Issey narrowed his eyes at Davenport.

"Maybe you were thinking, 'All this horse gear is good an' all, but what'll get me an even bigger payday is some grade A equine.' Stop me when I'm wrong."

Issey waited for more. Davenport looked down at his list of questions.

"We know you were there that night. That's a given. We have you on video here." He pointed his pen at the black television screen. "And we know you took the horses. How did you take them?"

Issey didn't respond.

"How did you get all three horses to go with you?"

Issey didn't respond.

"See, that's where I'm thinking three horses was above your paygrade. And this is where I'm thinking that that sister-in-law of yours enters the picture."

Here, Issey responded. "What?"

"Your sister-in-law," Davenport said. He looked at his legal pad. "Anissa."

"I thought you didn't know her."

"Yeah, I hate being deceptive. Regardless, look. It's from a newspaper down there."

He passed Issey a copy of the article with the photo.

The photo was about fifteen years old, early digital. The article was called "Herd Management Team Offers New Solutions for Pony Problem." In it, a group of Assateague and Chincoteague volunteers are moving wild ponies along a marsh. Anissa was probably in her early twenties here, in a brown tank top and all shoulders.

"There she is on pony patrol in a place called Assateague Islands. It's lotsa horses in the Eastern Shore, feral and semi-feral. If anyone knew how to handle three horses in the middle of the night, it's someone with experience."

Anissa, Issey thought. *Anissa?*

"And look, it's not the worst thing in the world. You know, buddy. You brought 'em back. They were fine. Talking about it would be to your overall benefit."

"Like I said," Issey rubbed his hands on his thighs. "I'm in the ingredients industry. We have a lot of new flavors of cinnamon in the works."

"Come on, man."

"I don't know anything about Anissa and this guy in your video. I've always liked the police, but I can't just make things up like some liar."

Davenport nodded and Issey asked, "Am I being charged with something?"

"You are not."

"Avi isn't pressing charges? I assume that's who gave you this video."

"No. He just wants to put this whole thing behind him and his family."

"Why'd he give you the video then?"

Davenport shook his head.

Issey asked, "So, I'm free to go?"

Davenport was disappointed in Issey. He nodded. "You are, Issey, but I hate to say that leaving isn't your best move. Just clear up some of this—at least for the paperwork."

"No, I think I'm gonna go."

Issey smiled apologetically—these two were doing a lot of apologizing to each with their faces. He stood and headed to the door. Davenport pretended to look at the legal pad with his notes, pretended to hide his feelings. But before opening the door, Issey turned, walked back, and sat down across from Davenport.

Davenport was relieved and he set the legal pad back on the floor.

"I appreciate it. It's a good move, Issey. It's the *right* move."

"Oh, no. I have nothing else to say." Issey said. "You brought me here. You're my ride."

CHAPTER TWENTY-NINE

Molly's pancake face drew up alongside him and then it was gone. There was the product pile, the stuff he had stolen. There was the gift pile, the stuff from his clients. And then there was the third pile. The third pile grew a little every day. These were the things that came back in, intensified and coiled, and had become a kind of shroud in the house. He could not control that pile, and soon life smelled like other people's laundry. Anissa knocked at the door fourteen times. Issey stood behind it, watching, afraid.

Molly had left a note on the kitchen counter. Issey kept the blinds drawn and the sunlight out. Darkness spread throughout the house like an advancing mask. The phone rang. Could be Berger. Could be Anissa. He let the answering machine get it. "My wife said you helped rescue those horses." He was hired for a job. Then another. How could it be? Yet he was hired and hired and hired. Smiles, hugs, handshakes. Money, small gifts in envelopes, heavy gifts tied together with a ribbon, all of which joined Molly's unread note on the kitchen counter.

Issey took efficient showers and ate hurried, uneventful meals. He drank water throughout the day and walnut juice before bed. His activities in town were limited only to client meetings and then it was straight home. Days bled together. Two lightbulbs had gone out. One in the hallway between the bedroom and the toilet; the other at the drafting table he didn't use. It always surprised him when a lightbulb went out. These stayed out. And where did that drafting table come from?

The general drift of his plan seemed to be working backwards. More clients came. He offloaded what felt like *two* holiday seasons as opposed to the one he had worked leading up to the horses, yet the inventory kept growing, doubling, tripling. He had run out of business cards or had lost them, had probably lost them, gone somewhere in these piles of things. Because the stuff and the clients—they just kept coming in. It was like he was going in half-blind to meet these clients and coming back home with the other half blind. A guy named Dan Vanetta called. He had a young-ish voice, was friendly enough, and wondered how his case was going since the family had returned from San Diego. Case? Family? San Diego? Issey pulled out his client list and saw "Dan Vanetta. Czechoslovakian chandelier." Right. The chandelier guy. From this view in the kitchen, he didn't see any chandelier in the horizon.

Issey said he would meet him at his house. He needed to refamiliarize himself with the place—was it a play or was it legit? Issey didn't know. The interview with Davenport had thrown him off his game. And the image of Anissa stealing horses, setting him up, and doing what, or how, or why—completely freaked him out.

The address wasn't one he knew automatically, and the drive took him into the upscale part of town, with the cement driveways and the *porte-cochères*. Sure. He knew this place. He had just passed this place for some reason. It was the house with the peacocking fanlight and witch window. And the guy—Dan Vanetta—was the tote man with the tulips. That's right—*this* was the chandelier house.

"Hey, Issey!" Dan Vanetta called out. Issey smiled and shook Vanetta's welcoming hand.

And the first thing Issey saw, staring at him from above the garage, was a surveillance camera. Issey pointed at it.

"That's new?" Issey never missed surveillance cameras and he knew instantly that one was not there on the night he had stolen the chandelier.

"Oh, yeah. Ever since the chandelier went missing, we had it installed."

"Ah," Issey said. "*Fait accompli.*"

Dan Vanetta looked at Issey. "I'm not sure that's the right way to use that phrase."

They went inside the house. Vanetta showed him the hole in the ceiling where the chandelier had been. That must have been one inspired night, Issey thought. The electrical wires dangling from the hole looked like the nerve endings from a missing tooth. Would he ever perform the same again? That hole in the ceiling could have only been pulled off by someone at the height of their artistry—and at the height of their insanity. He was jealous of old Issey. You need to be insane to do art good. Would that Issey ever come back or had the flash forgotten him?

"Anyway, I think I know where this could have gotten to," Issey lied. They were walking out.

Vanetta was good natured about it and also handsome. "No rush. We have holiday plans, so we're gonna be out of town again."

"Try not to broadcast that information." Issey pointed at the surveillance camera again. "And make sure you keep your camera on while you're away."

"Oh, yeah." Vanetta rubbed the back of his head and let his hand stay at his neck. "I just wish we had put up the camera before that night. We just don't—we don't feel safe here anymore. It's not right."

Issey thought about Anissa. He didn't feel safe with her out there. "I know what you mean."

He had one last look at the surveillance camera.

The surveillance camera. Suddenly everything that was supposed to bother him finally bothered him.

For all the things that worried him throughout the day—Anissa, the third pile, the general feelings of confusion—Davenport wasn't one of them. Issey didn't know why. It's not like he was callous towards the threat of arrest and he wasn't arrogant or even, for a change, stupid. He just didn't feel that Davenport had anything on him or even knew what he was doing.

Nothing was right about that interrogation.

That's because it wasn't an interrogation. It was an interview. An interview can lead to an interrogation. But that interview hadn't been moving in that direction.

Why wasn't Issey charged with anything? Sure, the surveillance video didn't get his face, but with his record and approximation in physical appearance to the guy in the video (debatable), there was enough probable cause to charge him. Davenport couldn't have been that stupid. Davenport wasn't stupid at all.

Issey drove past Garnett's woodlot. At the fork in the road, he took a right into a road wet with mud and snow. Caddy was right about Issey getting those snow tires, and Issey's dumb car was gaining animal traction in that mess of a road, confidently charging uphill towards Avi's horse farm.

He parked where he had parked Rohel's car the night he had stolen from Avi's tack room, which he knew wasn't as far as he should have parked. Should have been half a mile or at least a quarter mile. No, he was sloppy that night and there was no art in it. A true artist knows when those corners are being cut. You can't lie to yourself. It was the wrong steal. He knew he was lying to himself that night and all this time because he didn't put on his mask until he had reached the tack room. Not before it. His face was out the entire time. That naked seal face. He remembered his cheeks feeling pink that night. Then red with abandon. He knew this. *That* was arrogance so high that it was criminal! So criminal, in fact, that Issey needed to see for himself what he had indeed seen that night and hadn't remembered until standing in Dan Vanetta's paved driveway. It was the *three* surveillance cameras surrounding the horse farm.

The first one was planted among the trees, the one that tried to look like a tree but instead looked like a metal pole with a surveillance camera on top of it. Issey was so arrogant that night, he might have even stuck his tongue out at the camera, as if saying, "You think this fooled me, dummy? I know the difference between a camera and a tree." After returning to the tack room the second time and then coming back to the car with a new load in his hands and pockets, Issey might have also done a little dance with his rear-end facing the camera.

And that was just the camera hidden in the woods. The other two cameras, lens in plain sight of the horse farm's entry and exit points, he just ignored. He knew they were there. He just figured, the hell with it.

So there were three surveillance cameras with Issey centerstage. And yet, Avi had given Davenport the tack room footage. And in that footage, you couldn't really see what was happening. So, why didn't Avi give Davenport the footage from those three surveillance cameras?

Issey returned to the car. He was onto something and speeding home. It was almost a little too much for him.

There were three surveillance cameras. Yet Davenport only had the footage from the tack room. For reasons unknown, Avi was withholding the footage from the police. But Issey couldn't tell Davenport about the three surveillance cameras because Issey didn't want to go to jail. It was a situation.

At home, the third pile was out of control. Everything was a little out of control. Anissa. Molly. Avi. Throw in Dan Vanetta. Throw in Henry Hatch.

If Issey could just get control of the third pile, then maybe something resembling balance would be restored...

He pulled everything out. Every bracelet, Abenaki coin, ring, amulet, baseball card, baseball bat, baseball glove, earring, necklace, and handmixer. He separated ladies shoes from snowshoes, video game consoles from video game cartridges, ski poles from walnut canes from walking sticks from guitar stands. He fell on his knees, comparing blank canvases to estate blueprints to Sabra Field prints, an earthenware pitcher from the temperance era to a binderful of international stamps from the 1980s to the David Winter "collectible" cottages to the boxes of Lenox silverware, a *Le Château des Dames* puzzle, a "vine" rack, a Dutch oven. He used two autographed football helmets as an ottoman, one made out to Heather Baldwin, the other to Cheryl Xu. Leather belts and black wires and juggling pins spilled like guts from the fireplace. Something wooden broke under his shoe.

Was Anissa on one of those surveillance cameras? Was there a connection between Avi and Anissa? Did Avi own property or horses on the Eastern Shore?

Sweat poured from his fat face. His palms were wet. The house was swaying. He reached the kitchen counter. And there was her note. How long had it been there, he didn't bother asking. He just read it.

Heyhey dummy—

I know you were looking at me like I was acting weird the other day bc I was. I didnt want to tell you the decision I made after the hot air balloon ride bc I didnt know how youd react when you found out. Here it is—Im going away for a while to a womens yoga retreat. I want to wake up with the world and hike Mount Mansfield and do pilates and meditate and drink green juice and share positivity with other women. Its hippy dippy stuff, whatever. Dont judge me. Your ripping off everyone in town, fraudo!

Heres a brochure so you can see all the fun stuff youll hate. Its just for a little while but I all ready miss your stupid face.

Luv luv LOVE YOU!

Molly

PS Try and clear out all that shit by the time I get back. Namaste!

It was like the little hemphead was speaking directly in his ear, with her hoarse voice and boozy hair. He pressed the letter close and smelled her chubby handwriting, her pulpy skin. Molly was the answer. The house was a complete loss. It was a disgrace. What was this plan? Without her, his actions—the philosophy, the program, the client book—all of it was antics. She was the person or thing that was better than this new Issey, Bell River

Valley hero, town finder. She had been there all this time. Leave this town. Leave these people.

He'd pack. He'd go to her.

From the closet in their bedroom, he threw the indigo suitcase on the bed, unzipped it, and in it went the tweed herringbone jacket, the black nylon jacket, the gabardine blazer, the slimming black pants, the heightening turtleneck, the black wool cap, the black mask just in case. He'd buy toiletries on the way. On the top shelf in the closet was a second pair of ankle boots he had been trying to break in, so he packed them too. Next to the ankle boots was a book he didn't know. It was chunky and odd. And when he finally looked at its cover and saw its dervish clasp binding its pages together, he recognized it as a memento from their first night together, when he broke into her home and stole a few of her things along with her diary with the dervish clasp. "Perfect timing!" he said out loud and dropped her diary in the suitcase. The final thing on the top shelf in the closet was another suitcase. It was black and he didn't remember bringing it in the house. But wasn't that the house now? Everything was a lot of not remembering what it was or knowing what it is. The bedroom, though. The bedroom. Issey thought it through. Unlike the carnage in the living room and kitchen, nothing had entered the bedroom. Nothing had come in except his clothes. *He* had brought that suitcase in. And then he remembered: it was the black suitcase. Duh! The black suitcase from the airport—how long ago was that? Hardly over a month and he still hadn't gotten around to it. He and Molly would enjoy going through it when they reunited.

He threw the suitcases in the car's trunk. "Good," he smiled. "Good."

Inside the house, he looked at the letter again. It was undated. The brochure, which was unnecessarily lengthy, outlined the program and the housing arrangements and the work-for-boarding center and everything about the retreat. It gave everything except calendar dates. Molly was always useless when it came to details. She was sort of useless when it came to a lot of other stuff too. Sometimes her voice got on his nerves. Sometimes she blinked too much when she was telling a story.

There was a knock on the door. It was a new knock, had a kind of metropolitan swing to it. And it repeated itself. Knocky-knock, it went. Knocky-knock. Using his longest legs, Issey hiked over the piles to reach the door, to reach a most astonishing visitor.

"How did you find me?" Issey asked.

"Ha, ha, ha! You don't necessarily hide your light under a bushel, Issey! They're writing articles about you these days. Horse rescuer, hero—my word!"

The visitor brushed past Issey. He put his hands on his hips, standing in piss-position at the house overflowing with objects.

"Issey! You have certainly yielded yourself a fine harvest!"

Berger had arrived.

CHAPTER THIRTY

The valley broke into its weeklong holiday festival, and it was loud. Artisanal vendors and farm stands loaded into the common area while colorful food trucks lined its four corners. Musicians performed traditional folk shufflers. Unicyclists zipped between families. Jugglers tangled with gravity. The traveling balloon contortionists "Where the Rubber Meets the Road" recreated the nativity scene. Children see themselves one day as balloon performers. The dream transitions to caricaturist, then face painter, then dude. Meanwhile, Mom and Dad get similar whoozy ideas. They see microbrewing in their future, microfarming on the horizon, but town gossip didn't require as much training, and it was an occupation even the moodiest Bell Riverite enjoyed during the holiday festival, which made for the most robust of annual events.

Recent stories are told with the same juicy seduction as the organic avocados, fennel, and chicories retailed at a five hundred percent markup. There was Old Man Brill who was on house arrest for tax evasion and mail fraud and probably some other stuff. The gossips were all a little drunk on hops, and besides, no one liked Old Man Brill. But everyone liked poor Emma Pinhas. Poor, spongy, now dead Emma Pinhas. Her son Keith Pinhas spread her ashes throughout the valley from the heights of his hot air balloon. "Emma died while she slept," someone said, with a kid hanging on his arm, "She died doing the only thing she liked."

The population growth of the flatlanders continued. Many of the new people were circulating as if they had been part of the holiday festival all their loafery lives—slapping their thighs to the mandolins, sipping the cider, spouting off about local politics—slapping, sipping, and spouting—while those who had been generations in the valley held their breath in the attitude of a reluctant host.

But were the hosts really reluctant? And were these flatsos really all that new? At one point, outsiders were unknown quantities. Tourists at best. A drain on the land at worst. But the past twenty years had seen a new set of folks setting up their homes, arriving in the valley with their sleeves rolled up. They're city people, and while they might have put that life behind them, their expectations remain city high. They're tough and they expect more from their community than a local outhouse race. And good. Native-born Vermonters could be sold on a theme of resourcefulness. "The world is your cow so long as you do the milking." The flatlanders worked for it and it was hell getting there. Once they did, the community was more than willing to reciprocate their calloused hands and operator's jackets.

They helped the new pastor from South Carolina clean empty church pews and dust the cobwebs from hymnals.

They maintained the temperature on the roasting pig for a barbeque joint struggling to work with the northeastern palette.

They took turns bottle-feeding the kid goats, while the young and inexperienced farmers, recent Berkeley graduates, tutored at-risk teens and taught piano, articulating with dirty fingernails.

They offered to run the bike shop after the owner ran his car into a ditch.

They substituted at the yoga studio when the teacher had to put down her llama.

Hell getting there, but the outsiders are inside as a warmly welcomed, unquestioned part of the holiday festival. Their children run with painted faces. Their new farm stands cooperate with longstanding farm stands. Their pulled pork *tortas* get the same workout as the Vermonter's ham, cheddar, and apple roll. Meanwhile, Bell River had seen a rise in new tourism, the addition of hi-speed quad chairlifts, a multiplex theater, and an energetic shopping center that houses niche businesses like the youth yoga studio, the bánh mì café, the candle-making *atelier*, and the Belgian patisserie. And the flatlanders are out there volunteering in orange vests during paving jaunts—concrete replacing dirt roads, parking lots overtaking woodlots, and modern estates with the tennis courts and swimming pools and *porte-cochères* carving into hitherto unmolested mountain greenery. And then they make it out to the winter festival, when the sound they make is big. It's community, the new and the known for one big sendoff before the long winter and the even longer mud season. It's the cheer of a well-earned off-weekend, sets of families doing hula hoops, creemees in cones getting a good lick, money going into the holiday charity bucket, accents mixing, stories turning into anecdotes, handstands and headstands and dopes on a rope. Poor Emma Pinhas. Poor Old Man Brill. But have you tried Tanya's gingersnaps? She might be a maniac, but that bakery is really something wild! Come on, you'll stay the night and I'll take you in the morning. The "reluctant host" bit is less gatekeeping and more Bell River gruff. Oh, they might conceal their emotions like a set of championship lockpickers, but their doors were always open.

And it was above this holiday arena where Berger said, "You certainly rinsed these people of their money and possessions."

They were watching the festivities from a hilltop, with the December sun slicing through birch trees behind them. Berger mashed out his cigarette into meaty grass, joining a crew of four and the many others that he dropped during their longish uphill walk from Issey's home. Issey also smoked and dropped his cigarette near Berger's, and then Berger lit another, and then Issey lit another. Issey used to enjoy the recreational sex of cigarettes, but now he was huffing to keep up. His throat burned, felt made of plaid.

"What happened at Faneuil Hall?" Issey asked.

"You heard about that?"

Issey nodded.

"I took a bath on the deal. McCauley didn't do too good."

"He was killed."

Berger shrugged. "Like I said, he didn't do too good. You were right about him, Issey. He was too splashy with the guns. You had the right idea all along."

Issey smiled, but not too much. You never want to smile too much in front of Berger, who was pouring Prosecco into two flutes that he had taken from Issey's kitchen. "The whole thing was a bust. Before we even started, police were crawling all over the place. And once we started, police were crawling all over *the other police*."

Berger sipped his Prosecco then Issey did the same.

"I can't fly with a broken wing, Issey. You know what I mean?"

Issey didn't, but he fastened himself to Berger's French-cut face, which suggested that he had put the Faneuil Hall farce behind him even if it was an ongoing criminal investigation. He was "on the run," but his fine windswept hair, parted with farouche feathering, was paparazzi-ready.

Issey didn't know what to do with Berger. The last time they were together, Berger was kicking him out of the *Grüppe* and telling him to take a lobster on his way out. He had questioned his skills, rejected his stuff, criticized his heels. And he said they never called it a *Grüppe*.

Issey watched the festival instead, which was growing. Hairdresser Susan Gilmont and theater director Chuck Reed looked like they were swapping stories. Donya Clark was there, and she and Mrs. Robertson-Redeux were tearing down on a flatbread pizza. They were lively and jokey. Even blind Johnny Brin, who was normally in some kind of *mood*, was kicking up a storm.

Berger poured the last of the prosecco into his flute and dropped the bottle in the wet dirt. After gulping his prosecco, he also dropped the flute in the dirt. Issey placed his champagne flute next to Berger's. He thought about picking these up to bring home, but Berger was already walking ahead of him.

Issey caught up, and they were heading downhill.

"You're probably surprised by all of this. Here I am, after all. What am I doing here? Berger—of all people. Berger, you must be thinking. *Berger*."

"Oh—yeah. Of course."

Berger locked his hands behind his back.

"Breaking and entering capers usually follow a path from asportation to arrest. We know this. However, much like your unpaved roads that suddenly twine into the mountain and offer new uncertain roads—roads that certainly are *not* roads—so too is your career taking a rather circuitous route.

"Faneuil Hall was a mess. We went in the wrong direction, and it all comes down to my own stubbornness. You had good ideas, but I was too single-minded. Also coloring my judgement," Berger said cautiously, "you were one of Claudia's guys. And Claudia...well, she's hit or miss."

Issey didn't remember Berger talking so much in Boston. He put it down to nervous energy.

"Boston knows my face, B.B.B. is talking from both sides of his tits, the old network fell apart, and I'm running around. I'm in hiding. It's a total chore. And then one day as I'm checking up old cohorts—as you do—I see your face in your local paper, looking like the cat who got the cream! You rescued some horses, became some kind of local hero, even set up shop in someone's home. How did you get a house? How did you get all that stuff? Did you just back up a truck into town and load up?"

"I, uh," Issey began modestly, "I've always liked a hand truck. Good for quantity and mobility. I picked one up when I returned—from some barn or another. It's been a good tool."

"Issey," Berger turned to look at him as they were walking, "what you've done here is...*otherworldly*."

"Oh, sure. I guess." Was this right? Issey, still maybe dethawing, asked, "Really? You think so?"

"It's elegant and bastardly. A raging conquest." Berger drew his head back. "And now that you've set the market, Issey, what do you think about us getting the *Grüppe* back together?"

"The *Grüppe*?"

"*Jawóll!*"

"I thought you didn't like that."

"Lookit," Berger snapped, "I'm not trying to soft-soap you into a partnership. And it wouldn't be healthy to have bunch of nod monkeys on our team. It's always the wrong play, and I think now I'm at a point where I could use a fresh perspective."

Issey was slow to respond. Berger, this bigshot, this irresistible concept, was he asking Issey...

"Of course, Berger," Issey finally said. "What do you have in mind?"

Berger looked all around him, with hungry eyes.

"I don't see what's wrong with this."

"Here?" Issey looked at it. *Here?* "I don't know if there's any meat left on the bone here."

"There's always meat on the bone."

"Maybe, but..." Issey began.

"You know what? If you're not comfortable..." Berger shrugged.

"I just..."

They approached a busy creemee stand. Issey still couldn't believe that Berger was in Bell River Valley. Issey's little toy town!

But.

But this was also *Issey's* little toy town. This is where he had refined his skills. And he knew these people and their things. He had most of their things. The thought of sharing Bell River and its mountains and homes with someone else—even if it was Berger—no. It was Berger.

As if reading his thoughts, Berger asked, "This where you grew up?"

"Um... More or less."

The creemee stand was about fifty yards from the entrance to the holiday festival. Bodies were coming and going, decorated in face paint, Christmas rouge, and sleigh bells.

"No," Issey said. "Here will be good. The tourists have a lot of meat."

"There you go! We'll celebrate with an ice cream!"

Issey made a face. "It's a creemee."

"What's the difference?"

"One's an ice cream and one's a creemee."

A middle-aged couple in khaki shorts, showing off their pale winter logs, passed Issey and Berger.

"Hi, Issey!"

"Hello?" Issey didn't recognize these two. Berger watched.

"It's me! Brooks—Brooks Bosworth," he said with warm jowls, "You recovered my nesting dolls. Remember?"

"Something to do with your dead wife?"

"Hardly, but let me introduce you to Dotty Boudreaux."

"But we know each other!" she laughed.

"We do?"

"I hired you to recover my PS3."

"The video game player?"

"The video game *console*. But when we met"—grabbing Bosworth's hand—"suddenly my days didn't need to be filled with gaming."

"And I didn't need to fill my home with dead wife memories."

Issey was surprised. "You threw them out—after all that?"

"We're not maniacs, Issey. I gave my nesting dolls to Ms. Van Recklinghausen."

"And I gave my PS3 to Craig Kilby. But he said he didn't want it either, so I think he gave it away to someone else. Who knows?"

The couple smiled at Issey, nodded at Berger, who nodded back while licking his creemee. He said to them: "Shorts in December? Brave!"

"It's a summer's day for us!"

And they all laughed and then Boudreaux and Buttsworth took their thick pale rumps into the holiday festival while Berger, who had stopped licking, hung back.

"What was all that?"

Issey stared into the early bluish night. He stared into the holiday festival. Everybody was having a jolly old time and it was just getting started. There was only a small opening for the rest of the day to peer in, and then the day would be over, clicked in like a lockback knife.

"What was the deal with those two?"

Issey was trying to itemize what he had given away and what he had. And he had the nesting dolls. He had the video game console—lots of video game consoles. He looked into the festival again. He had the hairdresser's golden shears. And he had the theater director's copper

Abenaki coins. He had snowboards and skis. He had the tricked-out walking stick. Out with the old. In with the new. But who's left holding the "old?"

"Issey—I was talking to you."

"What?" Berger was there. He had forgotten Berger was there.

"I said, *what was that all about?*"

"Oh. I, uh, found some of their things."

"What do you mean *found?*"

"Stole."

"Ah," Berger said slowly. "And then?"

"And then I gave them their things back."

"No." Berger returned to licking his cone. "No, there's more."

"I also charged them."

"You charged them?"

"A small fee."

"Put me in the picture here. You stole their things."

"Yes."

"Then you returned these things to them."

"Yes."

"And you charged them for the service."

"Well," Issey placed his hand on the back of his neck. "More or less."

Berger wrapped his head around it.

"Sickening!"

"No." Issey replied quickly. "It was all done in good faith."

"Good faith?"

"Not good faith exactly. Those aren't the right words."

"They're the exact opposite of the right words," Berger said.

Lights from the festival glimmered behind them. Issey couldn't see Berger's face. "Like the cat who got the creemee..." They approached a large patch of field made out to be a parking lot for the holiday festival. Christmas songs performed by the elementary school's choir were squeaky and radiant.

Berger shot two fingers in the air. "'The greatest humbug of all is the man who believes—or pretends to believe—that everything and everybody are humbugs.' You're this town's *mala fide* P.T. Barnum, and you're as ludicrous as you are genius. Now, come on, let's go. There's a car we have to get rid of."

CHAPTER THIRTY-ONE

They drove separately, Issey following the tail of Berger's red lights. A few hours out, in Saratoga Springs, Berger nudged them in the direction of a dark forest shelter. He cut the engine, got out, and met Issey at his driver's side window. "Seeing as I don't know of any chop shops in this state, how about we toss it here?" Issey thought it was fine. Berger said they'd have to swap out Issey's license plates with the license plates of the car they were about to dump. Issey nodded and got to work. He then kneeled by a decaying tractor to unscrew the rear plate; he wheeled around and kneeled by a rusted No Trespassers sign hanging from a rusted chain to unscrew the front plate. He repeated the process, putting his plates on Berger's stolen car and then putting the stolen car's New York plates on his car. There was always a lot of kneeling and wheeling and more kneeling and more wheeling when you're in the employ kind of way, a lot of one guy smoking and the other guy screwing. Issey rarely got the smoking job, but he never complained. They then hefted and heaved the car into the forest junkyard, Berger letting out a salty grunt as the sedan joined vegetation and other garbage.

Berger tossed his suitcase in the backseat of Issey's car and joined it. "Mind if I rest my eyes?" And snoozed all the way until Issey's home fell into view.

Berger awoke in a daze. It was weird for Issey to see this handsome man semi-detached from his surroundings, a little confused and foamy. Issey walked him into the house. "Thanks, Issey," Berger half-smiled. "It's been a lot of rabbit-hiding."

Inside, Issey cleared some of the inventory on the couch for Berger. The couch? Despite having put on such a handsome face, Faneuil Hall had wrecked Berger. Maybe Issey was seeing him for the first time. Maybe he was getting used to Berger. But he looked smaller, maybe even shrunken. Issey showed him the way to the bedroom.

"Here, you take my room."

"Are you sure?" Berger looked inside. "Great." And then closed the door.

Issey stood facing the closed door. "I guess that's goodnight," Issey said under his breath.

Alone in the living room, with all of his piles, allowed Issey time for introspection. Berger. Here. *Berger*. Even if he seemed... *different* than he had remembered in Cambridge, Berger was still everything Issey wanted to be, both an acquired taste and a box office draw. Berger was a ladykiller, a mankiller, indifferent to human clichés and sour lips. After Faneuil Hall, most criminals would have crumbled after such a disaster, such a laughingstock, but Berger gave it his kiss-off cool. Yet, there was something different...

And then Berger, redressed in silk pajamas and holding a small jar of moisturizer, returned with full eyes. "I have to do my face before bed, but after that, I want to hear all about your adventures and all about of these wonderful *bibelots* in here!"

And so it was a slumber party. Issey whipped them up French press coffees and, with odd valley pride, served Tanya's pastries he had picked up during the week. He then read through his recent adventures to a guest spellbound from sentence one. There was his daring Yorke Program Architects thriller in Middleton, the raging payout for all the leather from Avi's tack room, the horse-hero parlay he had going on in town, the absolute pillaging of Bell River. He gave Berger a tour of the different piles in the house, curated by geography.

"The German stuff takes up the most space, but that spilled into the Austrian stuff," Issey said breathlessly. "There's a ton of Austrian stuff in Bell River. And it's hard to differentiate Germany from Austria or Germany from Switzerland or Germany from Mexican reproductions of German things meant to look like Austrian stuff, so the German pile is massive and I should've re-labeled it the Western European pile if I hadn't lost the label-maker in the German pile."

The night was winding down. Berger shared some bedtime skincare tips and some of his moisturizer, which smelled expensive. Through the opened buttons of Berger's silk pajamas, Issey could see Berger's ribcage sticking out. He could also see, and he pretended like he didn't see it, a shoulder holster and the grip of a gun.

They said good night. Issey made a bed on the couch. He worried about the gun. Berger slept in the room where Issey and Molly used to sleep, with the door closed. Issey tried thinking of Molly instead of the gun. Chatty and plump. Face not great with the truth. Voice strange. Hair in the middle of a torrential downpour and pieces of it in places you least expect human hair to be. Hair in with the spoons, hair stuck to the ice trays, hair draped over the kitchen faucet, hair on top of his hair. And she liked to walk a lot, mostly in the dark. They seemed to float through the valley.

"When you were... you know... doing what you did..." They were on a late-night, moonlight walk, and she was holding his hand. "Didn't you ever get scared of the dark?"

"Why would I be scared of the dark?"

"Um... Because you can't see anything?"

"Nothing bad can happen in the dark. Besides, they can't see anything either. No one can. And I got there first."

"Do you ever think you'll do it again?"

But at least with Molly and all of her questions and hair, there was never a gun under her clothes.

Berger slept until the very late morning and made his debut into the kitchen artfully disheveled, wearing Issey's pants with a belt squeezed to the last loophole. He wasn't wearing a shirt. His chest was tanned, hawklike, and strapped with a shoulder holster and gun.

"Morning, Issey!"

Issey nodded, tried not to look at the gun. He stood from his chair, back to Berger, and brought the French press while Berger smoked Gitanes.

"What's the Wi-Fi situation here?"

"I don't think we have that."

"Hm," he said. He looked out the window at snowcapped mountains. He had dead lobster eyes. When he finished the cigarette, he dropped it in the coffee cup. "I'm going to shower. You at least have hot water?"

Berger went in the bedroom, came out, still wearing Issey's pants, but missing were the shoulder holster and gun. While Berger showered, Issey took his moment and tiptoed like a cartoon idiot towards the bedroom.

He cracked open the bedroom door. He didn't know what he was going to do. The usual Issey plan, then. He squinted. He sucked in his tummy. He opened the door a little wider. He opened his eyes a little wider. When finally both door and eyes were open, a chill ran over him.

Everything was in its former life. But the room belonged to someone else. Berger's suitcase was on the foot of the made bed—made differently, tighter, meaner. The bed had lost weight. Reconciling the bed's meanness was Berger's Continental European cologne. It was a bright atmosphere, but it wasn't Issey's bergamot. It wasn't Molly's hemp body wash. Meanwhile, sprawled on the center of the bed, as if spreading, was shoulder holster and gun. Issey should take the gun. Would Berger notice it missing?

The shower ended. Now was the time. The holster looked sweaty. He didn't want to touch it. Berger would probably notice a missing gun. Shoot. He looked towards the bathroom. Now was the time, but not enough time.

Issey crossed from the bedroom back to the kitchen. He smoothed his pants and told himself it was going to be okay. Even if the gun and the slimy holster remained on the bed, it was going to be okay. What's the big deal? He had known plenty of criminals who had guns, what's one more? And hadn't he seen Berger with a gun before?

"That's some water pressure," Berger called in passing from the bathroom to the bedroom. "Better than Boston!"

"Oh, sure."

Issey started washing the dishes. Berger had used all the hot water.

No. Issey had never seen Berger with a gun. That's what he had liked about Berger. Berger was art. His hair was art. His talk was art. The way he moved with command, dressed with meanness, stole with poise—all art. And those cheekbones! But the gun was anti-art. Spaggiari had never killed anyone during his bank robberies in Italy. "Without arms. Without hate. Without violence." The only gun Spaggiari had used was a welding gun when he sealed shut bank vault doors. Spaggiari was art. Issey left the coffee cup, with its cigarettes and dregs, cold in the sink.

Issey sat on the couch. He stretched out and tried to get comfortable. Echoes of Christmas songs from the holiday festival below reached him, choir voices singing "Gloria." As soon as he entered the soul of a dream, the front door opened and then closed with a slap.

Berger reappeared, fully dressed in black, with bulging pockets. Probably bulging with more guns.

"I got us snacks. Courtesy of the General Store."

Berger unpocketed the hull on the kitchen counter, mostly junk food in plastic singles.

"How about we get to work?"

Issey wiped his eyes, still kind of in a dream.

"I've been pursuing new plans, but we'll need recruits. What about this guy?"

Berger dropped a folded piece of paper on Issey. He unfolded the paper and saw a "Have You Seen This Person!" flyer. Pieces of tape were on its corners; Berger must have ripped it from the window. The photo, a still from the General Store's CCTV, captured a rangy teen mid-snatch, his noodle of an arm sliding *Hungry Man* dinners down his baggy jeans. The camera zoomed in so intensely that the boy's face was nearly blue.

"Now that's a kid who won't croak."

Issey looked closer. "He's just some town punk."

"Exactly. You always need one guy who's a psychotic. Look at the boy's face. It has no soul, no connection."

"But isn't that what went wrong at Faneuil Hall?"

"What went wrong at Faneuil Hall was that *all* of those guys were psychotics. There was not a single voice of institutional sanity in the bunch—including mine."

Issey reviewed the kid in the photograph again. "Do we really need him?"

"I won't take no for an answer. Now, listen: we'll go out for a bit and then wing on up to St. Albans."

"St. Albans?"

"Apparently, that's where the little maniac lives. The woman at the General Store told me all about him. Big girl with a lot of teeth." Issey had a hard time picturing Pru melting all over Berger.

"She knew that?"

"She's a woman at a general store," replied Berger. "I'm sure she knows a lot of things."

Issey looked at all the piles surrounding them in the living room and kitchen.

Berger asked, "So, where is St. Albans—far?"

"Very."

"Good."

"But why would he come all the way down here to steal from the General Store?"

"Do the odds, Issey. It's far less risky than robbing from the place where you live. In our business, it's best we're risk averse."

Issey put his foot down.

"Berger—I—we have to talk about that gun!"

Suddenly, cold wind whooshed into the living room and the twanging of dueling mandolins from the festival below rattled between them. The front door was open. Anissa was standing there.

Where Anissa usually paraded through his house and touched all his stuff, today she stood in the doorway like some dog. Issey shut the door to the valley party.

"What can I do for you, Anissa?"

"I, uh…" With Berger and Issey waiting for her, she cleared her throat and removed tortoise-shell sunglasses. "I didn't know you had company."

Berger met her at the doorway, with a charming mask of a smile, and led her inside. "I'm someone who dips into different inks." He offered her his hand, and she took it like it was a gift in a small box.

They were a good couple standing together—she with the curved nose, expensive jeans, and Eastern Shore shoulders; he with the skull-face features of a catalog model.

"What do you want?" Issey asked again.

Her usual bravado was replaced with staginess—throat clearing, two made-up coughs, and a half-heard insult. "…at all this monkey shit."

Anissa's cheeks were pink. She was weird with her hands. Issey wondered if he should bring her one of the Japanese fans he had discovered under a pile he didn't know existed.

Berger *bon soir*'d, then cut the room in half, as if he were a sliding glass door, and was gone. She took his exit like a punch in the teeth. Issey worried what he was going to do in there with his shoulder holster and gun.

Issey ushered her toward the door.

"Who was that?"

"No one."

"You're getting something going, aren't you?"

"No."

She gave him some pushback, eyes like fluttering bluebells in the stranger's direction.

"We need to talk, Issey. There's been some recent developments."

Indeed there had been recent developments, he thought, remembering his last conversation with Davenport. Anissa and Avi, those three surveillance cameras, the missing evidence, the picture of young Anissa on pony patrol in Assateague.

But he didn't have time for it. There was a person with a gun in his house.

"Leave it alone."

He pushed her out and assured her they'd meet to talk about her recent developments, after the holiday, close to the holiday, on the holiday, whatever—just as soon as his visitor had gone. It was an easy promise to make because Issey never made a promise he couldn't break.

The sun had set, but an unseasonable heat kicked up. Issey was wearing a black nylon jacket. He rolled down his car window. The breeze, slushy and grassy, smelled like the day of the hot air balloon adventure. Keith's poor landing, Molly's hissing over eggy salad sandwiches, his walk where he said hello to neighbors, water conservationists, cute Old Man Brill. A Gitane broke the spell. Issey had almost forgotten that Berger was in the car.

"Every place looks closed." Berger took a long pull. "Let's break in one of them."

Issey said nothing. Before leaving the house, he knew what going out with Berger meant.

The flag with the honeybee came into view. The new age store where Molly worked. Issey parked the car and slumped back.

"Well," Issey began, "I guess we better—"

"Issey," Berger smiled at him, "I know your feelings about the gun."

Issey shrugged. "No feelings."

"I've been carrying this piece ever since the fiasco." Berger was downcast. He looked at the cigarette in his fingers. He flexed his knuckles. "It's ugly."

"There's just..." Issey thought about it. "There's just no art in it."

"It's not an art business."

Berger tossed his cigarette out the window. He then took off his jacket, unbuttoned his shirt, removed it, and draped the shirt over his legs. And once again there was his naked hawklike chest and once again strapped to it was the shoulder holster and the gun. Issey looked away while looking at everything.

"I don't need it."

He detached the holster from his shoulder, and, with the gun in it, handed it over to Issey. "Let's get rid of it."

The wet holster was in Issey's lap. The gun looked like it was a passenger dangling out of the open door of a helicopter. Issey got out of the car and wrapped the holster and the gun in a trunk blanket. For some reason, he pet the blanket, then closed the trunk.

Looking lighter, without all that meaty gun business, Berger was buttoning his shirt when Issey reached the passenger window. "I have this one," Issey said, pointing to the store where Molly worked. Berger nodded. This was art.

The lockpickers slid from leather case, found their targets, raked, clicked. Issey's lockpicking felt so fluid and precise, so *meaningful*, that he could put on one-man show on the art of the wafer lock. Instead, he stole all money from the register.

With cash and something extra for himself in his pocket—something that turned out to be a real treat—Bell River was looking easy again. When he got to the car, Berger was leaning his elbow on Issey's headrest. He looked somehow angelic.

"We did good, Berger!"

Berger agreed and took the cash. "Drink?"

"Of course!"

"By the way, who was that woman who came to your house?"

"That's just my sister-in-law."

"What'd she want?"

"She—she's in need of counsel."

"She's in need of a personality."

Issey was surprised. Anissa was *all* personality.

"Doesn't matter, though," Berger slid his arm from the headrest and pulled out a cigarette from his jacket. "She's seen my face. I'll have to kill her."

"What?" Issey jerked the wheel.

"Take it easy, soft serve." Berger laughed. "You'll believe anything they tell you!"

CHAPTER THIRTY-TWO

They took the party to the Sugar House, which was in high spirits from festival leftovers who were looking to extend last night forever. Berger moved his way through them and raised a hand to the bartender, who happened to be Eight Jeff.

"*Aqua vitae* for my partner!"

"Yessir!" Eight Jeff hooted with his big fat mouth, "That's water and... what?"

Issey turned away from this. The Sugar House, and its blooming winter beauties, was a hot date for the night. When Issey turned around, Eight Jeff and Berger were bumping fists and wasn't Eight Jeff acting like such a bigshot? "That's a really cool drink, sir!" Issey nodded towards a dark alcove table. "I'll meet you there," Issey said, and Berger slipped away.

Issey handled the drinks, the tab, and Eight Jeff who was absolutely *gushing*.

"He's my cousin," Issey lied.

"Is he in movies, and commercials and stuff?"

Issey wanted to throw up.

"Don't be so impressed. He's our age." Issey took the two drinks. "And he and I are going into business together."

On the way to the alcove with their drinks, he saw an older woman who was finishing the last drops of red wine by the fieldstone fireplace. He remembered she was paired with another woman in iron health and denim.

"Issey. Hello."

"Hello, miss...?"

"Baldwin."

"Of course—Baldwin. I knew—Baldwin." Heather Baldwin and the other one was Xu. Cheryl Xu. The football helmet ladies. And just the night before, during his slumber party with Berger, Issey had applied some cloth to the helmets' matte finish, careful not to smudge the autograph.

The good mood of the Sugar House must have baited him because he led with it: "Curious development, Baldwin—I'm in possession of your football helmet."

"Talk normal."

"I have your helmet."

"Okay," she said and eyed him suspiciously. "You have my helmet."

"I do..." Issey thought that this might clear things up, why they were in his home, but it did the opposite. "Actually, I have *both* football helmets."

She replied flatly, "So what?"

"But I gave them to you. I found them and *gave* them to you."

"Me and Cheryl went to war over those helmets."

"Don't you at least want yours?"

"I did. And now I don't 'cos all it does is remind me of our wretched friendship." Miss Baldwin pronounced "wretched" like "red shit."

"But wasn't the helmet pricey memorabilia?"

"Yeah. But we should've let 'em stay gone in the first place. That lousy bitch thought just because she had Jarius Harvin sign our helmets that they *both* belonged to her."

"But if I have both," Issey said, "this means she also gave hers away. Surely, this should count for something?"

"She can count it up her big fat ass."

"But why do *I* have them?"

"Beats me. Do you normally drink two at a time?"

This last line was said behind him, by red shit Cheryl Xu. She delivered a glass of red wine to Baldwin. "Here you go, doll. Eight's out of Cab; I got you Shiraz instead."

"Shiraz? Am I pledging to a fat girl's sorority?"

"You love it."

Issey was turned around.

"I'm turned around. I thought you said you were in a fight."

"That's right." Xu joined Baldwin by the fireplace. "We *were* in a fight, Issey. And now we're *not* in a fight. Once we got rid of that shit, our friendship got right again. And if you have them, you should sell them. That particular player didn't do autographs."

"And tell us again how you managed to get his signature," Baldwin asked.

"It was a pricey bill," Xu replied. "He charged me full freight, guys."

Issey finally reached the alcove, placing two brandy snifters on a round teak table. Berger leaned on the aluminum edging.

"Good stuff tonight." He congratulated Issey with a clink.

Issey gave a neighborly smile to Ryan Sweezy, who extended the gesture with a wave. Issey returned to the brandy. It was smokey and had gnarled snap. What was it with alcohol?

Berger smiled casually. "I've been thinking about Claudia Bünd lately."

"Oh?"

"I knew her about five years before you came to in Boston. It was like an unspoken thing, but she was..." Berger raised his eyebrows, "...difficult."

Issey agreed. "I thought it was because she was European."

"*Was* she European?"

Issey didn't know. He resisted saying anything.

"Whatever she was," Berger continued, "she was a genius. I never quite understood opportunity until she explained it. You can't just go in like a crazy person whenever you feel like it. You have to listen to what the situation is telling you."

The Sugar House was filling up and Issey was having a hard time hearing Berger. He nodded and smiled and said, "Of course!"

"This is what I'm getting to. I've been authoring this plan." Berger stopped. "How attached are you to the Vermont State House?"

Issey didn't know. "Not very!"

"Good. But after the fiasco with Faneuil Hall, you can understand that I need to exercise a little more caution."

Berger removed an envelope from his pocket. Issey leaned in.

"Sorry, but I checked your mail."

He handed a letter to Issey.

"I couldn't help but see that it was a tax bill. What's that all about?"

Issey cleared his throat. Berger shouldn't be going through his mail.

"It's just for my stupid house."

"Your house? Did you *buy* that house?"

"Of course not."

"Then why are you paying taxes on it?"

"It's my mother's," Issey said and then lied, "She died and left it to me."

"Hm."

"But it's only a house."

"Hm." Berger repeated.

"Is there something wrong?" Issey asked.

"It puts you in a vulnerable position."

"Really?"

"You know how it is."

Issey didn't and he nodded. "But the house is... a strategy. It's a Trojan horse."

"That's not a Trojan horse, Issey." Berger shook his head. "You should get rid of it. You never want to have more than what you entered with."

From across the bar, Eight Jeff smiled their way and waved. Thumbs up? All good? Another round? Yuck.

Berger asked, "Who else knows about your operation?"

"Which part?"

"Let's say—the buying and the selling. The *all* of it."

"No one," Issey affirmed. "Mostly no one."

"Who's in the 'mostly no one' camp?"

"My brother."

"Go on."

"His wife, maybe. Probably."

"The leggy dullard from earlier? And she can just walk in your house? Does she have a key?"

"I don't think so. Probably not."

"You don't lock your door?"

"Of course!" Issey shouted. "But not here. You don't have to here."

"Okay." Berger let it go. "Who else knows?"

"A recent friend."

"A girlfriend."

"But she's away on a yoga retreat."

"Even so, Issey, that's too many people."

"And maybe my brother's daughter. She's only eight, though."

"Because they don't talk to their friends at eight."

"She doesn't have the personality for it."

Berger put his drink down. The table wobbled.

"These are very strange choices."

"It's fine."

"It's not fine. All these people," Berger opened his hand toward the room, "they're all your.... They're your suckers, aren't they?"

Issey turned in his chair to a packed Sugar House. Now that he thought about it... "More or less."

"You've told your brother and his wife—her alone, Issey, she's unhinged."

"That's exactly the word I used!"

"It's risky decisions." Berger was fixed on it. "All these people."

"They're not bad."

"That's not the issue. If they know you're the guy who's broken into their homes and taken their stuff, and are now *selling it back to them,* then they're gonna roll you."

"Everything is fine."

"Issey," Berger said, "They're all your victims. The walls are closing in."

Issey shrugged. "I don't think so. I know this place. It's fine."

"I can fix this. It's workable." Berger was talking to himself, puzzled. It was the first time Issey had seen Berger lost. He took out a pocket notebook and pen, waiting for ideas to root out the mess.

Issey smiled. "I'll get us another round!"

He brought his smile on his way to the bar, passing his "victims." Caddy nodded, Donya Clark and Susan Gilmont waved, one older guy popped him on the shoulder, in the valley way. The Sugar House was like a roll call, a cast of characters with faces resurfacing in the possessions and junk that had overtaken his home. His home was loud. The bar was loud. It was all going to be all right. And there was Tanya on a stool.

Out of her messy baker's apron, she wore a fetching ivory blouse, with a cinquefoil print, cut-off corduroys tight in the thighs, and sporty slip-on shoes. Some of her chopped hair had grown in, unevenly. She was even wearing lipstick on her lips and some on her teeth.

"You're not with your little girlfriend," she said.

"Molly? She's on a retreat."

"I'll bet she is."

Her loopy voice was soothing.

"And you're not baking tonight?"

"I did the festival. I deserve a night off." She nodded toward Berger. "Who's the movie star?"

"An old—cousin."

"No. You're lying. Your mother didn't have siblings."

"Not in the family sense *cousin*."

"Lighten up, tugboat. I'm trying to get drunk. Here," she passed him a drink, "do a shot of tequila with me. I was gonna have 'em both, but sharesies is better."

Issey turned to check on Berger. Berger was scribbling something in a notebook. Big plans. Outfits. Props. Lockpicking. Night moves. A daring duo for all time.

"Hey," she said. "Here we go."

She clinked her shot glass onto his. Following Tanya, Issey took a swift belt. The tequila roared in his throat.

"To Bell River!" Issey cheered.

"What's gotten you so home proud?"

"Bell River's magic, Tanya. Don't you think?"

"It's lonely at night. Everybody goes home."

"But, tonight, everyone's here. It's the holiday festival."

"One night out of the year won't fill it. It's why people like me and you do our best work at night."

"Not that old shit again," Issey said. "I do all my work in the sun."

"No. You're lying."

Maybe Berger was right. Maybe everyone knew and the walls were closing in. Eight Jeff brought another round of tequila that neither had ordered. She took hers down immediately. "You're lying," she repeated, squeezing a lime onto her lipstick-stained teeth. "I saw you tonight. Drink your prove-it juice and prove it."

He shot it back, but held the tequila in his mouth for too long before letting it drop down the hatch. It burned in the places it shouldn't have burned, mostly in his nose.

"Where did you see me?"

"Coming out of your little girlfriend's store," she said. "You can't help yourself. I can't help myself either. It's why we do our best work at night. Don't worry, Isso, I ain't gonna *grouse*."

Then it was the tequila that baited him, and he pulled in close to her, channeling his next words directly into the part of her head that was missing the most hair: "And I won't tell if you won't tell either."

"Oh, yeah? What kind of secret do you have that I don't know?"

He unzipped his pocket and brought out the thing from Molly's store that he had taken for himself.

"I ordered these a long time ago and Molly said they didn't have them." In his hand, he showed her two pumice stones. "Turns out—they had those pumice stones all along!"

"What does that mean?"

"Something—I don't know what, but *something*!"

And they celebrated the next round like a couple of old hornets and the home team surged ahead. Tanya was all right. The night was all right. Issey turned to check on Berger in the alcove and found only the alcove.

CHAPTER THIRTY-THREE

Late arrivals crowded the bar, crowded the view to the alcove table. Lending extra volume was the tequila, a blackjolt to the organism: he could walk straight but not think straight or walk straight. Lacing his way to the alcove, good valley babes interfered, his name getting hey'd, his hands getting plied with other hands, questions about Molly, about their home, about finding something recently lost, about what he thought of the festival and the new wine garden and how his car was holding up, because "you need three cars in the valley just to keep up one" was what Caddy said, and Issey searched the big Southern toughie for answers, if he had seen—but by the time he got to the question Caddy was outside smoking a cigarillo, one leg leaning on a small retaining wall. Issey finally reached the alcove. The party was just starting.

Berger was gone. Berger's brandy snifter was gone. But the cologne hung around. Issey trained his nose in the direction of its cliff-side spritz and got a lead. A forming aromatic line led him to the bathroom. But, at that moment, speakers pumped to life, and nightclub music, as loud as the valley was deep, pounded four-to-the-floor goodies. This was the "Sugar Hour," and the effect was immediate. His feet were jacked by wobbly basslines. Treble made from tequila knuckled him in the guts. He wobbled and wheeled, and the wheeling was interpreted as dancing, and instantly, he was in a scrum of browns, greens, buffalo check, and Tiffany blue camouflage. Lavender valley dancers floated in white thermal tops and hardy down vests. Thick clogs, paired with even thicker mountain socks, battered the hardwood. Tanya folded alongside him. Her cinquefoil-print blouse was splotchy, her hands loose and destination-based. "You have a really doughy butt!" He twisted left and right, but roving bodies and Tanya's fastened hands held him in place. "Why are you freaking out!" Issey shouted in her ear: "Have you seen my associate!" "You said he was your cousin!" "Have you seen my cousin associate!" She got in two, three, four more squeezes. "Is that a roll of quarters in your pocket or is that a roll of dimes?" And then she freed her hands and lifted her arms for dancing. "Relax, Issey!" "But have you seen him!" She was bouncing to the beat, shoulders monkey, head choppy. "Have you seen him!" Bouncing. "Let it go! We're all here!" Bouncing. Steady beat. Prove-it juice. "These are one of those nights, Issey!" With one hand playing an invisible drum, she used the other to take his hand. Her skin was hot. She moved closer to the beat. "Find it!" Her breath was hot. "Find what!" Baldwin and Xu bobbed together, in iron health and denim, bobbing. Ryan Sweezy was all spilling vodka tonic and lionhearted hips. The river conservationists shucked around like streaky sediment. Caddy's smoking cigarillo, tipped with weed, traveled from hand to mouth, hand to mouth, hand to mouth. Issey started moving. "Feel the bassline. Fading left to right. Put it in your hips." The rust from his joints got so much oil that his mass became gooey. "That's it, Isso!" Names and faces, cut from his past, shot through a projector, moving and grooving like a shimmering disco ball. Tanya shouted, "Forget about your cousin! Feel the bassline. Fading right to left. Get in the groove!" He tried to relax. He tried to feel safe with Tanya, with her kissy face and deranged brains. The music was speaking directly to him. Free from Berger and the St. Albans boy. Free from the piles becoming bigger piles. Free from Molly, Avi, Anissa, surveillance cameras. All he had was sound and bodies and Tanya. The music was transformative, heaven-raising. Wait— was that? Was that Berger? Too many bodies. Issey grasped her hands up, up to the ceiling, up to the stars, and the crowd followed his lead, all hands sky high, sky high. A strobe light carved scalloping lines from one body to the next. Sky high, sky high. Neon red one moment, darkness in the next, seen, neon green. Streaky hands up, sky high, sky high. Hands up: Issey found a clearing to the bathroom and took it. The Sugar House was a good time to be alive if he had been someone else.

Urinals empty. Stall empty. Except for the young barista from the Post 'n' Bean, the bathroom was clean. Issey asked him if he had seen the man he had come with.

"Shoot, I didn't even know *you* were here."

He offered Issey some recreational drugs. Issey passed and the barista left. The opened door let in a heavyweight bassline felt all the way into the sleeves of his nylon jacket. His lockpicking rakes rattled. Issey waited at the sink for the door to close.

When it did, Issey ran water from a modern faucet onto his hands. He pressed paper towels to his face and neck. His fingers were buzzing. This adrenaline was different from entering people's homes and looking through their drawers and secrets and junk. Something felt changed, like there was a sudden absence of something. He wasn't sure if he liked it. The pursy face staring at him in the mirror looked happy, but mostly confused.

Adjusting his eyes to the flashing lights, the destiny of the party still had a long way to go, with more bodies bringing in more outside heat. No sign of Berger. Even his cologne was lost in grassy essential oils, sweaty shoulders, and sugary headwraps. Under the strobe lights, teeth dazzled. "Issey!" Tanya's waving hand. "Come back!" It was a good crowd. It was a good valley. Everyone had a touch of platinum in them.

He took the stairs two at a time to find a completely different setting. Upstairs was the soundproofed atmosphere of a rustic bed-and-breakfast. Good to be away from the music and the people and the tequila, even if some of it was still stuck on his shoe. To think that his mother had lobbied for the bar—what would she think today? He didn't know. He really didn't know her all that well, despite being such a good son.

The night was soaked in moonlight, and Issey searched for Berger in the hotel's shady corners—the gazebo, the lovers lane, the pissing hole, the koi pond. He looked in the gravel parking lot, under the cars, in his own car, under his car again, in the trunk. The results were predictable: gravel sticking in his palms, feeling hot on a cold night, and a missing shoulder holster and the gun. Berger even took the trunk blanket they had been swaddled in.

"Stupid," Issey said to himself. But then he looked at the situation: "The car's still here." He looked at the car: "He didn't take the car."

Did he replace Issey in the space of three tequilas and one Tanya? Did someone drive Berger to St. Albans, someone who didn't have all this valley baggage loving up on him?

Issey drove through town, to the places they had toured earlier. Issey knew that Berger's wiring was dangerous. Sure, he could be charming and thin, but he was a guy with a gun. And when Berger was in charge, people went to jail. People got shot and people died.

He parked at Molly's store, pressed his face to the glass, and once again pushed his lockpickers into the locking mechanism. Inside, he checked the single cash register (empty) and manager's office. Berger wasn't there. He hadn't been there. Issey stood, waiting for a thought. He walked through the aisles. The store smelled like Molly when she came home after her shifts. He found her hemp body wash, opened the top, and squeezed the bottle. Distant notes of yesterday were pleasant enough, he supposed, but also a waste of time.

Next, he parked at the winter festival, which was hitched up for the night. The grass was stamped and patchy. Trash flowered like tumors. Bottle caps. Raffle tickets. Little paper trays for French fries and tofu tenders. Mashed cigarette butts. Berger had been constantly smoking— French Gitanes—and the scene of their hillside watch, with its trashed champagne bottle and flutes, slashed the screen in half.

Issey followed it and hiked up the hillside where he was met by the returning smell of Berger's cologne. Berger's actions with the cologne and the cigarettes and champagne flutes and champagne bottle were untutored—especially for a pro, especially for someone on the move. Yet Berger was everywhere tonight, seen by everyone, using distinctive language that could be remembered for a police report. He even made friends with Eight Jeff, who was mister rules and mister police report mouth.

The general drift was in the direction of the St. Albans boy, but he needed information—information from wherever Berger might have gotten it. Issey returned to his car and drove to the General Store.

At the parking lot, he left the car running, and went straight to the counter.

Pru lifted tired eyes. "Hey, pal. Whatcha need?"

Issey asked about a recent shoplifter.

"Shoplifter. Blech."

Pru was wiped, but in a pleasant enough mood.

Issey showed her the flyer.

"Who is he?" Issey asked.

She was surprised. "I thought you were going to tell *me*."

"No. I have a flyer, taken from your store's CCTV camera."

"I don't think so."

"It was taped right up front." He pointed at the door.

"Couldn't have been here."

"But it was."

"I'm telling you it wasn't. Tanya said those signs gave off the wrong *vibe*."

"So you don't put up shoplifter notices?"

"I wish!" Pru said. "But I'd like to think Tanya's right on this."

Issey remembered Berger telling him he had spoken to Pru about the shoplifter. This is where all that St. Albans information had come from.

"Weren't you talking to a guy about this shoplifter?"

"What?"

"A cousin of mine was telling me—"

"You don't have any cousins, Issey."

"Whatever—he said you had a conversation about this guy in the picture."

"I don't think so."

"Handsome guy. Like movie poster handsome."

"You got a thing for this guy?"

"No, listen—he was saying you knew the shoplifter, that you knew he was from St. Albans."

"How would I know that?"

It stopped Issey. This very easy question: How *would* she know?

"Because... I don't know. You're the General Store person. You know everyone."

"*Everyone?*"

"I don't know," Issey rubbed his forehead. "I'm just a little turned around."

"A little?"

"Anyway," he said, on his way out, "It was good seeing Tanya tonight."

"She crushed it at the festival today. The bakery is *soaring*."

"No doubt about it. We ran into each other at the Sugar House bar."

"Please tell me she wasn't drinking."

"She wasn't drinking," Issey lied. Issey wasn't really listening. He focused on the window facing the street where the notice might have been taped before Berger swiped it. "Are you sure you didn't have a flyer up front?"

"What'd I just say?"

Issey was back on the road. It was a toothpick kind of night and he found two way down in his back pocket. He let it roll back and forth on his tongue like a real bad guy, a real scuzzo. Then it fell down his throat. It must have gone way down, down there with the tequila, because Issey was gagging so hard he couldn't see the road. He threw the car into a ditch, threw it in Park, and retched and retched until the toothpick came from out of his brains and into his palm. There were tears in his eyes.

He cut off the engine and got out of the car. The car was happy be rid of him. Where did Berger get the flyer with the St. Albans boy? And would Berger really murder Anissa? She wasn't *that* interesting.

Ever since he was young and got his first taste of the magic, with his chubby fingers wrapped around other people's mail, he had accepted the inevitable path towards trouble. That was okay. Life was okay, all about give and take. Something bad would happen. But not like this. Not with those piles, not with Avi's three surveillance cameras, not with Berger missing, someone setting him up, sending him in all different directions, like some dummy in this town where everyone wanted to wear the badge.

He stood in the middle of a road. The road was endless. He thought he could see the sign for the Misfit Farm, with its painting of broken goats, daffy calves and oldster horses watching daytime reruns of Fetlock. But it was an illusion, just the moonlight pooling off the car's hood, just the moonlight flickering through the arms of a hawthorn tree. In the distance was a single house banked into the woodland, a couple of lights still on. Issey pressed his hands to his eyes and made some binoculars with his palms. He zoomed into the entryway—a line of hooks on the wall, holding a line of weathered men's jackets. He panned to the other light. The kitchen. There was a modest wine rack next to the refrigerator. The kitchen table was also modest and cornered in, cottage-style, topped by a large and very immodest crystal bowl filled with a harvest of apples. The stove was standard. He yanked his lens back to the bowl. A sharp, thrilling wind ran through him. Was that a Lalique bowl? He could see from a mile away that it was—and more than that, from the circulating swallows, this was from the Hirondelles Collection. A Lalique bowl, from the Hirondelles Collection, with the satin finish and the goosey swallows—dynamite, delicious, in Bell River Valley!

He set his binoculars down on his hips. Why bother?

Then the light was turned off and all the remaining light then retreated to an unseen glade. Darkness surrounded him. It was a kind of totality, a kind of darkness he hadn't felt since the night he rescued the horses—or didn't rescue them. Issey thought he heard a child crying. What was it about the sound of a child crying that made him want to throw up?

Back in the car, Issey looked at the flyer again and focused on the series of numbers in the corner. Time and date. This was three years old. Did Berger bring the flyer with him?

Tanya was right about Bell River—it gets lonely at night. Issey hurried to the car. The sound of the car waking up was the only sound in the valley. You get so lonely you can finally hear what it's been trying to tell you. All the chitchat and clients and cheers and music and Molly in the mountains and Anissa in the entry and the stuff in his home swapped with stuff from other people's homes—fast from the valley depths Issey finally heard what it had been trying to tell him. And it wouldn't stop telling him and he couldn't stop hearing it. The champagne bottle and champagne flutes, the trail of cologne and Gitanes. Berger was setting him up. He had come to put Issey in the junk shop.

CHAPTER THIRTY-FOUR

Issey watched his house from a good distance. And it was just as he had expected—even if it made him sad. There was action in there, all right. Berger was waiting for him, pacing back and forth. He looked a little bulkier, but that was likely because he was wearing a shoulder holster and gun.

All of it—the reunion, the big plan, the new *Grüppe* in which Issey would be a select member—it was just a con. Berger didn't value his gifts, his fluid lockpicking, his sunnyside entry at two in the morning. No, Berger came with only one goal in mind. Destruction. It had to have been part of an endgame to bury anyone associated with the Faneuil Hall disaster.

But if Berger thought he could send up Issey, then Berger didn't know his target, and Issey was a moving one. He had home-field advantage, in the textures of the valley's darkness and ambient light. The town spread before him. He thought of Rohel, the soft card, Anissa and her critical cheekbones, the kid who had some kind of name that kids have these days, and soon Issey was driving into the neighborhood of a good idea, steering between the absurdities, and into the police station, occupied by only a single officer. The officer he came to see. Issey would be betraying nearly three decades of bad model behavior. But this was the only way. And someone should have told him it wasn't.

The reunion was something of a surprise for the hardwired Davenport, and Issey said he felt the sergeant needed a good "collar" in the books— "And boy have I got a whale for you!"

A pot of coffee later, Davenport asked, "Why are you doing this?"

"I have my reasons."

Sergeant Davenport set his pen down on his yellow legal pad and stretched his fingers. He had been writing a long time. The ink on Issey's boastful sentences was still warm.

"The coffee is good here, Clint."

"Issey, if what you're saying is true, then I'll have to arrest you."

"Of course. After all, I've given you a robust confession."

Issey had imagined a full-on gloat from the sergeant. He saw hootin' righteousness for Issey's life of poor choices, pictured a grin full of BBQ sauce and teeth made of okra. But Davenport got no joy out of it.

"It doesn't seem right."

"Be that as it may."

Davenport rubbed his eyes.

"It's all bad for you. You have prior convictions. You'll serve your sentence full freight."

"That's the second time tonight I've heard that." Issey thought it through, kind of. "I guess people are comfortable sharing their expressions here."

"You're not taking this seriously. Or maybe you are. Maybe you're deranged."

Davenport tried to laugh, but it was a flat tire kind of laugh.

"Clint, I imagine you'll need to see everything first, everything I stole from November all the way to the night of the horses. I was stealing that night, as a matter of fact. Or the night before. I can't remember. But it's all there."

Berger coming to his town and setting *him* up? Not on your life. With Davenport as an audience to his confession, Issey had crafted a perfect set up, even with its many, many flaws.

"So, let's drive together. To my house. I'll show you everything."

Davenport was slow collecting his jacket and keys and belt and gun.

They drove in the patrol car. Issey sat in the back. The balance between criminal and law was restored, comforting. In the cold backseat, Issey crossed his legs. Neither man spoke.

But he had talked a lot. Confessing didn't feel like confessing. Didn't feel like one thing or another, since none of it was real. Sure, he had authored those tales and, yes, they were all true crime romance, but Issey's words didn't hold any water. He'd be fine. Cut a deal. Never see the inside of a cell. They were just words. And if it became a federal case, Issey would steal Davenport's notebook and burn down the police station. Throw in Eight Jeff—why not? Issey would wear his black nylon jacket, which was always good for agility and breathing in the night.

Once again, staticky voices from the wideband radio cut the silence. Noise complaints from the Sugar House bar. A drunk driver. Somebody hit a deer.

"It's the girl baker from the General Store," the voice from the walkie-talkie said. "Should I put it down, sergeant?"

Davenport detached the receiver from the dash. "Junior Officer Fielding. Is that the girl or the deer?"

Laughter followed by feedback from the radio's frequency, followed by the crack of a shotgun.

The surrounding neighborhood was asleep for the night.

As if he was in the middle of a conversation, Davenport said, "But you never know with Fielding. We might have to go somewhere else for cinnamon rolls."

They continued driving. Issey's house edged towards them. Something wasn't right. The house wide awake. The windows roared with maniac lights. No, this wasn't right. The house looked as though it was in the middle of blowing its brains out.

"Clint."

There was no response. Davenport was staring at the house.

"Sergeant Davenport."

"What?"

"Radio for backup."

"What?"

"Radio for backup."

"Why—what's going on?"

"It's a lot of stuff inside. A real haul. You'll need help." Issey's lies sounded flimsy.

"What are you not telling me? Is someone on the other side of the door?"

Issey could see it. On the other side of the door was an ambush.

They were both out of the car, with Davenport starting his deliberate campaign towards the home. He looked imposing and enormous, but not enough for a maniac like Berger. Issey cut in front of him.

"Wait, Sergeant Davenport—"

"Who's in there, Issey? Who are you protecting?"

"It's no one—it was only me—I don't know. Radio for backup."

"Get back."

With surprising force, Davenport trucked Issey onto the ground.

Issey was dazed. Holiday festival, cozy comforts—these were from another time. He tasted blood in his teeth. Dirt lined the collar of his black nylon jacket. He heard his front door crack open. Issey got off his hump, wiped his hands on the hood of the patrol car, and headed towards the house. He really hoped, for the effort that was being asked of him, that Davenport was in there killing everyone.

But when the door opened, it opened with a great yawning echo. It was too late for guns. Issey expected an ambush and he got it.

"Why are we here?" Davenport asked, his uniform clean, his face clean. "There's nothing in your house."

"What do you mean? There's nobody inside?"

"No. There's nobody inside." He holstered his gun. "But there's also *nothing* in your house."

PART III

CHAPTER THIRTY-FIVE

Issey was a lousy thief, but a good son, and all the vases were gone. He was in his car now, driving on a road he had never driven on before, driving in the direction of Mount Mansfield. His high beams illuminated a deep forest shelter while in the rearview mirror darkness chased after him. There were only small openings for car lights to look in, and a deer, panicked by the high beams, shot into the path. Issey jerked the wheel to avoid killing it. The car twisted left and right. The tread sewed into the dirt. Eventually, he crested into a sloping shoulder.

He needed to stop. The deer told him so. The car hated his guts. He was driving too fast, driving away rather than towards, and he had steered through miles of up and down, miles of open clearings and fields, pastures and inns, mills and farms, far enough now to stop, to trace his map and the brochure. He got out of the car. Clouds scraped against a crepe paper moon. Fiery maples swayed with aggression. Deer mice and meadow voles skittered through silky vegetation. His neck and forehead, salty from sweat, were clipped by snow fleas. Pure black night surrounded him again and he held out his hands to find the car, to find the only two things important: the brochure and Molly's diary with the dervish clasp.

Berger had taken all the chairs. He had taken the sofa, the wingback, the stool, and the coffee table. He had taken all the items that were on top of the chairs, the sofa, the wingback, the stool, and the coffee table. The baseball cards, the baseball bats, the baseball gloves, the baseball plates; the snowboards and skis and video game consoles and Abenaki coins and Russian stacking dolls; the capelet, walking stick, production equipment; a hunting knife from Theodore Roosevelt, a collection of stamps, a collection of picture frames, a collection of boxes on top of boxes and boxes and boxes and shoes and things and boxes—and things! The football helmets were gone. Davenport joined Issey in the kitchen. The plates were gone. The utensils were gone. Everything—the pans, the pots, microwave, Dutch oven, the popcorn maker, the coffee maker, the French press Issey used for their slumber party, the garlic press he never used, the rice cooker he didn't know how to use, the vegetable steamer he refused to use, the blender for Molly's piña coladas, the egg slicer for Molly's eggy salad sandwiches. It was a soup to nuts cleanout, except for the soups and nuts left in the pantry and everything in the fridge. In the bedroom, all Berger left was a room. The bed was gone. The side tables were gone. The lamps were gone. The dressing table and standing mirror were gone. Berger couldn't fit into Issey's clothes or he didn't like them, so these were left behind. The clothes were stupid. They stared at him. Issey was stupid. And Berger's flattery played out: "Did you just back up a truck and load up?" He had even stolen Issey's hand truck.

Issey felt the sergeant's probing eyes. "Why are we here? You confessed—why?"

To trap Berger. To execute the perfect trap. But it wasn't the perfect trap. It might've been the dumbest trap and someone should have told him so. But he had no one. Someone had once told him he was stupid and easily confused. He had given them their stuff back. They were all at the Sugar House having a party. And now it was just an empty house staring at him. Fireplace and baseboards and wall outlets. Issey got rolled.

"Listen, Issey. There's nothing here to take you in for. There is just *nothing* here."

Issey smoothed the nervous fringes of his hair, "Apparently, Sergeant Davenport, a confession is good for the soul, but bad for the reputation."

"Where is everything?"

"I don't know."

Davenport walked towards the door, with searching eyes, when something under the dirty seagrass rug in the entry caught his eye. He picked it up, looked it over, and then handed it to Issey.

It was his tax bill. On the back, Issey read what had been written:

L'envoi—

Issey, I'm sorry. But I had to do it. I had opportunity. It wasn't personal. Just opportunity. It was a pleasure sharing this holiday season with you and I look forward to future collabs!

Ever yours,

B.

PS: Don't forget to pay your tax bill, Issey. They'll come looking for you!

Issey chucked it on the kitchen counter. He smiled a little and then frowned a little. Davenport picked up the envelope and read it too.

Davenport studied it. "Who's B.?"

"My brother."

"Your brother's name begins with an R."

"He has poor penmanship. You misread it."

Issey grasped for things to look at. There was nothing.

"I don't know what's going on, Issey, but this isn't good."

Issey shrugged and turned towards the bathroom

"You should've just kept your end of the bargain."

Issey turned to Davenport. "What are you talking about?"

"We shook on it, remember? You should've left on Wednesday."

Issey nodded. In the bathroom, Berger had stolen Issey's toothpaste and hair paste, the hand soap and the Art Deco soap dispenser. Issey opened the shower curtains. Berger had stolen Molly's body wash.

He was driving again. The rooflight was on. Resting on his right leg was a map with lines drawn towards his destination.

The missing body wash led him to his closet, where he reached into every pocket of every jacket, until he found, folded unevenly, Molly's letter about her retreat and the accompanying brochure. He was annoyed at himself for not having it on him at all times, annoyed that he hadn't read it the instant he found it, but this was a once-in-a-lifetime mistake. There were no piles obstructing the straight line to his only love. Molly. He had her letter smoothed open on the passenger seat. "Luv luv LOVE you!" He studied the ecstatic handwriting of her letter, heard her hoarse voice, saw the way she moved through the house, then studied the location of the women's yoga retreat, mastered the photos of the renovated barn, the open frontage, the nightly bonfire, the sunup horseback riding, the morning fruits and granola station. He read about all the things she had likely been doing—free form expression and Chakra self-discovery and mandala stuff. He imagined her sweating in tiger poses and drinking herself blind with spirituality juice and maybe thinking the whole thing was screwy. But they were screwy, screwy in the same way. He didn't need things. He needed Molly. Only Molly, his Molly!

He had arrived in the town where the retreat was held. There was another ten miles of mountain driving beyond the outskirts, but at least he made it to the town. He had never been here before, but it was like Bell River, with some small differences in the set pieces. Their General Store was next to the post office rather than across the street, and a tiny technical college took the place of the library. There were freshly painted fire hydrants and a green plastic box for the free town newspaper next to the blue recycle bin for the free town newspaper. There was the morning beanery with the Regulars Only sign next to the Closed one.

There was a lot of activity coming from an undecorated wooden *joint* called Krystal's Localfolk Bar & Lounge. What time was it? The car's digital clock read five minutes to midnight. Late. The brochure for the yoga retreat had outlined a strict ten p.m. curfew, roll call, and lights out in bold letters. So he hooked back into the center of the town and drove until he found somewhere to park himself for the night. The wheels crunched on gravel leading to a rusty motor lodge.

A sleepy old man with a white goatee, wearing denim overalls and nothing underneath, met Issey at his driver's side door.

"Sorry, son." The old man had a crispy voice. "We're full up."

"I just need to stay until dawn—pre-dawn, really. I could sleep in the boiler room."

The old man scolded him. "I said we're all *full up*. Turn around. There's a chain sleeper about two miles past the fallen water tower."

"And which direction is that?"

"When you leave here, turn right. Then head south. You'll see the water tower. It's fallen. Good night."

From the rearview mirror, Issey saw the old man directing a muscular arm, Right, Right, Turn Right, Leave Here, Right, Right, Leave Now, scooting Issey until he was out of sight. Issey turned right, then right, and then there was an intersection. Which way was south? South from what? Whose south? His south or my south? From the North Star? From Bethlehem?

Issey drove back to the open restaurant Krystal's. A bunch of excited young people came spilling out of the doors. Most of them carried acoustic guitars or mandolins. Some had hand drums. Others were carrying the wind under their long skirts. They also had tambourines.

"Hey, man! You're too late for last call, but we're going to the fieldhouse—c'mon!"

Issey got out of the car, thinking Molly might be among this late-night crew. He pictured her breaking out of the women's retreat, joining a late-night party, defying the curfew. But these people, with their tribal patterns and dreadlocks and flannel shirts and knee-length boots, were an anarchy too store-bought for Molly's taste. They were about twenty in total, piling into three vans and one pickup. One, a young drunk stocky girl, was doing some kind of dancing umbrella show for Issey's benefit. They were buffoons. Issey entered the restaurant. He was told to turn around and leave.

This town was sending him a lot of mixed messages, and the buffoons were still loading up. In the bed of the truck, an acoustic guitar buffoon and a mandolin buffoon were picking at the opening of "Maggie May." The truck started, the singing started, and soon old Maggie was leading the Mod away from home and into a tent. And then they were gone. Molly wouldn't have been with them, no. She preferred disruption on the scale of what Issey offered: walking down one step at a time as he stole her journal with the dervish clasp. He never got around to reading her diary. He wondered why.

He drove towards the yoga studio, probably. He figured he'd park on the perimeter and sleep in the car—if he could make it to the perimeter. He was tired and didn't know which way was north and which way was "true" north. After a few miles, he knew he was lost. He parked the car. He started the car. Within a few minutes, he found a road that was at least paved. Within a few hours, he found a secluded neighborhood buffeted by Lake Champlain. He parked his car for the night. The moon finally found its voice and, joining the deformed leopard frogs who were at full croak, it sang a midnight aria on the surface of the lake. Stretched in the distance, Issey could see Plattsburgh. He had driven a little too far, probably a lot too far, but that was fine. He'd wheel around and reunite with Molly tomorrow. He slept for a bit. When he woke up, he slept for a lot longer. Images drifted, of things and clients and the client book.

It had come fast, but it was now the next day and he found himself seated at a hip brunch *spot* where tap water was served in mason jars. All the servers wore loose tank tops. Issey didn't know where he was. He pushed his hands through his salty hair, combing through the clients, visualizing their names and their items. Half-eaten shreds of bread, like his half-eaten brains, were soaked in yolk.

He was in Burlington now, somewhere off the old North End. Yesterday's large-scale robbery of everything... "Just a drizzle," Issey said as he legged it from block to block, gumming the heels of his ankle boots. What better time to break them in? All was in high holiday bloom. Almost every other apartment had a turret and that warmed him, but taking a left turn on Loomis Street, the turrets ended and the chain fences began and this neighborhood looked like a cheaper, crueler version of the neighborhood with the turrets. This seemed to be the rag-end of an art district. The eaves were run down. A shutter was missing. Some doors didn't have numbers. Some doors had numbers in halves. A Jack Russell in the window was dirty. Issey looked at his watch. Berger had stolen his watch.

Berger had run him over. It wasn't "a drizzle," what Berger had done to Issey. Even if it "wasn't personal," Issey was left on the sucker side of life. It had been a complete dramatic raking. And these ankle boots were shredding his ankles.

And then suddenly it was night again and once again too late to coming knocking at the yoga retreat. So, like the night before, he found the guitars and mandolins spilling out of Krystal's restaurant. And like the night before, the guitars and mandos invited him to the fieldhouse for singalongs and reefers. The guitars and the mandos cheered. The tambourines, with the wind blowing up their skirts, collected a sedan of rich bozos visiting for the rich bozo season, and soon it was a bonfire of reefers, bottles, pills, and pockets. Pelvic pockets, rear pockets, rib pockets, appendix-pox, the small ones with the key inside, the big meaty ones in front with the stretched buttons. A Valentino raffia belt was thrown on top of a camo duffle bag; Salvation Army boots tramped a YSL scarf; crêpe de chine pants were smeared in an alphabet soup of CK numbers and slithery guitar strings. It was a feeding frenzy. A lumpy lunar cookout. One guy shaving cocaine-radishes over the embers was getting all the sweeties Issey would have had an opinion about. But he had no opinions on sweeties. The drunk stocky girl stood her big logs on Issey's hood and did her umbrella dance while he watched, protected by the security of his windshield. He didn't like this part of Vermont. He didn't like the people in this part of Vermont. The drunk stocky girl continued dancing. He clicked the windshield wipers and gave a couple pumps for the windshield-wiper fluid.

"What are you trying to say, man?"

"Who invited you anyway, buddy?"

"Why don't you get lost, creep!"

"Kick rocks, pervert!"

Issey could take a hint. He put the car in reverse. The crowd, wet and shifty, cheered in unison for the exit of this strange cretin who had been watching their orgy from his car for however long it takes to get a really good orgy going.

One of the tambourines broke ranks. She had sandy hair and freckles on her cheeks. She ran to Issey and, with the wind and bonfire behind her, called out, "Hey hey!"

Issey rolled down his window eagerly. "Yes?"

"Na na na na! Hey hey hey! Goodbye!"

Then the rest joined in. "Na na na na! Hey Hey! Hey! Goodbye!" And again. "Na na na na! Hey Hey! Hey! Goodbye!" The guitars and mandolins provided boisterous accompaniment. "Na na na na! Hey Hey! Hey! Good*bye*!" The car, who normally disliked Issey, nudged the transmission to change gears without giving him a hard time and sprayed a little extra windshield wiper fluid onto the windshield to protect its driver's sad face from all the young people who were having such a good time dancing in the road. *Don't let all this cheering hit you on the way out.*

And the cheering from the buffoons continued until the car's headlights disappeared. They got bored and Issey was forgotten, along with most of what happened under those creeping cottonwoods, in that tough part of town. Even though the activities were lost to alcohol and pills and soggy memory, the consequences that spread were generational and disgusting. It was no place for Issey.

CHAPTER THIRTY-SIX

When he lowered the yoga retreat brochure and put it on the passenger seat, instead of the high gloss estate from the photos, he saw a cavernous and chilly barn. He got out of the car and approached. The barn stank. It was years of sweat and skin and hair and breathing and clothes. It was soaking yoga mats and damp hard cots. Sounds were distinct but muted and came from unidentifiable areas. Was that someone speaking behind him? Was that primal screaming in the distance? Was someone's spine being cracked in two? Were those bones that were being chiseled?

The woman at the front desk had bright dark circles under her eyes and tea-stained teeth. She looked malnourished and happy about it. "Oh, Molly's a soaring spirit," she whispered, and led Issey to the visitor zone.

"And it's okay if I wear my shoes? I'm sort of breaking them in."

"Of course." The woman smiled sagely.

"And what about this gift I brought for her?"

Issey showed her the diary with the dervish clasp.

"Of course. It's fine."

"I've just never been to a women's yoga retreat before. I'm sorry about all these questions."

"In German, 'I'm sorry' means 'I inhabit your sorrow.'"

"Oh."

The woman looked at the diary closer. "That little clasp is funny."

They passed a running fountain that was broken. Moss had grown on the stone and a sour brine followed him to into the visiting room. A door closed behind him and the woman was gone. In the room was a table and two metal chairs.

When the door opened again, Issey was immediately decorated with Molly's kisses. By the time she was finished, she was out of breath. She pulled the metal chair next to him. She put her head on his chest, wrapped her hand in his, and purred.

Molly's hair had grown much longer and much lumpier. Under her big mess of brown hair was a vanishing body. She had lost a lot of weight. She looked like a person who didn't know she had lost a lot of weight, like the leftover skin was there by accident, with lots of give in the thighs of her yoga pants. He didn't know if this was good or bad.

After a while, she sat level to him, and asked, "Do you want a tour?"

"Really? I didn't think I'd be allowed."

"It's not a prison, Issey."

"I thought I heard screaming."

"There's screaming. But it's not a prison."

She took his hand and led him from the visitor's room to the other side of the barn, which was a surprising society of women of various ages, ethnicities, and body types. Many smiled at Molly and some of the women who had grown close to her showed genuine pleasure when meeting Issey. Many already seemed to know him, her Issey, her "person." They passed others who waved peace at her but were quietly tucked in their journaling nook.

From there, Molly walked him under a cathedral ceiling as high and as hopeful as Schröder's Gap. She roped her bony arm through his and they walked in stride like local worthies.

"It was really gross in the lobby," Issey said.

"It's the smell. It's still here. It's always here and it follows you around."

"I don't smell it."

"Then you must've acclimated to it already. You already started it. Smell is the outer journey. You're on the inner journey. It took me about a week."

"You've been here a week?"

Molly laughed.

"Let me show you my room."

"I'm allowed?"

"Still not a prison," she said.

Her room was windowless and spare, about the size of a prison cell. But Molly put some of her playful touches to it, like a yellow candy bar wrapper taped to the wall above the Garfield pillowcase on her bed. On her night table, there was a bracelet that looked familiar. Issey picked it up. Its feel was familiar. He felt the metal twine with his thumb. He was confused. It was like he had done this before.

"Our clarity coach said, 'To let in light, you have to crack open the skull.' She's French."

"I know this bracelet."

"Of course you do. It's yours. Well—*yours*." She used quotation marks. "It's Henry Hatch's bangle bracelet. And here." She got on her knees and reached far under her mattress. "We can't have lighters, but I keep it anyway."

He held it alongside the bracelet.

"This is the mechanic's lighter," Issey said. "The Ronson lighter."

"Caddy."

"Caddy's Ronson lighter. How do *you* have them?"

"You brought 'em home. And before I left for my retreat—I took 'em."

"*I* brought them home?"

"You brought them home."

Issey thought he was shaking his head at all this strange information. But he wasn't. He was just staring at these two items in his hands. "No, these were my clients' things...I gave them all back."

"Did you, though? They were on your kitchen counter when I met you."

Issey tried tracing the exchange, from one set of hands to the next. Whose hands were doing the giving and whose hands were doing the taking? He saw his hands doing both. His hands had always gotten a little too much action. When he looked up from his hands, she was waiting for him to say:

"It was me, wasn't it?"

"It was you, what?" She knew the answer already, but it was as if she needed *him* to say it, alone with his Molly, carved in this room at the end of the world.

"All that stuff that was coming in? That was me."

"It was you."

"But—me?" He was so disgusted with himself he could hardly say it.

"You were the one bringing everything in. I watched you. You were putting all the gifts those people gave you into a pile. And that pile got mixed up with another pile. You're really disorganized, man."

"There's no way. I watched..."

"All those people you stole from, they were giving it all back to you. But you were too obsessed with those piles to see that no one wanted that stuff anymore. There was, like, no talking to you."

He sank into his thoughts. The Cogsworths gave away the nesting dolls and the video games. Issey had these. Baldwin and Xu got rid of their helmets. Issey had these. How things were swapped or mixed up or traded down or passed over didn't matter. No one wanted their stuff anymore. Issey had ruined it. And they were better off with the memory. So they had given everything *back* to Issey as "gifts," gifts for services rendered, parting gifts to the lobster who pinched 'em for no real reason. He liked going through people's lives and taking their stuff, "stuff that didn't belong to them." His whole operation was patched together with chicken wire and dog fur. And no one wanted it.

He sat on her bed, with his head down. His thighs looked fat. Molly put her arm around his hump.

"But you're freed from all of it now."

"What do you mean?"

"Everything's gone, right?"

"How do you have all the answers?" Issey was indignant. "What kind of place is this?"

"Inner journey, buster." She tapped her head and then tapped his heart. "I didn't know it when I took the lighter and the bracelet. I just wanted a couple things that reminded me of you. But about two weeks in—"

"Two weeks!"

"Yeah, it's been about two weeks. Anyway, I figured the day you got rid of all that junk would be the day you came for me. You wouldn't be here if you still had everything."

"And I don't anymore."

"See," she winked. "I'm, like, totally self-transcendent."

With the two items in his hand, Issey suddenly felt small. She put her hands over his and kissed him on the cheek.

Issey asked, "Can I have them back?"

"Of course! I don't need 'em anymore."

He put the bracelet and the lighter in his pocket. Issey smiled—or tried to smile. He said he had something for her.

"Fer me?" Molly said in a voice. One of her comedy voices.

He pulled her diary with the dervish clasp out of his jacket pocket and handed it to her. Her smile was so big that the corners of her mouth reached into her lumpy hair.

Issey said, "I've had this for the longest time."

"Really?"

"I knew I'd eventually give it to you."

"It's so cool." She held it in both hands and looked at it front to back. "And what's this clasp thing all about?"

"What do you mean?"

"I've never seen a clasp like that before. Is it, like, some kind of little ballerina man?"

Issey rubbed his forehead. "This isn't your diary?"

"Well, I—what do you mean?" Now she was confused. "You're giving this to me as gift, right?"

"No, I'm giving it *back*."

"Back?"

"This is your diary."

"No," she said. "I would never buy a diary like this."

"But I... we know each other."

"Um. Yeah."

"No, I mean, we met before—before we met."

"Boy, you're really talkin' like an idiot."

Issey tried to untangle it and went over that night when he had "worked" her townhouse. He described coming down the stairs one at a time and her standing in the kitchen, watching his next moves. He told her about the roommate and the ricecakes and the television going a mile a minute. He talked about the long stare the two of them had shared as he crept out of the townhouse.

"I've never lived in a townhouse. Too *bougie* for me."

"Really?"

"I wish in this one instance I had." Her regret seemed genuine. "I always wanted to see you in action. You're just...you're a box-office draw, Issey!"

"So," he said, looking at her hands holding the diary, "you really *aren't* Rhonda."

"It's private."

"What?" he asked.

She shrugged into her wild mass of hair.

He asked again, "What's private?"

"I don't know." She sighed and looked around her little room. "These are the kind of problems you run into. You know?"

He didn't. She handed him the diary.

He asked, "How's the retreat?"

"Pretty stupid," she said, and kind of smiled at him and then kind of looked like she was going to cry some, maybe later.

Issey returned the diary with the dervish clasp into his jacket pocket. Molly didn't ask for much. She just asked for too much. He never saw her again.

CHAPTER THIRTY-SEVEN

For days, he and the Ronson lighter, bangle bracelet, and diary with the dervish clasp put a ton of miles on the car and the car was back to hating his guts. Issey had mapped all of the places Berger would have hocked Issey's stuff, particularly the high-end stuff—like a chandelier. If anything, he needed to find that stupid chandelier so he could give it back to that stupid Dan Vanetta and be done with this whole stupid thing. And he figured Berger would have set off homeward. Even if they despise the place, guys like Berger never let go until everyone calls him king.

Issey toured the pawnshops in the southern part of the state, then in Connecticut, then upstate New York. There were certainly many chandeliers in many of the pawnshops he visited and while Issey had forgotten some of the finer details of Vanetta's chandelier, he knew these weren't it. Most of the pawnshop owners knew of Issey or had heard of him. For some, Issey was trouble and they were fearful little mopes. For others, Issey was a myth come alive, a valuable and ruthless commodity. To them, Issey was regarded as a "tough guy." He was quiet and his eyes were empty. There didn't seem to be a mutual understanding between his actions and his brains. They let him see recent pawnshop tickets, and offered him their cards, with their personal phone numbers scribbled on the back. In New Hampshire, he actually *did* have contacts, as he had lied to his clients during the early days of his hero's post, mostly near the

Manchester airport, old guys who owed him a favor or who liked him for not getting in the way. Unfortunately, they hadn't seen the kind of chandelier Issey was looking for and also let Issey go through their tickets. One guy put him up for the night and recycled old stories about Cherry Addison and Bob Chicago and deaf Peppermill Harper. In a little dining room with a low ceiling and small cups, the old guy punctuated his stories with long rubbery laughs while Issey nodded at the right times. The guy was money-in-a-handshake, "something to help you, and don't you say nothin' about it," and Issey trotted on his way, continued his search, and took care not to think too much. He made a few stops in Boston and Boston welcomed him with some of the leftover crew who said Berger was a bum. The guys paid back old favors to Issey he didn't know were his to cash out. He didn't even know how many or even what kind of chips he had held. So, with his blank expression and friendly, psychotic eyes, he trusted the fair price of whatever they gave him. He had always kept his mouth shut and did what was asked, never got in the way, and sometimes got pushed around for another jerk's screw up. The conversations were quick. The guys were in the middle of their hustle outside the Terminator Pizza joint, or in the middle of the grind in their little corners by the Keno screens. For Issey, the trip was a good little earner. A complete waste of time, but a good little earner.

And when he finally came home, the mountains saw him coasting into Bell River Valley in the middle of the night. The road was empty and the night air gooey. He had been gone for so long that he had to rely on the feel of the valley to know what season he was coming into. It felt like the valley had experienced long and salty rainy nights and maybe a blizzard.

He parked and walked inside. The door wasn't locked and he had left all the windows open. Inside was the drafty smell a house has when a human hasn't been in it for a long time.

Or when nothing had ever been in it. Now that the house had time to settle into itself, its emptiness was transformative. Without things jamming up the walls, the house seemed to have restored dignity and character, and was now contemplating Issey, who paced from one room to the next.

Issey didn't know the house had a skylight and he slept under it. For a bed, Issey stacked various outfits in the center of the living room floor and burrowed his legs deep into slacks, turtlenecks, and shapewear. Sleeping on this clothes palette in the living room, in the company of this restored house, Issey was floating with moon and stars and calling mountains. A spray of pale blue light came from the skylight. Through opened, curtainless windows, came an aroma of breads being baked and cakes getting caked. Strange to think that Molly had lived here once. Strange to think that *he* had lived here once. Things were changing. He knocked off to Tanya's baking.

CHAPTER THIRTY-EIGHT

Stripped clean, the house was fresh and inviting, so ready for reinvention that it was almost like it had hiked up its workpants and said, "Let's do this!"

Stripped clean, the house was also a stale husk, with coal black squares on the walls where his mother's old pictures of geese and husbands used to hang. Issey set the bangle bracelet and the Ronson lighter on the kitchen counter and drummed his fingers. The echo in the empty house was immersive. The first thing he did was toss the dirty seagrass rug from the entry in the garbage pail. But there was no garbage pail because Berger had taken it.

He re-examined his plan to find the chandelier. The rasping of the map also echoed throughout the house. As unlikely as it seemed, maybe Berger had gone west. Maybe Berger had *kept* Issey's things.

The Ronson lighter and bangle bracelet kept him company on the kitchen counter. But they didn't really *go* with anything—or with anything the future design might need going with. Issey didn't feel like outfitting the house based on the vibe these two items were giving off. The windows were open. The front door was open. A pleasant December breeze brought in a memory—one he couldn't place. He remembered himself, but not a lot else. He returned to his plan and map.

Issey had returned everybody else's stuff except Vanetta's, and the chandelier wasn't part of the pile. He drummed his fingers on the kitchen counter. Echo. December breeze. Lighter. Bracelet. And the diary with the dervish clasp, but that was in the car and not coming in the house.

He waited for calls from pawnshop owners. There were none. No amount of bad news would diminish Issey's belief that he would find this stupid thing and he even thought in the two days since returning to Bell River that he had gained ground on it. He was somewhere on the case. The chandelier was somewhere in the area, somewhere closer to him. It wasn't "out there." Out there was gone. Out there was hopeless, a thing luxuriating in its own insignificance. And even if the stuff changed hands and went from house to house until it eventually landed in his house and then in Berger's possession and then who know where—all anyone would remember was that Issey couldn't find a simple chandelier.

His client book was nowhere to be found, but he wasn't looking for it. He had his memories of all the good thief-work he had accomplished that winter. Those were productive weeks, maybe his best, with gathering winter clouds and the black sky that knew how to keep a secret. Sometimes the nights were silky and sometimes the nights had a character that was a little rough. Sometimes the wind on the back on his neck was like a whisper, like a coded message that told him, "You have to buy a scarf."

CHAPTER THIRTY-NINE

Tanya, splashed with frosting and flour on her apron, hands, face, and hair, served a hungry morning crew. Issey was hanging around at the display case and chatting with her. Tanya made it easy to talk because it was easy to think about something else, everything else. She asked if Issey knew what a Local Arrangements Committee did. Issey said he didn't.

"Shoot. I was hoping you could tell me. None of us seem to know what we're doing—and this is our fourth meeting."

"What's it for?"

"Some bigshot author's doing a reading at Yellow Barn Books. And we're the Local Arrangements Committee."

"Hm," Issey said, thinking while eating a gingersnap. "I don't know."

"Then why'd you ask?"

Issey shrugged. In his pocket, he felt the bangle bracelet and the Ronson lighter.

"Anyway, I hope you don't mind, but I gave one of the girls your phone number."

"Really?"

"When you're around, Issey, there's not a dry seat in the house. That's what they say."

"Who says that?"

"I'm just sayin'. That's what they say."

Issey continued eating. Tanya continued working the line.

On his way out, Issey passed Sergeant Davenport and another, much younger police crony walking up the four steps to the General Store. Davenport fell back.

"Hey, Issey—you ever figure out what happened to all the furniture in your place?"

Issey shook his head. But Davenport knew Issey wouldn't tell him. Besides, Davenport didn't seem interested in that particular subject. He had eyes that were a mouthful of something else to talk about.

"I've been meaning to follow up with you regarding those horses."

"Again with that?" Issey groaned. "I don't think I have anything more to say."

"Come on, Issey. We're better than that." Davenport wrapped his hands across his forearms and shoulders. "Look, it's freezing. Why are we standing out here like jerks? Let's talk in the cruiser."

Issey shook his head. "I don't think so."

"What about inside?"

"*No.*" Issey was assertive. It seemed to have a sting and Davenport looked away.

The younger officer with Davenport pretended the conversation between these two much older men wasn't making him uncomfortable and he looked around at some air. He said, "You wanted a frappe, Sergeant? I can swing in."

Davenport shook his head without looking at the younger officer. "I'll meet you inside."

"I just thought—well, if I'm getting a frappe and you're getting a frappe, I can just get us both our frappes at the same time."

"No, Fielding," Davenport said bravely, staring Issey down. "I get my own frappes."

When the younger officer finally took the hint, and Davenport and Issey were alone, the odor of frustration coming off of Davenport was so stewed that it was almost savory. *What am I gonna do with you*? And they both thought this. *What am I gonna do with you*? It was relationship building time. They'd be work colleagues. Work on the opposite ends, of course, but work colleagues all the same, for these jobs they milled for nothing, the pointless inroads between cop and criminal. The world will be burning down, and Davenport knows he won't die with his other Okies from the pen, but instead chasing after a criminal like Issey who was trying to take advantage of this world's-on-fire opportunity.

Davenport finally said, "We arrested Avi last week."

"What? Avi? For what?"

"Insurance fraud."

"Insurance fraud?" Issey stood there still. "Insurance fraud for what?"

"Come on, Issey," Davenport sighed, not stewed at all, but frosty, and his frost was blowing on Issey. "We both know it."

"I don't. I don't get it."

"Think it through."

"I'm not good at that right now!"

"Take it easy," Davenport said. "He put a false claim on those horses."

Issey scrunched up his face. He couldn't figure it out. Calmly, with his leather voice, Davenport just told him:

"It was Avi who stole 'em."

"Avi stole them? The horses?"

"Uh-huh," Davenport nodded.

"Why didn't you tell me about this sooner?"

"Why would I?"

"I mean, I guess because..." Hm. Issey was stumped. "Because I found them...?"

"No." Davenport shook his head. "That wasn't you."

Prairie lines cut deep into Davenport's sad mouth.

"You know that, Issey. You know you didn't find 'em."

Issey said nothing. Davenport asked again if he'd like to sit with him in the cruiser and once again Issey shook his head. So Davenport stood outside talking to Issey, while the line of the morning crew of farmers and hotel workers came out of the General Store loaded with Tanya's treats. There was nodding in all directions when Davenport said: "Unfortunately, Issey, you kinda got rolled."

Issey gritted his teeth and thought, *Again.*

"Avi had been running that horse farm into the ground for about five years now. Up to his eyeballs in debt and no solution in sight. And then you came into town."

Issey tried to follow as Davenport continued. "Avi knew your habits and Avi took advantage. He filed an insurance claim for stolen horses a few days after you arrived. He must've shepherded them somewhere out of sight for a while. I'm surprised he didn't kill 'em—maybe that was in the plans. But I started asking questions and then all the new young people from the city started getting hot and the Chamber of Commerce started getting hot and the community developers started getting hot, and all this must've gotten Avi hot too. So he brought them back to the farm."

Davenport wiped his masculine lips.

"Did you know that Avi's horse farm has three surveillance cameras on the property?"

Issey shook his head, No. *Yes.*

"Okay, well, I think you do, and here's why: after you left our interview, I just followed you."

"Me?"

"I've been straight up following you for weeks now. Do you realize that every time you made a move, you brought us closer to figuring this whole thing out? I followed you on the night the horses were recovered. In the distance, I saw the truck coming back to the farm while you got caught in that storm."

Issey didn't respond.

"And then after our interview, I followed you to the horse farm where you tracked those cameras and I bet you came to the same conclusion as me: if Avi was giving us footage of someone burglarizing his tack room, why not provide the same footage to us of the exterior? He has three cameras. Got to be, those three cameras caught something. So why not give 'em to us? I'd say it was search warrant time, what do you think?"

Issey waited.

"So we get the footage for the cameras. And guess what we see?"

Issey shrugged. "I don't know."

"There's the tack room criminal in plain view, doing some kind of weird tiger dance with his rear-end pointing at the camera. Do you know any reason someone would do something so stupid?"

Issey said nothing.

"But then, right after the dancing criminal takes off in his car, we also see two of the cameras suddenly being shut off for roughly three hours. I mean, those cameras get shut off *real quick*."

Issey waited.

"That's weird, right? But, a third camera stayed on. And in that third camera, about twenty minutes *after* those two cameras are shut off, three horses are being led into one of those horse trailer hitches and then being driven off. And then the brake lights come on—as if the driver forgot his wallet and grocery list. And then here comes Avi running from the truck *painfully* to the barn. And then the camera footage on that third camera cuts out. Criminals always forget something. Avi forgot to turn off the third camera.

"And then once everything settled down and you became this town hero thing, he tried to throw us off. And that's when he gave us the footage of, well, someone doing a pretty good night's worth of damage to his tack room."

Issey thought about it. He said, "Hm."

Fielding returned with two drinks. Issey must've been fifteen years older than the younger officer, and Issey never felt older than the officers.

"They were out of frappes, sir."

"What'd I say, Fielding?"

"I just thought maybe it'd be better if I was in there and you were talking..."

Issey interrupted and asked, "But why would he give you the video of the tack room? Wouldn't it just lead you to the three cameras?"

"He probably figured once we had the criminal raiding the tack room that we'd never come looking for the other footage."

"Why not just erase the other footage?"

"Do you know how to do that?"

"Well." Issey thought about it. "No?"

"People are stupid, Issey. People *are* stupid—especially the smart ones. They're greedy and careless and too clever and too cute. It's like they want to get caught. That tack room footage is all one massive stupid bluff. Guys like Avi think they know more than some jerkwater police force. And good. We like to keep it that way."

"I thought he was...hm." Issey didn't know what he thought Avi was.

"Fact is, Avi's been our guy all this time. We had a woman from his insurance company who handles fraud—she saw it a mile away. The horses were seriously malnourished. I don't know if you know this, but you probably saved their lives."

"Oh. That's good I guess."

The young officer Fielding, with those two paper cups of something in his hands, said, "I guess I'm gonna sit in the cruiser, sir?"

"Yes, Fielding, yes—geez!"

Fielding's cheeks got warm.

"Sorry, son." Davenport put a hand on the boy's shoulder. "We're on the same team." Davenport winked at Issey. "All of us."

Fielding's cheeks went back to normal while Issey's got hotter.

"You still want your hot chocolate, sir?"

"Of course I want the hot chocolate." He took it and slugged it down. "That Tanya knows what she's doing. Bad driver. Good baker."

"Yessir!"

After he had gone and Issey had a couple of minutes to assemble himself, he asked. "You said you knew all along it was Avi. But you came to my party that night. Why didn't you say anything?"

"Everyone was having a good time. And we ain't here for a long time...You know how it goes."

"But I thought..." Issey was stumped. "And Anissa?"

"Yeah, no. Just pursuing some lines of thought. But I think my wife and her are gonna get together after her reading. Maybe they'll be friends!"

"Your wife is doing a reading?"

Davenport looked at Issey like he had lost his mind. "Where have you been? Your sister-in-law, Issey. She wrote a book. She's a writer. Remember?"

"Oh, yeah. All she ever talks about is her writing."

"Well, her book just came out. Seriously, though, where *have* you been?"

"I just...My girlfriend is on a yoga retreat."

"Okay," Davenport said, as if Issey's reply made sense. "Anyway, she's giving a reading at Yellow Barn Books next week. Hopefully, we'll all get together for a drink after. It'll be good if we all get a little toasty, right?" Davenport nodded in the direction of Fielding, who was in the police cruiser staring jealously at Issey and Davenport. "The kid'll drive us. It'll give him something useful to do."

Davenport headed to the cruiser.

"And you know what's funny? That dancing guy on Avi's security camera? We never saw his face. How about that? He just seemed to be doing some stupid tiger dance with his rear end pointing at the camera. Aren't people stupid?"

CHAPTER FORTY

The fact was Issey had opportunities to do some bad stuff. Plenty of opportunities.

The windows were open.

The front doors were open.

A breeze brought memories, of old habits, old impulses—those he couldn't take again.

Fiddlehead Inn left its doors open all night. The manager's office had no lock.

Issey said goodnight to Eight Jeff in the Sugar House. Eight Jeff said, "Have a great night, Issey! See you at Anissa's reading!" Apparently, everyone knew about Anissa's reading. Issey winked at Eight Jeff. Issey hated him. But Eight Jeff was happy.

The old houses, condos, bungalows, and barns—they had their doors open and they had their windows open. The single house banked into the woodland with the Lalique bowl from the Hirondelles Collection. He stared inside, from an unhealthy distance at 2:30 in the morning.

"The hustle's too much of a grind and the grind's too much of a hustle," he'd whistle, thinking of the old crew, thinking of Claudia, even Berger. They were duds, pointless duds, who had nothing better to do, he told himself, wandering outside, alone with a cold neck.

Almost every night, he visited these houses, condos, bungalows, and barns. He watched them from a distance. Plenty of opportunities invited him to do some bad stuff. Something held him back. He couldn't even blame it on the chandelier. He knew where that was.

Anissa had changed. She looked like Rohel. Isn't it dogs who are supposed to look like their owners? She looked like a dog.

"Well, look who it is." Her eyes dazzled on him. "I almost gave up on you. Come in, sugar cube."

It was late afternoon. Rohel was at a zoning hearing. Madison was at a sleepover. Both husband and kid were raging successes. Meanwhile, Anissa was home, and it was Anissa he had come to see. She was dressed for success, literature, and podiums. Anissa was always wearing success, always wearing *cool*. Today it was a tuxedo blazer and low V-neck t-shirt, white, expensive, completely inappropriate for Vermont.

She said, "I've been trying to get a hold of you with the big news."

But Issey interrupted her and said instantly: "You have the chandelier. You have it."

Anissa's author-y confidence shifted. Or maybe not. It's what Issey wanted to see. But it's not what happened.

She said, "Yeah. Of course I do. Why are you being *j'accuse?*"

Issey was confused. Issey was always confused and always wrong.

She looked at him. "Issey, you *have* known this, right?"

"Oh, uh, of course," he lied.

"Where do you think it went? You had it with you that night with the horses. I told you I took care of all that stuff. I put it in my trunk and drove it home."

"Really?"

"Issey, it's right there." And she pointed right there, towards the dining room where Dan Vanetta's chandelier was hanging and apparently had been hanging for weeks. But Issey had never looked up. The suckers always forget to look up. The suckers never see what's above them.

"You've had it all this time…"

"Yeah. I just put it up there myself. Rohel was no help. I'm starting to think he might be something of an idiot. Seems to be a family trait."

Issey thought about the chandelier. Anissa brought them two coffees. They sat on the couch with lots of birch pillows, and she had lots to say while Issey had lots to think about. They were in opposite moods. He was a little lost and she hiked one leg on the couch like a real dishy pal.

"Forget about that chandelier," she said, "I've been trying to get in touch with you forever because I wanted to tell you that my book finally came out and I'm doing a reading on Saturday."

"I heard about that." He then mumbled congratulations and smiled, but nothing was convincing.

He asked, "Why was it so important to tell me?"

"I don't know," she said, shrugging, smiling, "we're both kind of outsiders."

Issey nodded. Strangely, he never knew it. He was an outsider. They were both outsiders. And so, in an uninterrupted stream of thought, he told her everything that had happened to him. It didn't come out in any kind of chronological order or with enough specific details to make sense, but Anissa was always on the inside—being an outsider will do that. So could being a writer. And Issey figured that's why he told her. Not because she was his brother's wife but because she was a writer and she could remove her emotions from these events and assemble a story out of all this dumb material because that's what writers like Anissa do.

"So that Berger was the guy from the Faneuil Hall shooting? He seemed so…"

"Handsome?" Issey said, "Like a Hollywood model, right?"

"Um, no, Sandra Dee. I was gonna say creepy."

"Creepy?"

"Yeah, he was gross."

Gross? It would be an argument they could pursue later, but on this point Issey knew she was wrong.

Anissa asked, "And he just stole *everything*?"

"Yes."

"Like all of it?"

"Everything."

"He just didn't seem capable."

"No, Anissa—he's *really* good. Like *haute cuisine* good."

Anissa thought it over, like she wanted to spend time with it.

"It's just remarkable."

"What do you mean?"

"I mean, one after another, item after item—you stole everything. You took from these people and then you gave it back. And then somehow you brought it all back in. And now it's all gone."

Issey shrugged and she continued:

"I'll bet you that everyone knew all along. I bet you they all knew it was you."

Issey put his coffee cup on the coffee table and she continued, happily engaged:

"Maybe it's because you're so stupid and brain damaged, but it's just quite magical. You don't seem to have a clue about your own motives. Do you even know why you do these things?"

"Of course," he lied.

"You ransacked your brother's former employer—and what happens? It all comes out that Yorke alone was responsible for the Tower collapse and Rohel gets a new job. You use Madison in your little game of three-card monte—then she builds her confidence, then she makes a friend, then she makes two friends, then three, then she's having play dates and sleepovers. You come into town like a raging criminal—and the Oklahoma police sergeant makes a big arrest. And you got me a friend—I'm gonna hang out with his wife after the reading. And shoot, you even helped your creepy criminal buddy from Boston."

"Berger? How's that?"

"He stole all your stuff, dummy. He got his confidence back. His self-esteem is probably shooting through the roof!"

Issey thought about it. "I guess all along I was doing something kind."

Anissa laughed at him. "You're nice, Issey. But you're not kind. And you're not even all that nice. I'd say you have no past and you have no future and even in the present you're something of a tourist."

"Geez," Issey said, annoyed at her, Anissa, his stupid best friend.

"I will tell you one thing, something I've been wanting to tell you since you came into town," she said. Her voice was straightforward.

"Oh?"

She nodded and looked towards the floor. "I am *so* jealous of that Cuban heel. It is superb. *Where* did you get those boots?"

Issey gasped, "They're stunning, right?"

"Exhilarating!"

Issey melted in the couch. "Tell me about this book and your reading tonight."

"Oh, well!" She threw her hands up. "It's a big book, Issey. It's called *500 Dog Names*."

"What's it about?"

"What do you mean?"

"I mean, what's in it? What's it about?"

"It's about 500 different names for a dog."

"And that's a book?"

"Yeah," now she was annoyed at him. "It's got writing and a spine with my name on it. It's a book."

"I thought you wrote stories about relationships and strangers or something."

"I keep telling you I'm not that kind of writer."

"And they paid you for this?"

"Yeah, Issey. It was a huge advance. So are you coming to this reading or what?"

"What would you even read?"

"The dog names, stupid. The dog names. What don't you get about this? It's the different names for a dog. Baxter. Rex. Spot. Winston. Rodeo. Christoph. Bistro. Fleur-de-Lis. Caprese..."

CHAPTER FORTY-ONE

At Yellow Barn Books, to a packed standing crowd, Anissa was on her third encore. They don't usually do encores at book readings, but she was on her third one because it wasn't one of those kinds of books.

Yellow Barn Books was one of the rare round barns in the state. About a decade ago, when it had been retired as a working barn, new owners Heather Baldwin and Cheryl Xu converted it into a bookstore and small printing press. At night, they cleared the History & Biography displays, which were units on wheels, and turned that area into a performance space for readings, one-person shows, duets, improv challenges. The smell of pages was always crisp. And Yellow Barn Books, though situated deep in the state, was no stranger to readings from Big Name Literary Types. This season had already seen Gabriele Käsebier from Berlin read selections from her award-winning novel *Bulletin!*; the poet Calvin Capeheart was enormous in reputation, size, and beard, and he shared unpublished poems read through the husk of his wooly-bully beard; even the hot literary sensation Janey Asp squeaked through her book everyone seemed to be buying. But it was Anissa's *500 Dog Names* that really made the barn shake and she was on her third encore.

On stage, under string lights hung from the barn's peak, Anissa was all bracelets and cheekbones and height. Behind her, a projector shot the faces, paws, bodies, and fur of the dogs from her book. Once the crowd got a good look, she then revealed the perfect name for the dog—the name which she had researched, organized, and felt compelled to write.

An unremarkable cocker spaniel was "Jeff," and Eight Jeff, who was in the back serving concession wine in plastic cups, said, "Hey—that's kind of my name!" The gigantic fur monster Komondor was "Henry" and Henry Hatch's snorts sent ripples through his blubbery face and oversized clothes. The Labradoodle was paired with the name "Rohel," and Madison yelled, "That's my daddy's name!" The Pitbull was obviously "Caddy," and someone shouted, "Word up!" and Caddy said, "Shut up, stupid." The Pomeranian was "Cheryl," and Heather Baldwin shouted, "Do more fact-checking" and when "Heather" was revealed to be a Golden Retriever, Cheryl Xu shouted, "She wishes!" "Pru" was a Shi Tzu, which was met with wild guffaws. Meanwhile, "Tanya" was a patchy Border Collie mix and the crowd said, "Ohhh." Things got a little dicey when the Dalmatian's name was "Clint." The Oklahoma sergeant was booed. But this likely came from Avi's children, a long line of rats who still came to book readings. When Anissa showed a greyhound and read "Avi," the other section of the crowd booed at the "Clint" booers and then there was a spray of hissing, a fluttering of popcorn, and a wet pipeline of "SHHHHH!" from the Yellow Barn Book Club Members who wore badges. Before a book reading of dog names could get any more hostile, Anissa pivoted like a real show-woman and clicked onto the following dog on her projector. It was an overweight and waddling Corgi and Anissa raised a finger to the crowd—"Shut it!" Her bracelets clinked and she looked into her book, looked at her audience, and then read the name "Issey." And everyone laughed and cheered and booed and laughed and cheered. It was that kind of night and everyone was a little roasted by the end of it.

Issey missed Molly. He missed the way she smelled. Her fragrance was like a grassy afternoon. He couldn't remember the sound of her voice or the exact words that came from her pancake face.

Issey mingled a little and walked outside for some night air. Outside, Caddy nodded at him, said Pitbull was right, and then told Issey it was about time for his tires to get rotated. Issey didn't know what that meant.

"Isn't rotating what they do on the road?"

But then something unexpected happened: Caddy removed a cigarillo from the front of his mechanic's overalls and *lit it with the Ronson lighter.* But Issey had the Ronson lighter in his jacket pocket. He tapped his jacket pocket to be sure.

"Caddy, how do you have that lighter? I gave it back to you and then you gave it back to me. Right?"

Issey was a little shouty and when he pulled the Ronson lighter from his jacket pocket, he rattled it in Caddy's direction.

"You need to settle down. I put that in your car after I fixed your door window because *I thought you would like it.* I guess I thought wrong."

"Oh," Issey replied, tone normal, face warm. "I thought it was the same one."

"I ain't gonna give you my best lighter."

Issey smiled a little. "Well, I can't take it. I have to give it back."

"I don't want it." Caddy shook his head at Issey. "You stupid asshole."

When Henry Hatch passed, conversing like a ham with theater director Chuck Reed, Issey had the same idea. Why do I have your sister's bangle bracelet? What is it doing in my life? But Hatch and Reed were too involved for bracelet talk, so Issey left it alone for the time being. Maybe it would be best if he just left it alone altogether. It would just amount to the same thing. It didn't matter how Issey had it now. Issey had it now. That's all there was to it.

Issey walked to his car. He had a hard time finding it. Cars and pickups spilled beyond the carved perimeter of the designated lot. But Issey—night animal, prowling sightseer—knew all along where he had left the car. Of course! When he saw it, he said, "Of course!" He opened the door, which wasn't locked, and dumped the Ronson lighter and the bangle bracelet on the passenger seat. But something wasn't right. Something was missing. He looked out, over the scatter of cars and then around, to the lights and bodies of Yellow Barn Books.

When he squinted, he could see it, that restless glimmer of a thing in the crowd. Rhonda. She looked nothing at all like Molly. The clues always buffed out to something, but she looked like nothing at all and exactly like who she was when he had broken into her townhouse. In her hands, she was holding her diary with the dervish clasp.

ACKNOWLEDGEMENTS

All novels have their "secrets," and these are the people who are part of this novel's secrets. Open sesame! To Cassie & Bobby Rangel and Beth & Thom White for nearly three decades of inspiration, art, music, and camaraderie. To Manoli Kouremetis for optimism and hours of shoptalk. To readers John Navarro and Emma Jones who thankfully stayed pals with me after reading early drafts. To Tagore Hernandez for Tempo con Popo and Sisia Daglian for always asking good questions about the book's progress. When are we reforming Soup Club? To Chelsea Gardner Courtney Jennings who hates books and still listened to me while I talked about my book. To Suzy Gilmont for endless joy. Somebody tell her to charge her phone. The battery is at 1%. To Craig & Hannah Kimberley: from Norfolk to Boston, we kept the party going! Love always, babes! To Breena and Mark Stuart for creating a space for 12s in Boston. What a party! To Tracey MF Vaughan for hair and dishing at the salon. To the absolutely brilliant Raúl Lázaro and those fingers lifting the C. To the heroes, Dan, Marc, Gregg, and Chris. Heed the call! To all the staff at the Hadley Hilton.

Thank you to everyone at Black Rose Writing. Reagan Rothe, Mary Ellen Bramwell, Minna Rothe, Justin Weeks – thank you for believing in this book. A special thank you to David King, who showed incredible patience for the 172 line changes I asked him to make.

Finally, a special thank you to the state of Vermont, where I lived for four years. Thank you for being a good sport about all of this.

ABOUT THE AUTHOR

Gregory Grosvenor grew up in Ansbach, Germany. He moved to the US, eventually earning an MFA from Old Dominion University. Ever since, he has taught writing and the art of the short story at various colleges in Virginia, Maryland, and Massachusetts. Grosvenor currently lives in Cambridge, Massachusetts, with his three cats, Dinah, Theo, and Bramlet Abercrombie.

NOTE FROM GREGORY GROSVENOR

Word-of-mouth is crucial for any author to succeed. If you enjoyed *Second Pocket First*, please leave a review online—anywhere you are able. Even if it's just a sentence or two. It would make all the difference and would be very much appreciated.

Thanks!
Gregory Grosvenor

We hope you enjoyed reading this title from:

BLACK ROSE
writing™

www.blackrosewriting.com

Subscribe to our mailing list – *The Rosevine* – and receive **FREE** books, daily deals, and stay current with news about upcoming releases and our hottest authors.
Scan the QR code below to sign up.

Already a subscriber? Please accept a sincere thank you for being a fan of Black Rose Writing authors.

View other Black Rose Writing titles at www.blackrosewriting.com/books and use promo code **PRINT** to receive a **20% discount** when purchasing.